Shattered Dreams

CARRIGAN RICHARDS

Shattered Dreams
A January Dreams Novel
By Carrigan Richards

Published by Carrigan Richards Publishing, LLC

Cover design by C.R. Graphics.
Edited by Lindsey Alexander.
www.readinglisteditorial.com
Proofread by The Literary Vixen

To learn more about author Carrigan Richards, visit her website at www.carriganrichards.com

Also by Carrigan Richards
Standalone Novel
Pieces of Me

Elemental Enchanters Series
Under a Blood Moon
Under the Burning Stars
When Darkness Fell
Under the Winter Sun
Under an Onyx Sky

January Dreams Series
January Dreams
Silent Dreams
Shattered Dreams

ACKNOWLEDGMENTS

In 2012, Megan appeared to me. She was telling me about these dreams she kept having. I wrote her story during National Novel Writing Month (NaNoWriMo) that year. The story poured out of me. At first, I thought that was the end of her story. Years passed and I still could not think of how her story continued. I prematurely published January Dreams. Then life happened and as I was dealing with my own issues in the form of emotional and mental abuse, I knew how Megan's story would continue, but I couldn't quite write it. I wasn't ready to face it. I got to a good place in my life and cranked out Silent Dreams. It took me a while to figure out how Shattered Dreams would come into the mix, but when she did, I couldn't believe it. This series has taken a long while to write, but she was worth it. I love these books and I'm so proud of myself.

With that said, I want to thank all of my readers and fans. Your patience, understanding, support, and love over the years has helped propel me to keep this dream alive. You are truly amazing.

There are so many people who helped me through this process and helped me in life that I want to thank. First of all, my editor, Lindsey Alexander. Without you I wouldn't have been able to bring these characters to life and realize what was missing.

Thank you for challenging me and pushing me to become a better writer.

To my bestie boo, Laura Trujillo. Your friendship has meant the world to me, and I don't know what I would do without you. Thank you for keeping me straight and focused and for being there no matter what. Your encouragement keeps me from falling into that deep, dark well of doubt.

Angie Rivera, I don't know what I'd do without you either. Getting me through the meerkat days with fun gifs and memes and just letting me vent. I know it can't be easy, but you truly are amazing and have the kindest most genuine soul.

Jennifer Watts, your unconditional love, and friendship has gotten me through all the years – even the ones dealing with "Ron."

Nicole Hoffmann thanks for letting me complain about work and for helping me through times when I get stuck. Keep up the glitter, girl.

Thank you, Stephanie Wooddell, aka flower child, for my endless medical questions and for being awesome. You make me laugh and you truly are amazing. Thank you to Sarah Rutledge, Gina Morgan Moody, and Caitlin Denman for all your excitement and continuous support.

And of course, to my family for cheering me on. I love all of you. Patrick, you are the best brother a girl could ask for. Thank you for believing in me, for the awesome book talks, and for spreading the word about my books. Your support truly means the world to me. Finally, thank you Brandon for always understanding and for believing in me and my dreams; for always answering my random questions and for putting up with me.

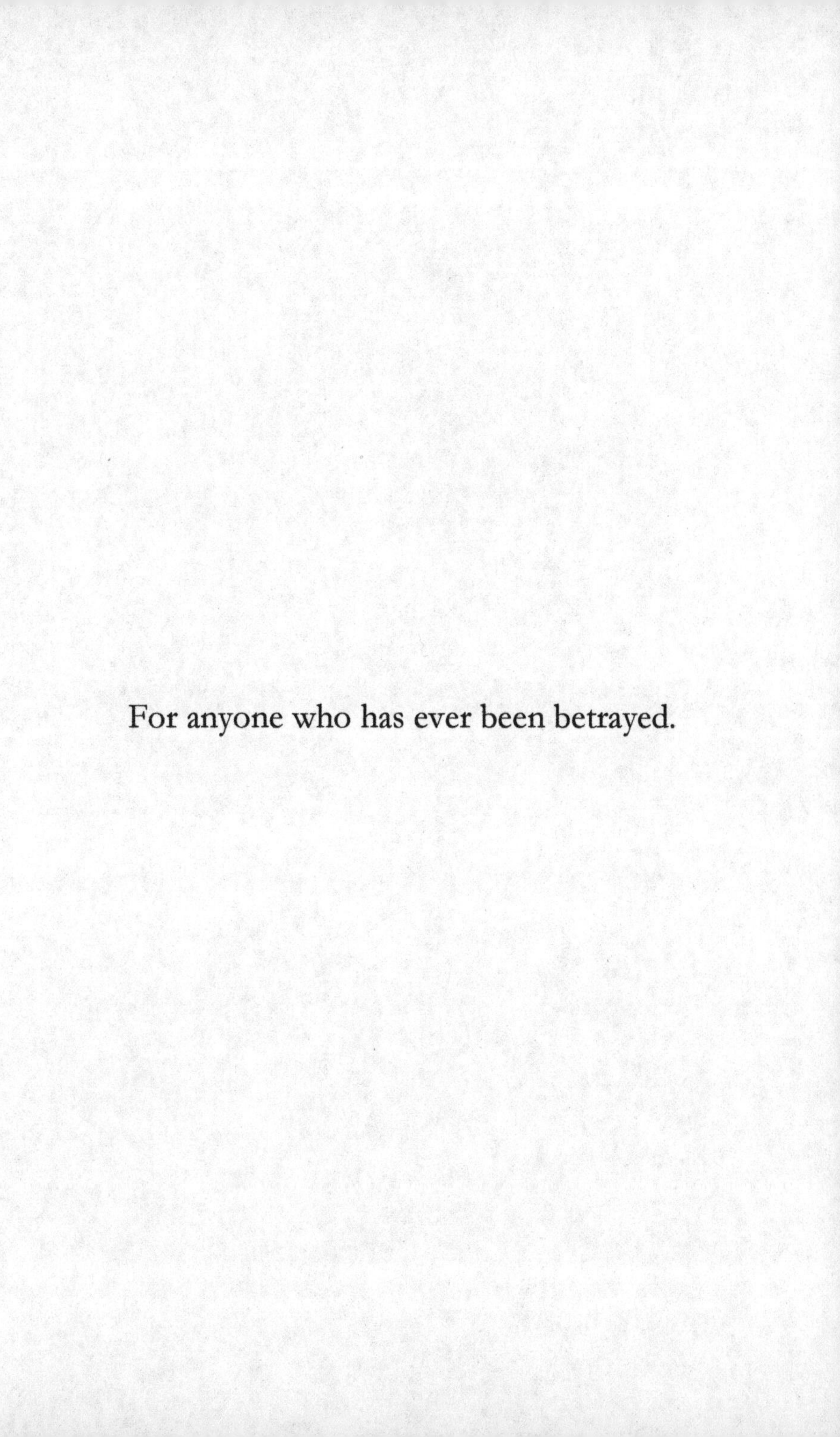

For anyone who has ever been betrayed.

*When he shall die,
Take him and cut him out in little stars,
And he will make the face of heaven so fine
That all the world will be in love with night
And pay no worship to the garish sun.
— William Shakespeare, Romeo and Juliet*

One

A constant beep drags me from a deep sleep. It's a soft beep. Not like the one that usually annihilates my sleep when I have to go to school. When I try to open my eyes, they fight with me, resisting, almost as if my eyes are telling me, it's not time to wake up. I wince as I try to move my arm. My body aches like I was hit by a freaking freight train and there's a perpetual throb inside my head. Then I feel the excruciating pain shooting up my spine, twisting its way to my heart. It's almost too much and I want to give in.

I moan and slowly open my eyes. Warm, piercing light makes me squint and when my vision somewhat sharpens, I see the IV stand next to me. The room is dimly lit, and I can barely make out a TV jutting from the wall. I still can't figure out what the beeping is.

IV. Beeping. Hospital. I remember. A bald man told me I'd been in a coma for a month. I'm trying to recall everything he said. Something about being shot. Was I shot again? Images start flooding my mind of me giving Casper a potion to sleep; me drinking a potion to make me appear dead. Florence selling me out and Vincent holding Joffrey's head as he entered the cave. The memory makes me nauseous. He used the Nuummite Jewel to return me to the human world, threatening to kill Casper and leaving me here.

Oh God what did I do?

I messed up. Bad. Now I'm in the mortal world while Casper is still in Arvada.

On my left, I see a figure in a chair, with his head in his hands. He has blond hair and for a split second my heart palpitates thinking it's Casper. But the shape of the figure is wrong and he's wearing pale blue scrubs.

I start patting around and I feel the cold metal bars of the bed.

The man stands over me. "Megan," he says my name and I freeze, losing my breath. My heart drops to my stomach.

"Vincent?" I wince. My throat is on fire. My voice sounds terrible. It feels worse than when I had strep.

"Oh, I'm so glad you're okay." He lets out a relieved sigh and squeezes my hand. "I love you so much, Megan. I was so scared I lost you."

He looks wrong. Bleach blond hair that reaches his chin and brown eyes. Did he change his look to be like Casper or have I lost my mind?

"Lost me? What happened? Where am I? Why-why are you here?" I recoil from him, but I can't move very far without the pain ripping through me.

"You're in the hospital. I couldn't bring myself to leave you. I had to know you were okay. How do you feel?"

My vision clears and I notice how messy his hair is and his bloodshot eyes. A rough beard and mustache have appeared on his face. He looks like he hasn't slept in days or longer. His dark eyes are laden with guilt. He should feel sorry. I'm hoping my stark fear isn't showing on my face. I want my mom and brother. Casper. Cherry. Not this deranged lunatic feeling sorry for me.

Except I did plan to kill him. Does that make me just as deranged?

I clear my throat, which feels like someone shoved glass shards in it. "I thought you left." Did he go back to Arvada and kill Casper? Has he returned? I refuse to believe that.

Vincent hands me water and I take it. The cool liquid feels great as it moistens my throat and mouth, but the burning is still there, and I can barely get the water down. "I don't have much time. I wanted to see you."

"Where's my mom?"

"You have to forgive me."

"Forgive you? After you killed those people and brought me back here leaving me." Why isn't he upset with me? I concocted a plan to kill him. He was so upset with me that he brought me back here. Now he wants *my* forgiveness? "Why am I in the hospital? The doctor said last night I was shot."

He watches me almost as if he's waiting for me to recollect everything. "You don't remember anything?"

"I remember everything," I snap. "You turned into the dragon and killed so many people. You burned their homes. You brought me back so you could leave me here."

"I never wanted to leave you."

"Did Jacques make you do all of that? I know you are not that cruel, Vincent." He can't be. I refuse to have fallen in love with such a monster. What would that say about me?

He looks away, ashamed.

"Your mom loved you, Vincent. She wanted me to tell you. She never meant to hurt you. Jacques used you against her."

Blood drains from his face. He stares at me for a few seconds and recovers.

"It wasn't your fault. None of it. You're not a bad person."

He looks like he might break down and cry.

"What happened once we came back from Arvada? How did I get shot? Who shot me?"

"Megan, calm down. Don't get so worked up. You're okay."

"Why are you here?" My chin quivers, and a tear rolls down my cheek. "You said you were going to leave me here."

Vincent keeps glancing at the door like he's waiting for someone to come in. He fidgets with a key card. He's nervous about something and clearly can't focus on what I'm saying.

He furrows his brows. "Your mind must be a bit muddled."

"My mind is fine." I think.

"I made the biggest mistake of my life and I'm so sorry. I never meant for you to get hurt." He leans over and presses his lips to my forehead. "I messed up, but I will make it up to you."

"What happened?" I ask again though I know he won't tell me. He's holding something back. And his constant fidgeting is driving me crazy. "Would you stop? What is wrong with you?"

"I did something bad, Megan. I'll fix it. We'll get out of here and everything will be fine. I have some things to do before we can leave together. Plus, you need to get better. I'll see you soon." He gives a small smile. "You have my word. You just have to wait."

I snatch his hand. "Vincent don't leave me here. I wasn't trying to kill you. Florence got it all wrong." I have to make him believe me. I have to save Casper. "You have to get me out of here. Please. I promise I'll be good. We have to go back to Arvada."

He squeezes my hand. "We will, Megan. I promise. Just rest for now. I'll come back for you, and we'll leave. I promise. Please don't hate me. I'm not a bad person."

If that's what he has to tell himself to feel better. "I don't hate you." Except I do.

He nods. "I love you, mon trésor. I promise. I'll come back for you." He releases my hand.

"No, don't leave."

Vincent frowns. "I have to, Megan. For now."

More tears fall down my face. "Please." I'm desperate now.

"I will come back." Vincent replaces his hat and walks out the door leaving me once again.

Thoughts of him killing Casper invade my mind. What more does he want from me? Why won't he just stop? Why won't he let Casper and me be happy? I don't understand it and I never will.

Tears roll down my cheeks like little droplets of pain running for freedom.

How could Florence sell me out like that? What was she really trying to gain? I can barely remember what she said.

I miss Casper and I long to see him again. I can only hope that Silvyr kept him safe.

Two

No matter what position I'm in, agonizing pain twists its way all over me. Why was Vincent here? He said before he was going to leave me here. But he came back. I never wanted to kill him, but after what he did to the Elves, how could I not? He wasn't ever going to change because of his dad.

My mind is so foggy and my head hurts. I've been in and out of sleep, and nurses constantly check on me all night. That potion from the witch seriously did a number on me. She never warned me about the intense effects from it. It's frustrating and I hate it.

Although I should've known something that makes me appear dead would do something like this.

The hospital room reminds me of the one Casper was in when Vincent ran him off the road causing him to be in a coma. Vincent seems to be really good at that.

There's a green, leather-looking chair next to me. IVs and tubes attached to the wall behind me. Lots of buttons and flashy lights. No windows. Which is a shame because I would love to see if it's sunny or rainy or night or day. I don't even know what time of year it is. We left the mortal world in May. A small TV is attached to the corner across the room.

The door opens and the bald man and a brown skinned woman walk inside. Why hasn't Mom or Jonathan come by? How did Vincent visit before them? He probably mind-controlled people.

"Good morning, Megan," the nurse says. Her voice is high-pitched and hurts. She's short and has a pretty, bright smile. Her perkiness reminds me of a cheerleader. "How are you feeling?"

How do I even answer that? I feel like a freaking train ran me over. "Okay."

She hands me water urging me to drink. I do while she checks my blood pressure and other things. "Good. You were a bit agitated last night."

"Wouldn't you be?" I ask.

She lifts an eyebrow, while the bald man chuckles.

"I see you haven't lost your sense of humor," he says, but I'm not sure it was funny.

"Who are you?"

"I'm Doctor Ellis. Do you remember me?"

"From last night, yeah." I want to sit up, but no matter how hard I try, I can't. "How did I get shot? What happened? Vincent wouldn't tell me."

"Vincent?" Dr. Ellis' expression darkens. "Vincent Young?"

"Yes. He brought me here and left me. I have to save Casper."

"Megan, your mind is confused. A lot of different things are going on. You're getting agitated and it's not good for you," the nurse says.

"Then tell me what happened."

I hear nothing for what seems like forever. Then a sigh. "You should rest."

"I don't want to. Why am I in the hospital?"

"Vincent shot you."

I look at the doctor. What is he talking about? Vincent shot me again? He looked super remorseful last night. Did he seriously shoot me the second we returned to the mortal world? Why would he do that?

"He shot me a while ago, too." I try sitting up again but can't. It's like I'm tied down which is the most frustrating thing. "I-I took a potion that makes you appear—" I stop. It sounds ridiculous no matter how true it is, and I can't let the doctors know about my immortal world. They would definitely lock me up forever.

"It's okay, Megan," Dr. Ellis says. "Don't force it. When you were shot, you lost a lot of blood causing a coma."

What did Vincent do to me? Why would he do that? Okay yes, I was going to kill him. Was he trying to kill me in the human life so I would be reborn immediately without memories of anything? None of this makes sense. My head throbs, my body aches, my throat is killing me. I need to get back to Casper.

"It's okay that you don't remember much. Comas take a toll on memories. But you're showing great progress."

"Great. I have to get out of here."

"You will soon. You still have quite a bit of rehab ahead of you."

"I don't need rehab. I need to get out of here. I'm fine." Even though I'm far from fine. Everything hurts. I'm exhausted. Irritated.

"Megan, you've had extensive tissue and muscle damage. The bullet stopped right at your kidney and luckily didn't penetrate the entire kidney. It did cause slight paralysis, but it seems to have faded. You will need physical therapy from the coma."

"Where is my mom? How was Vincent able to visit me before her?"

Dr. Ellis narrows his eyes. "Your mom is on her way. You just woke up last night. I know he's caused you a great deal of pain, but he wasn't here last night."

"What? Yes, he was. He sat in that chair." I point to it.

Dr. Ellis and the nurse exchange a look. Do they think I'm crazy?

"Only doctors and nurses are allowed in here at night, hon," the nurse says. "I'll ask the nurse last night if she saw anyone, but she would've said something to me at shift change. Especially if he was here."

Did I dream it? Is Vincent in my dreams now? He's in Arvada and has found a way inside my dreams. What does she mean especially Vincent? Probably because he shot me. I still don't get it. Did he shoot me so that he would return to Arvada and kill Casper without me interfering?

Blood drains from my face.

That's exactly what he did. He shot me on purpose so that I would be incapacitated then he could kill Casper.

No. Casper isn't dead.

If Vincent has a way into my dreams, then I can find Casper in them. I have to. He has to be alive.

Tears roll down my cheeks like little droplets of pain running for freedom. Vincent always wanted me to forget Casper and somehow, he's done something much worse.

Three

An oak tree rustles in the warm breeze. Birds sing and tweet to each other as they hop from branch to branch. The bright, high sun warms my skin as I inhale the sweet scents of lilac and lavender. Thin, wispy clouds scatter across the immaculate blue sky. The grassy field is lush. It's peaceful here and I know I'm dreaming. It's too perfect to be real.

I don't know where I am though. Seems like a perfect place to lie in the grass watching the clouds drift by. I seem to recall Casper and me doing that once.

"Megan!" I hear him cry for me. His voice dissipates any agony. Turning around, I scan the field, my heart knocking against my ribcage. When I see a shadow of a man near the tree, I rush toward him. My eyes focus on his shaggy blond hair, angular face, and his deep, brown eyes.

"Casper," I say with such love. I dart into his arms, and he wraps me into a tight embrace. I can feel his heart pounding through his chest, matching mine.

"It worked," he says with relief in his voice. His lips sweep across my forehead. "I've been trying to see if this would work."

"I've been searching for you, too. I didn't think this could happen." Casper is alive. Elation overwhelms me and tension releases from my body allowing the tears to free fall.

Everything fades away as he pulls me into his arms. I breathe in that crisp clean scent of his. When I pull back slightly, I gaze into his eyes. I can see his love in his eyes. It's fierce, beautiful, and only for me. My body hums with anticipation. I need him. I want him. He is my everything.

Casper sweeps my hair from my face and leans down. The longing is unbearable. He presses his lips to mine, filling me with warmth. I have never felt more alive. His lips move with a fervent urgency, and I match his pace. It's like we've not seen each other in ages, and the kiss feels that way. And if this is the only way we can be together for right now, it's good enough for me.

Together. We are together.

Even if it is just a dream.

"Where are we?"

"This is one of my favorite places."

"It's beautiful. I wish this were real, Casper."

"I know. Me, too. It's better than nothing."

Drawing back, I frown. "I'm so sorry. I never wanted to put you to sleep, but I had to. I thought I was saving us. I thought I could do it. I didn't think Florence would betray us—"

He lifts my face, and his eyes meet mine. "It's okay. I'm here now. I found you." He pulls me to his lips. Soft, warm, and just the right amount of pressure.

Taking my hand, we sit beneath the oak tree tangled in each other's arms watching the vast field.

"You don't hate me?" I ask, weakly.

He tilts his head and gives me a knowing look. "I could never hate you. I love you, Megan. I know why you did it even if I may not agree with it, but I understand."

I tell him everything that's happened so far.

"He hasn't been back to Arvada," Casper says.

"He hasn't?"

"No. As soon as you left, Silvyr and some others made Florence a prisoner. It's been calm since he's gone. Even King Jacques hasn't touched us."

"Why did Vincent shoot me again?"

"I don't know. If I ever do see him, I will kill him. He deserves to die, Megan."

I know this, even as hard as it is to realize. "I thought I saw him in the hospital, but it was a dream."

He tenses. "He's coming to you in your dreams?"

"I think so. I don't know. It felt so real, but all my dreams do. The nurse said there's no way he'd be there." I freeze.

"What is it?"

"Unless he was there and compelled everyone to forget they saw him." *Of course.*

"I thought he was going to leave you in the mortal world. Do you really think he's there?"

"Maybe. He said he had to do some things before we came back here."

"What is he planning?"

I shake my head. There's no telling what Vincent is planning. I don't understand his motives anymore. Why hasn't he returned to Arvada?

We spend as much time as we can together catching up on what's happening in Arvada and the mortal world. Though not much is happening on my end. At least my mind doesn't remember.

It feels good to be in his arms again. To hear his voice. To see his beautiful face. To taste his lips. To smell his woodsy scent. This is my heaven.

"I want to be with you, Casper. Not in a dream. Not in a mortal life. I have to figure out how to come back to you."

"I'll talk to the witch. She must know a way."

"You have to hurry. I don't know what Vincent has planned. He said he was coming back for me. He says he'll bring us back, but I don't believe him."

Casper gazes into my eyes. I love the deep brown color of his with a speck of gold. "We will find each other every night in our dreams." He holds me tightly against his strong body. "You know I love you and that you're the only one for me. We will get through this."

I meet his eyes and as I search them, I know he's right. "Promise you'll meet me every night in my dreams."

"Always. I promise." Casper crushes his lips to mine. It isn't a sweet kiss. It's heavy and undulating and soul baring. No matter how many times this man kisses me, it always feels like our first.

Four

The door opens and the second I see her reddish-brown hair, a flood of emotions hit me.

"Mom."

Mom, Jonathan, and Ron, my stepdad, come into the room. Emotions overwhelm me and once Mom starts crying, I follow. She rushes toward me and wraps her arms around me, holding me so tight. My real mother and father disowned me under Vincent and his father's manipulation, and it feels amazing to have a mother love me, even if she is my human mother for this lifetime.

I missed her more than I thought I ever would. And Jonathan. He awkwardly puts a brown teddy bear in the crook of my arm and shoves his hands in his jean pockets.

I've wished for this for so long I can't control my tears.

Jon's brown eyes look bloodshot, and his hair is a little longer than usual. He's let the stubble on his face grow a little more. He doesn't look like my nineteen-year-old brother any longer. He looks much older.

"You look like crap," he says, and I know he's only trying to lighten the mood.

"Jonathan." Mom says his name like a warning.

"Damn. I thought all that beauty sleep would've helped my appearance."

"Good to see you, Sis."

"You, too."

"How are you feeling?" Ron asks and I almost forgot he was there. I can't decide if I've missed him or not. He gives me a weird hug. It's probably weird because we hardly ever hug each other.

"I'm okay."

Mom hugs me again. "Oh honey." She continues to weep as she holds me, and I let her.

"Really glad you're awake," Jonathan says.

"Me, too."

"I was getting tired of the hospital food."

I roll my eyes.

"Jonathan be nice," Ron says.

"It's okay." I don't mind at all. I like that he's trying to cheer me up. Maybe I can talk to him alone.

Dr. Ellis comes into the room, and my family looks toward him. "Good morning."

"Is she going to be okay?" Mom asks.

"With the right amount of rehabilitation, she will recover fine and be back to normal soon."

Mom squeezes my hand.

"Normal?" Jonathan raises an eyebrow. "She was never normal."

Dr. Ellis chuckles at the same time Mom glares at Jonathan.

"There are some forms to sign if you don't mind doing that now?" he asks, and Mom nods.

"I'll be right back." She kisses my forehead and smiles. She and Ron follow Dr. Ellis out of the room.

"Whew...do I know how to piss her off or what?" Jonathan lets out a whistle.

I chuckle. "Where's Dad?"

Jon frowns and I know that means Dad isn't here. "He's called every day. I told him this morning you're awake. He wants to talk to you."

Part of me is hurt that Dad never even came. But that's how he is. He's always hated driving from Atlanta to here.

"I need to get out of here."

"I don't blame you. You've been lying there for a month. Can you even move your legs?"

I let out an annoyed groan. "Jon, I really have to get out of here. Vincent's here and he's going to come back to get me."

The look on Jonathan's face changes to confusion and worry. "What? He's not going to hurt you. He wouldn't even be able to walk in this hospital. Everyone's looking for him."

"Why would everyone be looking for him? Because he shot me?" That would make sense and explain his shady behavior the other night.

"Uh...yeah. Don't you remember anything?"

I sigh. "Yeah. He shot me, but—" I almost let it slip that he brought Casper and me back to Arvada, but no one knows about it. I'm not sure I can tell Jonathan the truth. Maybe I can tell Cherry, my best friend. I can't wait to see her.

"There's kind of a manhunt going on after what he did."

"A manhunt? Are the police offering an award? Why would he come here if there was a manhunt?" What has Vincent done? Shot me, hasn't returned to Arvada, and has police searching for him. Though not like anyone will find him. He can compel people. And he can return to another world. So, there's that.

"Uh..." Jonathan frowns and stares at the ground.

"What is it?"

He lets out a breath. "I didn't want to be the person to tell you. Was kinda hoping your memory would come back."

My memory is fine, but okay. "Tell me."

"Not now. You just woke up and I think Cherry's coming later."

"Jon, tell me." I stare at him willing him to tell me whatever it is on his mind.

His shoulders slump and he sighs. He sits in the chair next to the bed and his leg starts shaking worse than Savannah, my mini-Jack Russell. I swear it looks like he's about to have a panic attack. All the blood drains from his face. "Megan...Vincent." He stops and shakes his head. "Vincent didn't just shoot you. He shot several people at Spring Valley killing six people."

I was not expecting that. "What?" Why does Jonathan think that? Have I been back longer than I thought? Did Vincent bring us back and shoot up a school? Why would he have done that? "When was this?"

"It happened at the end of October. It's November now."

November. I'm trying to piece everything together. "Vincent shot me after prom in May." We returned to Arvada. Were we in Arvada for five months or have we been back here longer, and he erased my memories? Did Vincent make up some ridiculous story so that people thought we had been here the whole time? All of this is making my head hurt. I don't get any of it.

Jonathan furrows his eyebrows. "No. You guys broke up around prom. Dr. Ellis said your mind would be a little messed up. It'll all come back."

So, I've been told. "Yeah."

"There's more." His voice shakes. "C-Casper was one of the casualties."

I guess it makes sense that humans think Casper died since he returned to Arvada and hasn't returned. But what do they think happened to me? What a crazy story Vincent has concocted. It baffles me.

"Did you hear me?" he asks, softly.

I nod. I should probably feign tears. Casper's not really dead, but they don't know that. Maybe since Vincent erected us from the human world, he had to return to devise some insane story for people to believe.

Jonathan places a hand on mine. Despite all the insanity, it feels good to be comforted by him. "I'm really sorry, Megan."

Tears well in my eyes. How could Vincent do this? How could he make people believe such a lie? I feel so lost, like a large chunk of my mind has been erased. Like Vincent's done to me so many times before. I wish he'd leave my head alone. He said he didn't want to mess with it when we were in Arvada. What changed? Except that I was going to kill him.

When we came back to the mortal world, he grabbed me, and I knew he would erase my memories. But what exactly did he erase? I remember everything that happened in Arvada.

Part of me wants to find Vincent to figure out what the hell he's done, but I don't want to see him. Unless he's the only way I have to return to Arvada. This is messed up. Why would he create this insanity for me to live in? What game is he playing now? Is this all because I planned to kill him?

I need to hurry up and heal so I can leave. I have to save Casper before it's too late. Vincent can still return.

Cherry. My heart starts pounding. "Is Cherry okay?" If Vincent hurt her, I don't know what I'll do.

"She's fine."

I let out a breath.

Mom, Ron, and Dr. Ellis return. When Jon gives her a knowing look, Mom breaks down and hugs me. It angers me that Vincent put these people through so much unnecessary pain. What is the point? What kind of sick game is he playing now?

"How are you feeling?" Dr. Ellis asks for the thousandth time.

"I'm fine. I feel good." Which is a total lie. Everything hurts. Every muscle aches. My head feels like there's a balloon inside inflating and deflating. My back feels like someone keeps stabbing me in the same spot. And I'm so groggy. Especially my mind. It's like a constant cloud of muddled memories. I can't find my way through them. "How long do you think it'll be until I'm well enough to get out of here?"

"You've had substantial damage and you've just awakened from a coma. It could be weeks."

I let out a frustrated sigh. I don't have weeks. I have to figure out a way to get back before Vincent comes back for me. He kept talking about taking us back. Can I fake a front again with him? Am I up to playing his game so that I can be with Casper? I thought coming back to the human world would be better, but so far, it's just a long nightmare of confusion. One of Vincent's amazing parting gifts I suppose.

Clever trick, Vincent.

I don't know how or when, but I will make him pay for this.

"You should get some rest."

"I'm tired of resting," I say, remembering when I was sick with mono. At least then I had something to pass the time. "Do you have my phone?" I ask Mom, really needing to talk to Cherry.

"I'm sorry, dear. We haven't gotten you a new one yet. Jon and I will go do that now and come back. I know your dad has been wanting to talk to you."

"A new one? What happened to mine?"

She looks at Jonathan.

"Why don't we give Megan some time to rest?" Dr. Ellis suggests. "She's had enough action for the day."

Mom nods and kisses my forehead. "I'll be right back, okay? I love you so much."

"I love you, too."

Jon reaches in his pocket and pulls out his phone. "Here. Call Dad."

My family leaves with Dr. Ellis, and I'm left alone and confused.

This whole thing is crazy. It's like I'm stuck inside some messed up shattered dream. No matter what, it feels like being with Casper will never happen. There are so many obstacles preventing us from being together. Like the universe is so against us. At what point should we give up and give in? Should we even consider it? I don't want to, and I know Casper doesn't either. We fight so hard to be together, yet we've hardly been together.

It's exhausting and I don't know how much fight I have left in me.

I hate this. I've wanted to return to the mortal world for so long and now that I'm here I don't want to be. I'm so relieved to be here, but everything is different. Will I ever feel like I fit in anywhere I am? Is that something I have to deal with no matter what?

Though I feel slightly safer here than Arvada. At least there isn't a war going on.

I have to escape Vincent. I have to be with Casper. I miss him and I will do whatever it takes to return to him.

Five

Dad and I had a heartfelt conversation. It felt great to hear his voice and he apologized so many times about not coming to visit. He hates being inside hospitals, though who doesn't? He didn't think his car could make the drive. No surprise there. I love my dad, but sometimes I wish he'd try harder.

It was so comforting talking to him though. We didn't even have to talk about my injuries or the shooting or any of it. He never pushes.

I want to know more about this supposed school shooting. Using Jonathan's phone to search, maybe there will be something I can find. I don't even know what I'm looking for. I type in "Spring Valley school shooting."

Tons of articles and pictures pop up. Pictures of an aerial view of the school. Pictures of Casper and the five other victims. Pictures of the injured, including me. Why would Vincent choose this as his story? How did he have time to convince all of them of this? There is so much that doesn't add up. I skim through article after article but end up being disgusted over all of it.

Did Vincent really shoot up a school? I shake my head. It doesn't make sense. Although Vincent did say he did something bad. That he messed up but will fix it. Did our coming back to this world mess up events? I remember the witch mentioning something about how the Jewel can mess with time.

What did you do Vincent?

I click on the first article dated November 1, 2018.

Armed student shoots ten; kills six.

November 1, 2018. Birmingham, AL. Yesterday, Vincent Young entered Spring Valley High School shooting ten people, killing six.

"It was the scariest day of my life," says Amber McLaughlin, 17.

Like many students, Amber was just doing what all teenagers do – go to class without anything to worry about except relationships, studies, college. But October 31 changed their lives forever.

"I thought it was some prank because it was Halloween. But it wasn't. I was face-to-face with Vincent, but Megan Devereux saved me," Amber says. Megan Devereux, 17, was shot in the back and is now in a coma. One of the victims, Casper Truitt, 17, her boyfriend perished. Tyler Graff, Amy Burress, Hayden Davis, Ray Pearson, and Jason Bell were killed.

I click on another one.

Where is Vincent Young?

After Vincent Young gunned down fellow classmates, killing six on that fateful day in October, police have yet to find him. Young, distraught after his mother's death, shot and killed six people, injuring ten. One of which is his ex-girlfriend who has been in a coma ever since. Many parents are furious that police have not found him.

"He's a teenager. He can't be that hard to find." Dr. Burress, father of victim Amy, says. "Police have just given up. I want justice for my little girl."

The parents of the victims are growing anxious every day that justice hasn't been served.

Most of the articles say the same thing. Vincent was a troubled youth. Came to school. Shot a few kids, injuring some, killing six including Casper. My name is in the articles too, which is weird to see my name plastered all over them. I pause on one particular passage when I see mine and Amber's names in the same sentence.

"Megan saved me. I have no doubt that Vincent was going to kill me, but she kept talking to him, and I escaped."

What?

After clicking on several articles, I put Jon's phone down. Wow. Vincent really did mess up. But did he really leave me here to deal with this? Is he actually going to come back or is this part of his torture? Am I supposed to pretend that I really am a victim of a shooting?

Mom and Jon bring me a phone. When I open it, I roll my eyes at the Homer Simpson background that I know Jon put on it. We all hang out in the room talking. More like listening to Mom talk, but I don't mind. I actually enjoy hearing all her stories that I've missed since I've been gone. She's much more vibrant than my mother in Arvada. Jon's leaning against the wall on his phone, watching videos or scrolling through Facebook. Every so often he makes little witty comments only to annoy Mom. She usually gives an exaggerated sigh and I know she's playing along, too.

"You got an apartment?" I gasp at Jonathan. "When?"

Looking up from his phone, he furrows his eyes at Mom. I hate that everyone seems to exchange looks because they don't want to hurt my feelings or whatever. Makes me feel like a total outsider.

"What?"

"I got an apartment in July. You helped me move."

Wow. How much does the Jewel change events? I have absolutely no memory of these things. How can I continue on so that they don't think I'm so messed up in the head?

"Oh," I say, bringing the room to an awkward silence.

There's a knock at the door and I'm grateful. Cherry Stimm pokes her head inside, yelps and runs to my bed. Her brown curls bouncing. Her eyes wide as she wraps her arms around me.

"Cherry be careful," Mom says. "She's hooked up to a lot of things."

It's so good to see her. It's the first time I've smiled since waking up. It's like she brought the sunlight with her. Her excitement is contagious.

"Ugh. Too much estrogen up in here. I'll be back." Jon walks out the door and we laugh.

"I'll let you two catch up," Mom says. "Do you need anything?"

"Nah, I'm okay, Mom. Thanks."

She kisses my forehead before she leaves.

Cherry sits next to me on the bed. "Omigod, I missed you. I'm so happy you're awake."

"I missed you, too."

"I'm so happy to see your eyes. I hated seeing you..." Tears well in her eyes and she shakes her head. "Nope. Sorry. I'm not going to cry."

"It's okay. Are you and...?" I can't remember her boyfriend's name.

"Luke."

"Right. Still together?"

"Yes. He's been amazing. He's really helped me through this. I love him so much. I told him the second you woke up he may not get to see me much."

I chuckle. "Don't push him to the curb for me."

She shrugs. "I'm sure he's tired of me anyway."

"I doubt that."

"Ugh. I'm an awful friend. Here I am talking about my boyfriend when..." Her chin quivers and tears fall down her cheeks.

I shake my head. "No, stop. It's okay."

"I'm so sorry," she says through thick tears. "I really tried to be positive and happy."

I squeeze her hand. "It's okay."

"How can you say that? Your mom told me your memories are messed up and that you haven't really reacted to much. It's a lot to process, I'm sure."

"I guess."

"Ugh, these hospital gowns are so depressing," Cherry says. I know she's trying to lighten the mood.

"I really thought I could handle this."

"What do you mean? Being in the hospital? I don't think anyone can, really."

"No. Being here."

Cherry wrinkles her eyebrows. "Um. What?"

"I spent so much time wishing I could come back so I could see you and my family. I know Vincent's messing with me. He does this all the time and I'm never ready for it. It's like I'm just one of those girls who no matter how bad her boyfriend treats her. She always falls for his games."

"This isn't your fault at all, Megan. You haven't fallen for any of his crap. Not since you broke up with him. You're not one of those girls. You saw what a terrible person he is and left him."

"He's going to keep messing with me. This isn't over for him. Not unless I go back to him and pretend like everything is okay or unless he's dead."

"The police will find him and lock him up then he can't ever mess with you."

"I have to tell you what happened."

Cherry wipes a tear. "What is it? Do you remember anything? I'm sure the police will want to know. They've talked to the other victims, but there really isn't much to go on. It's like he legit snapped one day." She inhales a deep breath.

I hate seeing the pain and confusion and sadness in her eyes. Vincent has to fix this. I don't know how, but he has to.

I shake my head and take her hand. "I have to tell you the truth, Cherry, but you have to promise not to say a word. Not to anyone. Not even my parents."

She furrows her eyebrows. "Megan, if you know something, you need to tell the police. They are out there looking for him."

"You have to listen to everything I say. Hear me out. I need you to believe me and I know this is going to be so far-fetched and ridiculous sounding, but you are my best friend. I have to tell you."

"O-okay. Is everything okay?"

"No. None of this is okay. Everything is so messed up. The police will never find Vincent because he escaped back to Arvada. Look, everyone seems to think this school shooting happened, but it didn't."

Cherry gasps. "What?"

"Right after prom Vincent held me hostage in his basement."

Her jaw drops as a horrified look crosses her face. "What?"

"I escaped after setting his house on fire. He got out and followed me to Casper's. Then he shot me." I take a deep, shaky breath. "Do you remember my dreams at all?"

"Yeah. The ones that consumed you. About you and Casper falling in love and breaking up with Vincent. Then something about Elves and Sprites."

"All of it is real."

She cocks an eyebrow. "Um." She looks at me like I have seriously lost my mind.

"I know it sounds crazy, but it's real."

I take a moment, briefly considering the implications if I actually tell my best friend the truth. "I'm a Sprite. I am an immortal being. Vincent and I are both Sprites and Casper is an Elf. Those dreams were the story of my life. Casper and I fell in love and found a witch. She made us a potion so we could escape to the human world. We were born into human lives, given only dreams to find each other in each life.

"After Vincent shot me, he took Casper and me back to our immortal world, Arvada, by way of the Nuummite Jewel."

I try to ignore the baffled look on Cherry's face as I explain everything to her. "The Jewel is to keep Vincent from becoming a dragon and the Sprites and Elves have been at war for centuries because of the Jewel. But neither side knew the truth about it."

She slowly nods. "Yeah. I remember you talking about a jewel."

"I haven't been in a coma. Vincent took us back to Arvada and it was terrible. He tried killing Casper and took me back to our home. He made me think Casper hated me and never loved me. Gave me up for the Jewel. It was awful. I saw so much death and blood." I shake my head as if to make the horrible images in my head vanish. But they stay. They're always there. And I can still smell the coppery scent of blood.

I continue my story and watch her face become more and more horrified especially when I talk about the dragons and pretty much all of it. I feel embarrassed telling her because it all sounds like something on TV.

"Because we came back here when we did, the Jewel messed up the time-space continuum. I have to go back to Arvada, Cherry. Vincent will find Casper if he hasn't already, or he'll come back for me."

Her face lightens up. "Man, either they gave you amazing drugs or your dreams are scarily vivid. You should definitely write this down. This will make for an amazing story." She gives a nervous laugh.

My heart sinks. She doesn't believe a word I've said. Not that I blame her. If I were in her shoes, I probably wouldn't believe me either. I don't know what I can do to convince her.

"I just mean...it could make a good book. With dragons and witches. Fairies and elves."

"Cherry, I know how it sounds. Do you understand what I'm saying? Casper isn't really dead."

She clears her throat, and her eyes fill with tears. "Vincent..." She swallows and wipes a tear from her cheek. "Vincent killed Casper." Her voice cracks. "He's been missing since the shooting. The police are tracking him. I have to believe they'll find him."

I shake my head.

Her face drops. "Megan, I...I think you need some rest. They said sometimes when you wake from a coma, your mind is a jumbled mess and that what you dream you really think happened."

I can feel my temper rising. "I have to rescue Casper. What if Vincent gets to him? Of course, everyone here thinks so because of this strange, concocted story Vincent made everyone believe. I need to get back. He's made me forget things again. He messed up everything making everyone believe he did this horrible thing."

"That's because he did, Megan. He took it upon himself to walk into that school and kill people." I can hear the anger and sadness in her voice. "And he will pay for this."

"He's going to pay for a lot of things. I'm going to make sure he does."

"How?"

"I'm going to kill him."

She gasps and her eyes widen. "I know he deserves it, but you can't just take it upon yourself to do that. That's not who you are."

I shake my head. "He will never stop. You should've seen all the horrible things he did in Arvada. I can't imagine what else he will do here if he's still around."

"The police will find him."

I look at her in disbelief. "Not if he's in Arvada."

"It isn't real!" she shrieks. "Vincent didn't shoot you right after prom. That isn't what happened."

I let out a frustrated groan. I want to hit something. The police and everyone else are wasting their time. Vincent's probably long gone by now.

"Why can't you believe me? I know it sounds ridiculous, but it's the truth." My chin quivers and it takes everything I have to keep my voice level. I know I have no right to get upset with her and I don't know why I expected her to believe me like it was nothing.

Her face reddens. I shouldn't have brought up Arvada or anything about my true self. She thinks I'm a crazy person. For a brief second, I think maybe I can use my magic on her, but I'm a human now, at least I think I am. I'm so weak it feels like I am. I don't even know anymore. Either way, Vincent has messed up so badly. She wouldn't have known he shot me after prom because we left right after that.

"I know everyone told me to tell you things in bits and pieces, but you have to know what Vincent did. You have to remember it."

"I remember everything he's ever done to me."

"Then remember that he killed several people and injured several. Including you. That day will always be with us, but you act like it never happened. I don't know if you're avoiding it or what."

"I told you what happened."

She closes her eyes for a few seconds like she's counting to ten. Maybe she is. Maybe I'm frustrating her beyond belief. I wish she would believe me and not Vincent.

She takes my hand again. "You broke up with Vincent the night of prom and a couple of weeks later, you and Casper started dating. You two were inseparable. It was intense. He really loved you. You had the summer of your lives, not to sound cliché. You kept telling me how scared you were to go back to school and face Vincent. Especially after his mom died at the beginning of the summer."

"No. None of that happened."

"Casper told you he'd protect you because we all knew how dangerous Vincent had been. I mean, he drove Casper off the road." Tears overflow and run down her cheeks. She lets out a curse. "I hate crying."

She takes a beat. "Casper saved you. No one knew what Vincent was going to do. He even talked to you prior saying he was going to leave you alone and that he was going to move on. But clearly he didn't."

What a horrible thing to make them believe. "It's awful what he did. I swear to you I will fix this."

"This isn't up to you to fix."

"Someone has to."

"Yeah, the police."

I roll my eyes.

We're quiet for a moment, probably trying not to anger each other any further. We're both being stubborn, and I know I'm not helping at all. I missed Cherry so much and I don't want to ruin our time by arguing about what's real and what's not. But it doesn't look like she's going to help me.

"Have you told anyone else all this?"

"No. No one else would believe me. I mean, I told Dr. Ellis that Vincent was here when I woke up and he brushed it off."

Her blue eyes widen. "Whoa. Vincent was here?"

"Yes. Said he needed to fix everything. That's why I have to get out of here. He said he was coming back for me." My pulse edges higher.

"Omigod. You need to tell the police. Are you sure he was here? I mean, it wasn't a dream, was it?"

I roll my eyes. Then it hits me. Vincent messed with everyone's minds here so that no one would believe they saw him.

Great. There is a psychopath roaming the streets who can compel people. How am I going to be safe from that?

"Amber called me the other day," she says, and I know she wants to change the subject.

"Why?"

"She was asking about you. If we heard anything. She's really changed. I mean, we all have. She's definitely a lot nicer now. It's weird that she calls. We mostly talk about the shooting."

"One of the articles I read said that I saved her."

Cherry nods. "Yeah. She says Vincent was pointing the gun right at her, but you stepped in. People think he was looking for Casper and others were just in the wrong place at the wrong time. I know a couple of guys tried to stop him, but they were shot." She wipes tears from her eyes. "Sorry. I didn't want to bring you down."

"It's okay." It really happened to Cherry, and I know she needs to get through it. I hate all of this. I can't believe Vincent would put so many innocent people through this. "You're not going to tell anyone what we talked about, right?"

She shakes her head. "No. I can bring you some notebooks so you can write all this out. I know you and Vincent were working on a story before and you were writing about the dreams. Maybe this can be a new story or something."

She sounds so hopeful, and I don't want to let her down. I don't want her thinking her best friend is a crazy person. "Yeah. Sounds good."

Cherry bites her lip. "You should rest. You've been through so much. I'll come back tomorrow."

"I don't want to rest anymore. I need to get out of here." I need to be with Casper.

She starts crying and wraps her arms around me. "It's going to be okay. I promise. We'll get through this. Together. I'm so sorry."

I let her comfort me, but something feels off about it. She doesn't believe me. She thinks I'm a psycho with a messed-up mind.

Granted, if someone told me all of this, I would think the same. To be fair, when I started having those crazy dreams, I felt the same. How can I convince my best friend that this is the truth so I can leave this place and save Casper?

Six

 can only imagine each time my family or Cherry talks to me, they all update each other with a progress report about me. *Well, today she didn't sound crazy. Today, she seemed off. She can't remember that. She needs to do this.* It's all a blur of pain, medication, and strange looks. I feel like I always have to be perfect since they're watching me so closely.

Mom and Jonathan have been here every day after they get off work and talk about their days. I never thought I would ever miss that. Even the dramatic animated way my mom explains whatever happened that day.

"And then she had the *nerve* to tell me the report was wrong." Mom throws her hands up in the air and lets out a dramatic frustrated groan.

I chuckle. It's funny how much we talk now and how close we've become after I told her about my attack. Now it's like she wants to get to know me or spend time with me. I'm not used to it, but I really like it. She actually listens to me now.

"I'm sorry," I say. "Hopefully tomorrow will be better."

"Well let's hope so. How are you feeling today?"

"I'm okay. Tired of being here."

Mom frowns and moves a strand of hair behind her ear. "You won't be here much longer.

"So they say. It gets kinda boring during the day." I've had a speech therapist work with me as well as helping me relearn how to eat and drink. It's the strangest thing. Something that was once second nature you have to relearn. I never thought I would be someone who would have to do that.

As promised, Cherry brought me some notebooks. I've written some, but I can't concentrate. Another side effect of being in a coma, I guess. Or being shot. Or being through a vortex. Or drinking a potion that makes you appear dead. Could be any number of things.

I've checked my social media and it was strange to see because it's filled with pictures of Casper and me together. Cherry and I are in some and there are a bunch of pictures of Savannah. There are so many dated from this summer. I don't understand it. I've even researched space time continuum, but it was way over my head. What is even more bizarre was when I looked at my Facebook. So many people from school posted on my wall wishing me a quick recovery and talking about how sad they are that I'm in a coma.

It's baffling because these people never said two words to me. Maybe I'm being too harsh. I got some private messages from some. One from Amber and one from Casper's friend, Brad.

Amber wrote an entire novel and I skimmed through it. She apologized and expressed a lot of feelings. It's so sad that everyone believes it happened and I guess to them, it really did. Brad's message is not friendly at all. It's filled with anger and resentment because I chose Casper over Vincent. Had I not done that, Casper would still be alive.

I haven't responded to any messages or comments. I don't even know what to say to anyone. Glad it took me getting shot for you to acknowledge my presence?

"Are the pain meds helping at all? Does your back still hurt?" Mom asks.

"Yeah." It's a constant nagging ache and it sucks because it never hurt when I was in Arvada. "Physical therapy is kicking my butt right now."

"I know, honey. Just keep powering through it. How do you feel about talking to someone?"

"What do you mean?" I ask her.

"Well, Dr. Ellis thinks it would be advisable if you talked to someone about what happened or about anything you wanted to."

"I don't know. Wouldn't they think I was crazy or something? Knowing what was inside my head?"

"No. They're there to help."

I mull it over in my head. It could be good to get rid of some of these memories that are embedded in my head. If that's even possible. I know I'd never be able to tell the therapist the complete truth, otherwise they will for sure send me to a nut house. If therapy is what it takes to leave here, I'll do it. I just hope it won't be too late by the time I return.

"I've been seeing someone."

"Really?" I ask, surprised. I never thought of her needing therapy. I always thought she was too good for it or something. Maybe it's helping her change and be more understanding.

"Seeing you here for weeks and knowing what happened to you…I just…I needed someone to talk to. I felt guilty for so long. Like I couldn't protect you at all." Tears well in her eyes, and I want to hurt Vincent even more for making my mom feel like something so traumatic actually happened.

"Mom, it wasn't your fault."

She nods. "I know but you're my baby girl. Of course, I'm going to always want to protect you. You've been through so much because of that monster."

That's the truth. I'm not even sure how I've managed to still be somewhat sane after all he put me through. Or Casper. How many times has he tried killing Casper? I've lost count and that's really sad. What is it about Vincent that makes him want to torture people? Is it because he's not getting what he wants or what he thinks he deserves? It has never made any sense to me, and I know a lot of it is his dad and how much control he has over Vincent. There are so many people out there who could break that control. But not Vincent. He's just like his father. He has to be in control in his own way. And he left me here to clean up his mess.

"How are your dreams?" Mom asks. "Or are you having any?"

"I can't really remember any of them." Except I dream of dead bodies, dragons, and Vincent. It's been a couple of nights since I've seen Casper in my dreams. I hate it. I miss him. I never dreamt about him when I was in Arvada either. I hate the twisting ache that hits me whenever I think of Casper and how much I miss him. I hate how we only have small moments of happiness before Vincent ruins them. And I hate that we're apart, yet again.

"Hey." Mom pulls me to her and holds me tight.

I didn't realize I started crying, and now that I've started, I can't stop. It's a full-on ugly cry. All the pain and heartache I endured while in Arvada, and even in this human life, comes to a head. It feels endless.

"It's okay," Mom says. "Cry as much as you need, sweetie." She starts rocking me, and I just let it all out. There is nothing like having your mom comfort you. A mom who would never turn her back on you or abandon you. I'm very lucky and I don't want to take advantage of these moments. Because right now she's the only thing keeping me together.

Seven

made a mistake," I tell Casper. It's been a few nights, but we finally found each other again. I'm not sure why we've been having trouble. Unless Vincent is interfering. Casper and I hold hands as we stand in a meadow. Long grass with wildflowers scatter to the edge of the horizon and beyond that are beautiful, sprawling mountains swallowed by blue smoke. Tall trees surround the meadow as butterflies dance in a delicate manner here and there. As the clouds drift across the sky, shafts of golden sun illuminate the meadow in patches. I inhale scents of evergreens and clean air.

Somewhere nearby I hear a stream of water like a creek.

I know this place. Casper and I had come to the mountains in one of our lifetimes. He must have been thinking about it.

"What happened?"

"I thought I could trust Cherry and I told her everything. It's insane what Vincent has done." I explain everything about the shooting and as always, he listens intently.

He shakes his head. "I can't believe this. When do you get out of the hospital?"

"Soon."

"I talked to the witch. She says you have to find the Jewel in order to return."

Of course. I tip my head back and peer into the sky. "The only way I can do that is if I find Vincent."

"You can't do that."

"Why? I mean, not that I want to or anything, but he's my only way back home. Did you ask the witch if you could return?"

"She says there isn't a way. It will kill me. She also says you and Vincent shouldn't have returned the way you did. You're right about the time space continuum. It messed up everything. She told me we can't keep meddling in the human world."

"If we return, will it right everything?"

"Yes. You have to return during a celestial event. She said if we can bring the Jewel to her, she'll destroy it."

"Won't that turn Vincent into the dragon permanently?"

"She wants us to kill him when you return."

I nod. "I'll find Vincent and convince him to return us both. Then the second we get back, we kill Vincent."

He shakes his head. "No. Megan, you can't find Vincent. You can't."

"Why?"

"It's too dangerous. He shot you and you almost died. Before that, he was going to hang you."

"I know. But when he came to see me, he was very remorseful. He won't kill me. He's not a bad guy. His father—"

Casper pulls away from me, anger flashing in his eyes. "You never see it, Megan. You never see what he's done. You're still trying to save him and for what? Why do you still defend him?"

"I'm not defending him! What choice do we have, Casper? Am I supposed to stay here without you?"

"How would you even find him? How could you take the Jewel from him? You know what it did to you last time."

I remember. The Jewel possessed me and made me bring it back to Vincent and Jacques. It was the most bizarre feeling. "I can do this, Casper. I'm not weak anymore. I know what he's done to me."

"If you find him, what's to stop him from killing you?"

"He won't. He still loves me. I can pretend again. I can play his game."

"This is ridiculous. You're going to get yourself killed."

"You did this before. Don't you have faith in me? You think I can't do this? Why do you think I put you to sleep before?"

"Am I wrong for wanting to protect you? Damn, Megan. I love you so much and it's killing me that I can't be there with you or that you're not here with me. All I want is to be with you. But no matter what, you're still fighting something."

"You're not wrong. You know as well as I do, that we will never be happy if he's alive."

"What if you die?"

"I'll come back in another lifetime, and we'll try again."

He lets out a curse and runs his hands through his hair. "Do you even hear yourself? How can you say that? What if he takes you hostage again? What if—"

"We can't focus on the what ifs. I want this to end just as much as you do. I'm miserable without you, but I don't see another way." Why is Casper being difficult? There isn't another way to do this. "If you can come up with another way, I'm all ears. Trust me. I don't want you anywhere near Vincent. He's destroyed us too many times."

"What am I supposed to do?"

"I'm stronger than you think. I can do this. You have to believe me." It's time for me to do what's right. Casper's sacrificed enough for both of us. It's my turn to do the same. Grabbing his face in my hands, I force him to meet my eyes. "I will find the Jewel. I will do this for us."

I kiss him and he relaxes slightly. We're quiet for a long moment as we enjoy each other's embrace.

Casper lets out a sigh. "I don't want you to do this."

"I have to. I can convince him. He won't hurt me. Especially if he thinks I'm in love with him. It won't be easy." The words leave a sour taste in my mouth. I don't want to do this again, but I have to. For Casper and me.

He grasps my face in his hands forcing me to look at him. "Are you sure."

Peering into his brown eyes, I nod. "Yes. I would do anything for you." I reach up and press my lips to his, kissing him with a passion that warms my entire body.

Eight

Trees whizz by in a blur of colors of green, orange, yellow, and brown. I grip the door handle praying that I won't get sick. I don't even know the last time I've been in a car. It's definitely different than being in Arvada and I'm not used to it. I'm trying to ignore the sickening feeling inside my stomach that threatens to escape. I'm not sure if it's from being in a car or the medication cocktail that's still buzzing through me.

After being in the hospital for almost two months, I'm finally going home. Physical therapy helped, but I'm still in crutches which is weird. All the doctors and nurses were so happy for me when I pushed myself and didn't give up. They don't understand the urgency. I have to get better so I can find Vincent. I can't be hobbling around trying to find some psycho.

Another thing I'm happy about are the jeans and sweater I'm wearing. They are so much more comfortable than corsets and dresses. It's a little chilly outside, but we can never prepare for fall weather in Alabama. We never know if it's going to be overcast and eleven degrees or sunny and seventy.

Being home feels bizarre. I haven't been there in so long. All five of my dogs greet me and I never thought I would be so happy to have all of them licking me, crawling all over me and freaking out. Especially Savannah. She immediately climbs on my shoulder and stays there. The simple gesture almost brings that lump of sadness to the base of my throat, but I'm able to shove it away. I won't be here forever, and I guess I need to make the best of my time here. To make sure I spend as much time with these furballs as I can.

When I return to my room, it looks different than I remember. The aqua comforter is new on my bed. There's a silver pattern lining all over it and my bed is made. The walls are a grayish-purple color, and above my bed are pictures that make a large rectangle shape. I move closer and my heart slams into my chest.

Pictures of Cherry and me. Pictures of Casper and me. Pictures of my dogs and family. I don't even know where they came from because I didn't take them. Is this all some big joke? Would Vincent really have gone through this much trouble? Why would he make everyone think that Casper and I were together all summer? None of this makes sense. Is that what the Jewel did?

Climbing awkwardly on top of my bed, I get a closer look at the pictures and my fingers brush over one of Casper and me. We're smiling, our faces together and in the background a band is playing at what looks like a day concert. My hair is pulled back in a ponytail and I'm wearing a tank top. Casper's wearing a simple white T-shirt.

But I have no memory of it.

Savannah jumps on the bed next to me, pawing at me to pick her up and I do like she's a toddler. I snuggle her close and look at more pictures. Cherry and me posing for our senior year pictures. I almost don't recognize myself. I'm wearing a simple necklace with a swan pendant and a black velvet drape that shows my shoulders. My dark hair is straight, and my smile looks genuine. Almost like I was really happy.

Have Vincent and I been back in the human world longer than I think? Did we escape to Arvada in May and return shortly after and live our lives until he shot up a school?

No. I haven't been here since May. What did he do to me? What has he done to everyone? Someone had to have photoshopped these pictures. They aren't real.

"I contemplated whether or not I should take those down," Mom says as she enters my room. "But I just couldn't bring myself to do it. Casper was a good man. He was good for you."

"He still is," I mumble.

"What?" Her voice moves closer.

I have to constantly watch what I say around everyone. They all think Casper is dead. Now that I'm home, I can concentrate on trying to figure out where Vincent is. Casper says he's not in Arvada. Where is he?

"Are you hungry? Do you need anything?"

I shake my head and turn to face her with Savannah still in my arms. "No, I'm okay." It's weird to have Mom constantly be at my side. I'm not used to it. I like it though.

"That dog missed you so much."

"I missed her, too."

"I'm cooking your favorite tonight."

Lasagna. For the first time in a long time, my mouth actually salivates. Hopefully, I can eat it without getting sick because seeing these pictures and how much my room has changed is kinda making me nauseous. And I'm still reeling from all the drugs in the hospital.

"That sounds great."

She lets out a sigh and watches me for a second before her eyes well with tears. "I'm so glad you're home and you're okay." She gathers me in her arms and holds me tight. Savannah wriggles from the tight grasp but stays in my lap.

Mom kisses my forehead and closes the door as she leaves.

I'm exhausted but I have to start. I open my laptop and wait for it to boot up. Savannah stays in my lap as I comb the internet. I don't even know what I'm looking for or how to find it.

I type in his name. Tons of articles and pictures pop up. Police statements. Eyewitness accounts of seeing him. Most turned out to be untrue or a case of mistaken identity. An hour passes and I lean back in my chair, needing to stretch. Savannah hops down and I stand. My back is stiff, and it hurts.

Where are you, Vincent? He likes the mountains and parks. His family here is pretty limited. He had a friend, but I never met him.

God, what a dumb girl I was. I dated a guy and never even met his friend. Never met his mom and only saw his dad once. Granted, his human family isn't real, but I didn't know it at the time.

If Vincent erased my memories, why did he only erase some? Usually, he erases everything, and I still remember Casper. What happened when we returned? Where were we? Examining my mind for anything, I search for a clue or something I can use.

It was dark. Wooded. There were lights. Then I woke up in the hospital. What did he do?

Savannah whines. I look down at her and she's shaking with her tiny paw up by her chest. I didn't realize I had been pacing and I know she senses my nervous energy.

I take a deep breath and try to bend over to pick her up, but I can't. It's so frustrating how limited my body is now.

I'm so angry that he shot me again and left me to deal with this. I can't believe any of it. Why would he do it? How could he kill all those Elves, bring me back here and make everyone think there was a shooting? Whether he meant it or not, he brought us back here and really messed up everything. Didn't he know what would happen?

I inhale another breath. Sick of asking the same endless questions. Sick of trying to figure out Vincent and his motives.

"Megan, are you okay?" Mom asks, peeking inside.

"Yeah."

"What is it?" She crosses the room.

"I was just thinking. That's all."

"I know all of this has to be frustrating and confusing. Unfortunately, I don't think anyone will ever make sense of these things. I'm so sorry you're dealing with this." She gathers me in her arms the second she notices my chin quiver. "I'm sorry."

"I miss him."

"I know."

We stay like that for what seems forever.

"Are you hungry? Let's have a family dinner."

It's been a long time since I've sat with my family. Mom helps me out of my room and to the dining room table. Jonathan and Ron are already there. The dogs are under the table hopelessly waiting for any one of us to drop something. It's so hard not to give in to those adorable puppy dog faces.

I'm not really that hungry, but I want to be here. I've missed my family and I want to enjoy the time with them, while I'm here. I don't know how much longer I'll be here.

Mom scoops out some lasagna and for once, the topic of conversation isn't Vincent or the school shooting or me being in a coma. We laugh over how Savannah refuses to touch the ground when it's raining or when Radar takes over Jonathan's bed like it's his own or how they dip their entire heads under water and blow bubbles. I've missed it and I love that it gets my mind off what's happening in Arvada and everything else.

After dinner, Mom and Ron go to bed and Jonathan and I end up hanging out in in the living room barely watching some weird movie on TV.

"What have you been up to?" I ask. It's been since May that I've seen him, though he thinks I've seen him more than that.

He shrugs. "Working. School. Or was." Last I knew, Jon was working as a programmer intern at a fairly decent-sized company and getting his bachelor's degree. He's always been into that nerdy stuff, but it pays well and he's so good at it. I remember when he was in high school, he created an actual platform for people to make interactive online games. From the looks of him, he's like the gazelle version of a human. Very lanky and not at all athletic. I swear he eats as much as a rhino but never gains a pound. While I on the other hand even dream about eating Cheetos, I gain a pound.

"How's all that going?"

Another shrug. "It's okay. I ended up withdrawing from school this semester."

"What? Why?"

"Uh...because my sister was in a coma? It's been hard without you."

"Really?"

He looks at me confused, then returns his gaze to the TV. "Why do you sound so surprised?"

"I don't know. Everyone always seemed like they were upset with me all the time."

"That's just Mom and Ron. You know how they are. I was never upset with you."

I nod. "Yeah, but now even Cherry is."

"It's been tough on everyone, I guess. We've been through a lot of emotions. I'm glad you're okay."

"Me, too." Jonathan's never really been the kind to talk about his feelings or even say things like this, so I know he means it and I can tell it's had quite an impact on him. I hate that. I hate what Vincent's done. He needs to fix this, and I have to make him. Somehow.

Jonathan and I finish the movie and I return to my room with Savannah. I thumb through my new phone and see Casper's name in the list of contacts. I long to text or call him. Anything. I miss his voice. I know I'll find him in my dreams, though as soon as I lie down, I'm wide awake. The throbbing, stabbing pain in my backside isn't helping. I have prescription pain medication and I take one. Then wait. Eager to see Casper and feel him again.

Nine

an you describe your relationship with Vincent Young?" Officer Freeman asks. He's completely bald, a little overweight, with kind blue eyes, but I bet they could turn cold in an instant. He seems a little bored asking me questions, almost as if he knows I won't be able to help him much.

We're sitting at the dining room table in our home with a couple of officers. Mom sits beside me trying to chew a hole in her lip and Ron's at work or whatever he's doing these days. It's almost noon, so I'm sure he'll be home soon.

"Um. He was my boyfriend."

"How long were y'all together?"

I don't even know how to answer that. "Six months?" I take a guess.

"Did you ever see any kind of signs of violence or anything?"

"H-he drove Casper off the road."

Mom gasps. "That was *him*?"

"He killed a guy who...attacked me."

"How do you know it was him?" Officer Freeman asks.

"He told me."

His eyebrows raise. "And you didn't think to tell anyone?"

Blood creeps to my cheeks and I intertwine my fingers over and over. "I couldn't."

"What do you mean you couldn't?" He's getting frustrated now and starting to scare me. I don't want to say the wrong thing and end up in jail. I haven't done anything and maybe I should've kept my mouth shut about this. But really, what's it going to hurt? They won't catch Vincent.

I guess I can finally tell everyone this part. "He locked me in a basement."

"Megan? What?" Mom's jaw is wide open as she stares at me in horror. "When?"

"The night of prom. He kept me there for days." I tell them both everything that happened once we got back to Vincent's house and the days that followed.

With the exception of us returning to Arvada. I tell them all of the things Vincent confessed.

Mom furrows her eyebrows. "You were here, Megan. You came home the night of your prom. I would've known if you had gone missing."

"Did you report any of this?" Officer Freeman asks.

"No. I knew that if Casper and I reported any of this, Vincent could potentially hurt us again."

He cocks an eyebrow. "He *did* hurt you and several others."

"Okay what would you have done had we told you? There was no proof of either incident."

Mom shakes her head. "That doesn't matter."

"Megan, you should always report such incidences. The police can always help you."

"I'm sorry. I was just really scared." Not that anyone could've done anything to Vincent had I told them. He would've gone back to Arvada like he has now.

"Do you know why Vincent went to school that day and shot people?"

Yeah, because he messed with things and now you think it happened. "No."

Officer Freeman narrows his eyes like he knows I'm lying. He's learning forward, his huge forearms resting on the table and a small pad of paper in his hands with a pen. I don't like the intensity of his stare. I can't exactly tell him the truth, but I'm a terrible liar.

"Is there something I should know? Anything that will help us find Vincent?"

"I don't have any information." There's no way I can tell them that he may be in another world. I'm getting agitated and I want to lie down. Being questioned by the police is tiresome because I can't exactly help them out. Or can I? "I want to help find him though."

"We have a whole team of people looking for him."

"They're obviously not looking hard enough. It's been over a month, and no one has found him. What does his dad say? Have you asked any of his friends?"

"His dad moved away, but he's been talking to police and cooperating. Do you know any of Vincent's friends?"

I frown. "No. I never met any of his friends. Vincent was always secretive. I never even met his mom."

"Do you think he will contact you at all?"

"I don't know. He visited me in the hospital, but the doctor thinks I dreamed it."

"It's highly possible that you dreamed it. It would've been very difficult for him to get passed nurses and security."

"Not if he changed his looks and stole scrubs."

"What did he look like?"

I tell Officer Freeman everything I know about that night whether it was a dream or not. I feel like I can figure out what's a dream and what isn't. I'm not that far gone like everyone apparently thinks I am.

"Is there anything else you can tell me?"

"That's all I know. How are you going to find him? Do you have any leads?"

"I understand you want to find him. Everyone wants justice. We are doing everything to find him. If he does contact you, you have to tell us."

"Is she going to be safe?" Mom asks. "She's been through so much because of him. Does she need protection?"

"I'm fine, Mom. Really."

"I think she will be fine. He would be stupid to contact her, but we've seen it happen before. I think we have all we need for now."

"Will you let me know if you have any leads?" I ask him as he stands from the table.

He exchanges a look with Mom. "We'll let you know if you're in any danger. Thank you for your time."

Mom walks him to the door and comes back into the dining room with a strange look. I can't decide if she's mad, sad, or what. "Why haven't you told any of us anything? Why are you so afraid?"

Because it never mattered to anyone here. "It's not that big of a deal," I say, immediately regretting the choice of words.

"Not that big of a deal? Megan, he put Casper in a coma. And he killed your attacker? When did that even happen? How do you know he did these things?"

"Because he told me. Vincent is obsessed with me."

"You're not safe here."

I roll my eyes. "Mom, I'm fine. Besides, he's long gone."

She shakes her head, and her chin quivers. "I have to keep you safe."

"You are." I hobble on one foot and gather her in a hug. "It's okay, Mom. I promise."

I never thought I would have to comfort my mom like this, and I know she thinks it's strange that I'm being so calm about everything. But the officer is right. Vincent would be stupid to show his face anywhere near me. I still don't know how he got into the hospital room or where he is. I have to get through physical therapy so I can get out there to find him.

GABRICA NICHOLAS

Ten

I've never been to a therapist's office. I've only read about them or seen them in movies. Fancy leather couches. Weird knickknacks on their desks. Degrees plastered across the wall. Dim lights for ambiance I assume. Dr. Brown's office is not like those at all. It's bright with windows that lets the sun filter through, glinting in a beautiful way. Drawings and sweet notes from little kids thanking her cover the beige walls. She has a simple floral couch and a green chair across from one another. Both look like she got them from a garage sale.

It's December and while it's cold outside, Dr. Brown's space heater is set to a thousand degrees. I'm starting to sweat underneath my sweater.

I haven't had time to start my search for Vincent because everyone is practically attached at my hip. I still can't drive so I'm kinda at everyone's mercy until then but I'm no longer in crutches and I can walk normally, except for my slight limp. Casper and I see each other every night in my dreams. It's the only solace I have. I keep searching online and I've found actual forums praising Vincent for what he did. How on earth could anyone praise that?

"There are many sick people out there," Dr. Brown says. "Same ones who praise Charles Manson or others like him.

I shake my head, disgusted.

"Your mom tells me you don't really believe the shooting happened. That you live in another world."

I stare at her shocked. How does Mom even know that? My heart falters. Cherry told her what I said? I can't believe this. First, Florence betrays me, now Cherry? I can feel the blood drain from my face as I let the betrayal of my best friend stab me. I don't know who to be mad at more, my mom for telling the doctor or Cherry for telling my mom.

"I guess you want to hear all about how crazy I am now."

Dr. Brown and I have been talking about everything that's happened since I came out of my coma. Mom filled her in with everything that happened before I guess. Not really sure what all she told Dr. Brown. She seems pretty interested in what I have to say, though she is getting paid so I'm sure I could recite the dictionary and she'd be fascinated. She jots down few notes, but for the most part, she watches me which only makes me fidget more. I've never been a fidgeter, but ever since I woke up from the coma it's like I can't stop.

"I don't think you're crazy," Dr. Brown says. "We can talk about anything you would like."

"I'm not sure how all this works. I've never talked to a therapist before."

"Well, this is your time. We can talk about anything."

"Anything?"

"Yes."

"Do you have to tell my mom or anyone?"

"Whatever you say in here is completely confidential."

"Yeah, but I'm sure you'll have to tell my mom and lock me away somewhere."

"Why do you think that?"

"Because it's true. Isn't that how it goes?"

"Not necessarily."

I nod and look away, unsure of what else to say. I want to tell her about Arvada and Casper, but she already doesn't believe me. I can tell by the way she mentioned it. No one does. Why would they? If I were human and someone told me all about such a place or anything like that, I wouldn't believe them either. Humans would never believe in something like that. Maybe a select few. I wonder how much Cherry told Mom about Arvada. Thinking about everything I told Cherry makes me cringe. Of course, no one here would believe that. Dragons? Elves? Sprites? I feel stupid and embarrassed, but most of all betrayed. Didn't Cherry think that would hurt my feelings?

"Why don't you tell me about yourself? Maybe we can start with that."

"Like what?"

"What do you like to do? What do you hate?"

"Um. Well." Clasping my hands together, I try to think of what I like to do in general. Not as human Megan. Just me. "I like to write. I used to write all the time."

"Have you tried writing at all since being home?"

I tell her that I tried in the hospital, and we talk about how much I've written and when I started. It's something that's always been ingrained in me. I love it. We talk about aspirations for the future, and after experiencing King Jacques and everything he did, I tell Dr. Brown that I want to do something with social work or maybe work toward nursing. I've seen so much death and couldn't save a single person. I always felt so helpless.

"Before all this I was so ready to leave because of how strict my parents were. They've changed though. I feel like my mom understands me more and we're closer."

Dr. Brown nods. "Tragedy tends to bring people together. Has your overall goal changed? Are you still eager to leave?"

"Yes and no. I love being here, but..." I miss Casper, I want to say. "I need to explore what's out there," I tell her instead.

"That's a fantastic goal." Dr. Brown smiles.

The room is suffocating, and I don't see how she's okay with her turtleneck and jeans. Her cropped brown hair has bits of silver in it, and she isn't wearing makeup. She seems confident and I wish I could be that way without makeup. Anytime I go without it, I swear people think I'm sick. Casper always tells me how beautiful I am with or without it.

We sit in silence a few minutes. "I hate what Vincent did."

"Do you remember what he did?"

"I guess he shot up a school." Or at least he's made people believe that.

She looks at me. "You don't believe he did?"

"I don't know. I could see him doing something like that yet at the same time, I can't."

"Why can't you?"

I shake my head. "He's just so messed up because of his dad. Not that that gives him an excuse. I always told him he could be better, but he never listened."

"Not everyone will listen even if it's in their best interest. Sometimes people have to follow their own paths to learn themselves."

"I want to help the police find him. He has to fix this."

"Sadly, there isn't much he can fix. Do you remember any details?"

I shrug. "Not a single one." *Because it didn't actually happen.* "You should ask my friend, Cherry. She seems to have told my mom everything and seems to be an expert about my life."

"You seem bitter toward her. Has she hurt your feelings?"

"She doesn't believe what I say. What I know to be true and what she thinks is the truth are two completely different things."

"How do you mean?"

I let out a breath. "Nothing. They're right. I don't remember anything."

"If you remember something differently, you can tell me. It's a safe environment."

"My mom has already told you, apparently, but I'm not crazy or a psycho."

"You aren't crazy, and I don't think that."

"Apparently everyone else does."

"Who cares what they think?"

"Easier said than done."

"Say it back to me. Tell me you're not crazy."

"I'm not crazy," I say it like a question unsure of where she's going with this.

"Now, say it like you mean it." She winks.

I bite the insides of my cheeks to keep from grinning. "I'm not crazy." I say with conviction.

"Good. Do you feel better?"

I don't know how I'm feeling. "Yeah." I look away and stare at the weird pink floral design of the couch. It looks like something from someone's grandma's house. It's comfortable enough I guess, though it has a stiff texture. I think about all the people who sat here before me. Did they ever get the help they needed? Thinking about all the pain and tears shed on this couch. What if someone from the school shooting sat here? Pouring their heart out over something they believed happen. The more I think about it, the angrier I am at Vincent.

"Are you having any dreams? Flashbacks?"

"Dreams yes. No flashbacks."

"What kind of dreams?"

"Of Casper. He's always in them. We talk. We cry. We hold each other." *Until we can be together again.* I expect her to start talking about how he's dead, that people always dream of loved ones when they die blah blah blah. But she doesn't.

"Those must be comforting." Her words take me by surprise, and I feel more comfortable with her.

"They are. As sad as it may sound, it's almost like I can't wait to fall asleep so I can see him again."

"That's only natural. It's the only time you get to see him."

"I wish I could text him or pick up the phone and call him."

It's only the first session and the more I talked to Dr. Brown the more she made me relaxed. I don't feel on edge like I do with my family and Cherry. It's like everyone has to walk on eggshells around me like I'm going to explode. I don't know what it is or why they feel that way. With Dr. Brown, it's almost like I can breathe. I don't have to watch my words as much. I noticed I stopped squirming and playing with my hands.

"How was it?" Mom asks as we both buckle our seatbelts.

I shrug. "It was okay."

"It was the first visit. It took me a couple of times to get used to my doctor before I unloaded on her."

"Yeah."

When Mom and I leave, we're quiet on the way home. It's another overcast December day. Freezing and windy. Mom has the radio on and instead of her usual blaring and singing loudly off-key, the volume is turned down low and she's not singing along. Her hands grip the steering wheel like she's super concentrated on driving. Usually, she's just relaxed. I wonder if I make her feel so on edge. Does she think her daughter is a crazy person? I don't want to drive my mom to the point of thinking she did a bad job raising her child. The thought makes me feel bad. I wonder if that's what Vincent's dad felt. I understand now why the witch told Casper he couldn't return to the human world. We're born into these lives and we're messing them up. We should never have come to this world, but once I fix everything it will be okay.

For the time I'm here, I should just play my part so as to keep everyone else happy and believing that I'm fine, which I am. The longer I play the part, the quicker I can start looking for Vincent. I've been thinking about signing on to those forums and playing along to see if someone can give me a clue, but I don't want the police to be tapping in to my every move. Can they do that? I need to figure out if Vincent really had a friend. Maybe I can start with his house.

Mom pulls to a stop at a red light, and I look to my left and see the Waffle House. The same one Casper and I ate the night we found out we shared dreams. I can't wait to get home so I can go to sleep and see Casper. Sounds pathetic if you think about it. Like I'm some forlorn love-sick girl. Which, I guess I am. I know he can't be my only fixation right now, but he is.

"Mom, I don't want you to worry about me."

She glances at me quickly, then turns her eyes back to the road. "You're my daughter. Of course, I'm going to worry."

"I mean about what Cherry told you. It's just all in my head."

"Does this mean you believe what Vincent did?"

"I don't remember any of it. But I trust you." Even though everyone's minds are so messed up right now because of us returning. Including mine.

"I think Dr. Brown can help."

I nod. "Sure. I'm sorry if I made you crazy. I never meant to."

"You've never made me feel that way. I wish that I could've been there that day to protect you. No one should have to experience that. No one should have to get a call saying their daughter has been shot at her own damn school." Her voice shakes and rises with anger.

I squeeze her arm. "It's okay, Mom. I'm okay."

Letting out a breath, she wipes her cheek and shakes her head. "It's not okay. None of this is okay nor is it normal."

She's right about that. I don't know how to comfort her, but I guess with time she will be okay. I wonder what happens when I return to Arvada. Do they all just move on? I wonder if the witch can give me a potion for them to make them forget me once I leave, like Hermione did in Harry Potter. Tears cloud my eyes at the thought. Once I return to Arvada, I won't have parents. They saw their only daughter betray them. Maybe I can talk to them and convince them that they were manipulated by Vincent's father, King Jacques.

Too many thoughts swarm my mind, and it hurts my head.

"School starts back the second week of January," Mom says. "They've renovated it. Hopefully they've also amped up the safety," she mutters under her breath.

"And?" School seems like such a waste of time.

"Well, I need to know if you're ready to return. I'm not saying you need to give me an answer right now, but we do need to think about it."

"Okay." Pretty sure by then, I'll be gone from the human world. That's only a few weeks away. I have some serious planning to do when I get home. I've already wasted too much time.

Mom pulls into the garage and shuts off the car, but she doesn't move. "I want you to return to normal. I know there's no such thing. I'm sorry for what happened to you, and I wish there was something I could do to help you."

"You do enough. I promise."

"I know I'm not the best mother, but I really do try."

"I know you do. Let's go inside and cook dinner. I don't want to cry anymore."

She nods and wipes her cheeks. "You got it."

"I love you, Mom."

"I love you too, baby girl."

Eleven

After dinner with Mom and Rob, I take the dogs outside and watch them run around in the wooded backyard. The cold always makes them frisky. I laugh watching them play and realize how much I've missed this. They tease each other; chase each other; bark; act like total goofballs.

It's peaceful here. No war. No dragons. No fires. No burning flesh. Although, I still smell the coppery scent of blood. I don't think I'll ever not smell it. Vincent is here. Am I truly safe? Will he risk coming back here?

Something catches my eye at the far edge of the yard. Blue almost wispy looking. Like a floating ball. My heart throws itself against my chest. It's an orb.

Casper? Did Casper find a way here? Did the witch help him? I take a step toward it.

"Megan," Mom calls. "Are you okay?"

I twist around to face her. "Yeah. I'm fine. Why?" I turn back to the orb.

"The dogs have been scratching to be let in. Didn't you hear them?"

I can't stop staring at the bouncing orb. I know that's Casper and I have to go to him.

"Megan, what are you looking at?"

Looking back at my mom, I tell her nothing. When I turn back to the orb, it's gone. I follow Mom back inside and head to my room. Did I really see the orb? Is someone really messing with me? I can't calm my beating heart or the anticipation that charges through my veins. I have to investigate. If this is a way to Casper without my dreams, then maybe I won't have to find Vincent.

It seems to take forever for my parents to fall asleep. When they do, I creep down the hall to the back door, hoping like hell none of my dogs wake up. Nosy little pups.

Miraculously, I manage to get outside. I'm still in my pajamas and it's cold, but I want to know if the orb came back or if it will. I wait in the cold. Peering at the cluster of stars above, enjoying the quiet night.

As I'm about to give up, I see the orb appear once again. I march toward it, not caring that I'm leaving the house. I have to get to the orb. The further I walk, the further it seems to get from me. Maybe it's leading me to Casper. I don't know how far I walk when the orb stops. I keep going until I'm standing in front of it.

Glowing blue wispy colors grow into a sort of pathway. I can't see through it, but it's calming, pulling me to it.

Once I step through, it's silent. Like the orb Casper and I travelled in. I feel the peacefulness and it relaxes me. I scan my surroundings. I'm in a forest, but something is different about it. The tallness of the trees and the intense smell of pine. Then I see a flicker of light nearby. Then another. Then several. Thousands of tiny yellow lights glitter throughout the forest. Fireflies. Some land on me and it makes me smile. I keep walking until I reach a meadow with a great tree that has a trunk twisting its way to the branches looming over. Hundreds of fireflies congregate in the branches lighting it up like a Christmas tree.

"Megan?"

Twisting around, I see Casper and run to him. He catches me in an embrace.

"Is this real?" he asks. "How did you get here? Did you find Vincent?"

"Where are we?"

"Arvada."

I inhale sharply. "Th-There was an orb. I followed it."

His eyes widen. "It worked? I talked to the witch, and she helped me. How did you find it?"

"It was in my backyard."

He pulls me against his chest and lets out a breath. "We're safe. Maybe you won't have to find Vincent at all."

"You mean, I'm back for good?"

"I think so. The witch didn't go into details. She just told me how she could help. She said she can only help so much." He takes my face in his hands. "You're here."

I exhale, but something doesn't feel right. It was too easy for me to return. "This isn't a dream?"

"Does it feel like a dream?"

"It all feels real. The dreams have always felt real. You know that."

He leans in, pressing his lips to mine. "Does this feel real?" The way he moves his mouth with mine in a heated passion feels real. More real than any dream could provide. It's more intense, almost like our first kiss as humans in that library copy room. Just like then, my skin is set ablaze and my body throbs with a want. This is real. He's really here and we are together.

I run my hands through his hair loving the way his hands grab my hips, pulling me closer to him. "I've missed you," I say between kisses.

"I've missed you."

I let out a moan when his lips trace my jawline to my neck. He slowly unbuttons my pajama top, and I help him remove his shirt. I swear it feels like our first time. We're clumsy. Mouths are everywhere. Hands wander. We're together.

Twelve

tear through the forest. Passing trees, branches, leaves. It's dark, cold. The moonlight barely gives off enough light for me to see. I'm starting to hate the dark. I don't know what or who I'm running from, or why I'm out here. I'm shaking uncontrollably. My pulse races and I'm breathing hard. I have to get out of here. Am I dreaming? Am I starting to have the dreams of Vincent chasing me again?

I look behind me. Nothing.

My heart is thrashing in my ears and my lungs ache.

I don't know where I am, and I hate the feeling of someone chasing me or watching me. I hear no sounds and it frightens me more. I don't know how I got out here. I have to be dreaming. Except I can't wake up. Analyzing my surroundings, I see nothing but trees. My eyes are wide open, the cold making them water.

I stop for a moment, trembling and sucking in deep lungfuls of air, trying to ignore the pain in my back and all over my body. My legs are weak, and I don't know how much further I can run.

I don't know why I'm scared or what happened. Nothing comes to me. I start seeing images of Casper and me. I found him in Arvada. I went back. We made love and fell asleep. But what happened after that? Did someone find us? Where am I? The woods look familiar like they are part of the human world. How did I get back here?

A chill touches my neck. Fear slams into me. I start running again, hopeful I'll see something like civilization soon.

Seeing the road ahead, I relax a little. Maybe I can get someone's attention and they can help me. Once I reach the road, I glance behind me for a second. Someone is after me and they're about to get me. The squealing of tires forces me to look forward. A car skids to a stop right in front of me, smoke billowing behind it. Headlights blind me.

My heart jumps to my throat. I can't breathe. I swear I just saw my life flash before my eyes.

"What the hell are you doing?" the driver asks.

"I-I." I glance toward the forest.

The driver steps out and I block the headlights so I can see him. His light brown hair is short, and he wears glasses. He looks familiar, but I can't remember where I've seen him. He turns his head toward the woods and back to me. "Are you lost? Is someone chasing you?"

"I-I..." The words are stuck in my throat.

"Do you know you just ran out onto the road? I could've hit you." He's yelling at me, but he doesn't seem upset with me, more to himself. He takes a beat. "Are you okay?" he finally asks.

"Um. I don't know." My voice shakes and I can barely comprehend what's happening. I hate how much I'm trembling.

"Is everything okay? Is someone after you?"

I don't even know. Tears rush to the surface, but I push them down.

"Do you need to go to the hospital? You're miles away from everything." His eyes rove over me, not in creepy way, more of an assessment. "Were you out camping somewhere?"

I look down and see that I'm wearing my matching flannel pajamas. I'm dreaming. This has to be a dream. "N-no."

"What are you doing out here?" His voice is frantic yet concerned.

I wish I could answer him. I wish I knew why I was in the middle of nowhere. I don't even know where I am. Anxiety grows inside me.

"You're Megan Devereux, right?"

"H-how do you know me?"

"We go to school together. I'm Spencer Peterson."

The name rings a bell, but I still don't know. I'm too freaked out by why I'm out in the middle of nowhere right now.

"Can I give you a ride somewhere? It's freezing out here."

I don't have my phone on me, and I have no idea where I am. There's also a chance that once I get inside his car no one will ever see me again. Why can't I remember anything?

Ugh. This has *to be a dream*.

"Do you want me to call anyone?"

I shake my head. "I'm fine. Thanks." Crossing my arms in front of my chest, I start walking away.

"You're kidding me, right? I can't just leave you out here. I'll give you a ride."

"It's okay."

"Look, I'll take you wherever you need. Just please don't make me leave you out here."

I stop and turn around, meeting his eyes, wanting to take him up on his offer. His high cheekbones and cute face make him attractive and there's an innocence and a kindness about him. "Spencer Peterson?" Vague memories come forward. "I remember you. You were in my math class last year." He always sat in the back of the room and never said a word. But he's smart at math. I'm terrible at it and because I never understand it, I'm usually writing or texting Cherry in class.

"Yeah."

While he seems harmless, I'm still a little wary. I agree to let him give me a ride. He opens the passenger door for me, and I slide into the seat. Heat blasts from the vents and when he gets in the car, he turns it down thankfully. It was drying out my contacts.

Spencer starts driving and we're quiet for a few minutes. I'm praying he won't do anything to me. Nice doesn't always mean nice.

"Can I ask why you're out here?"

I shrug. "I really don't remember." I'm not sure why I tell him the truth. Maybe my mind is spinning too much to come up with a lie. I expect him to laugh or start teasing me. Anything.

But he doesn't.

"Are you cold? I have a jacket—"

"No, I'm good. Thanks." I glance at the clock and my heart stops. Two thirty-four. I curse internally. Why am I out so late? Did I really see an orb and find

Casper or was it a dream? Did I sneak out? Mom is going to kill me. "I'm sorry for running into the road."

"You're lucky I was able to stop in time."

"I said I was sorry," I snap. I'm not really angry with him. Just the situation. It's scaring me and frustrating.

"Were you drinking? Partying? Playing a prank?"

"What? No. Why would you ever think this was a prank?"

"I just know how a lot of you popular people are. Although, I've never known you to be mean."

"Popular? Please."

"You dated Casper Truitt."

I don't miss the past tense he used.

"Sorry. I didn't mean to bring him up."

"It's okay. I'll see him again soon."

He clears his throat. "Um. Hopefully not *too* soon."

"Of course, not," I tell him, recovering quickly. I can't even remember if I was dreaming about Casper. I know I saw him. It wasn't a dream. It was real. What is happening to me? Am I messed up because Vincent ripped me from the human world and brought me back?

Spencer keeps giving me a sidelong glance almost like he's curious about something. The green and red dash lights illuminate his face and reflect in his glasses. I'm so embarrassed by the whole situation. Why was I running? Why can't I remember?

"Did you suffer a head injury? You know, before?" he asks.

"Before what?"

He hesitates. "Before, at the shooting."

Shooting? Oh right. The supposed school shooting. "No." I wonder what else Vincent did to me when he visited me in the hospital.

"What's the last thing you remember?"

I sift through my mind searching for anything. "I had dinner with my family. Then I went to my room." Found an orb. Found Casper in Arvada. "What day is it?" I ask, hoping I haven't missed days or whatever.

"It's Saturday. December fifteenth."

I let out a relieved sigh. Okay, I haven't missed days. I've missed hours. Which scares me. There are at least six hours missing from my memory. I'm too young to start forgetting things.

"I take it you don't have your phone on you."

"No. It's at home." At least, I hope it is.

"You really don't remember?"

I shake my head. "Please don't tell anyone. I don't need any more evidence that I need to be locked up."

He lets out a short breath. "Not that I have anyone to tell, but your secret is safe with me. For what it's worth, I understand that fear."

"What?"

He waves me off. "It's not important. I just know the feeling of having to say or do the right thing, so they don't strap on a straitjacket."

"I'm sorry."

He shrugs. "I'm sorry as well. I know you're probably dealing with a lot of crap right now."

"Yeah. Everything's a mess."

"And they still haven't found him."

"Vincent?"

"Yep. I really don't understand how he still hasn't been caught. Most of the school shooters kill themselves or are caught within seconds. But he's still out there. Probably laughing and being proud of himself. Fucking asshole."

I want to ask Spencer his story, but I'm scared. I don't think I can handle hearing more stories about it. "I'm sorry."

"Why are *you* sorry?"

If Casper and I hadn't escaped to the human world, Vincent wouldn't have followed, and we wouldn't have interfered with the humans. Vincent certainly wouldn't have lashed out on them. Or changed history or whatever he's done.

"You know this wasn't your fault."

I nod. But it is my fault. "I've been trying to find clues to find Vincent. I've been online and I have some ideas to start, but I haven't been able to drive yet."

"Shouldn't you tell the police these things?"

"They won't help. I know there are a lot of people opening their homes to him."

"What?"

I tell him about all the forums I've seen online like some crazed obsessed person.

He shakes his head. "What the hell is wrong with people?"

"I don't know. It's messed up."

The thought of asking Spencer to help me find Vincent crosses my mind, but I barely know the guy. "Do you live around here?" I ask him. I like talking to him. His voice is soft yet relaxing which is helping ease my anxiety.

"Not exactly."

"Why are you out here so late? Coming home from your girlfriend's house? Or a friend's house?" I ask but regret it. Why am I so nosy? "Sorry." I want to keep him talking, I guess. It gets my mind off the fact that my mom is going to kill me. Not that it will matter. None of this life matters. Once I return to my real world, they won't remember me. I won't even be a blip on their radar. I tried returning tonight, but something happened.

He hesitates and as I sneak a peek at him, he's gripping the steering wheel and his teeth are clenched.

I softly clear my throat. "I'm sorry. I didn't mean—"

He shakes his head. "It's not you. No girlfriend. No friend. My friend Tyler was killed that day."

"I'm sorry." I swallow the lump and return my gaze to the window. I don't know what to say. Even if I had the right words, it wouldn't matter. They're just words. Words can't really bring comfort. I'm not sure what can bring comfort for such a tragedy. Certainly not me apologizing every five minutes.

We're quiet for a while.

"I don't know what to tell my parents." I wring my hands together, trying to figure out a way to get out of this. I can't just show up to my house, especially if Mom found my bed empty.

"Tell them you needed some air or something."

"You don't know my parents."

"Aren't they asleep? Can't you just sneak back in? It's okay, you can relax." He nods toward my shaking leg.

But it's not. I know Mom's probably called a million times and she's worried. Did Casper and I find the witch? Did she make me forget the last several hours? My mind is a blank void. Like a black hole.

"Was there someone else out there? You looked scared out of your mind."

I know he wants answers, but I have none. "I don't know." I can feel his eyes on me for a few seconds. "You probably think I'm crazy, don't you?"

"Considering what all we've gone through, no. I've never thought you were crazy. I saw how much you changed when you were with Vincent. I hated it, but there wasn't anything I could've done."

"What do you mean?"

"Come on. A beautiful, popular girl like you? Don't pay attention to guys like me."

My cheeks feel warm. He thinks I'm beautiful? What? This has got to be the weirdest dream I've ever had.

Spencer rolls the car to a four way stop and looks to me. "Well?"

"Well, what?"

"Where am I going?"

I look around, but there's nothing. It's dark and it's just barren outside. "I live in Irondale near the library."

"What, no fancy mansion?"

"I don't know what you heard but no I don't live in a mansion."

We're quiet the rest of the way, and when he slows next to my house, only because he refused to drop me off at the Waffle House, I start to panic. The lights are on in the house.

"I don't know what to say to them. I don't want them knowing I don't remember." My stomach twists in knots. "Um, thanks for the ride." I open the door, and Mom bolts outside toward me with Ron in tow.

She rushes up to me, gathering me into a tight hug. I don't expect this. "Megan, where have you been? I have been calling you."

Ron eyes Spencer as he gets out of the car. "With some guy," he says with an undertone of judgement.

"Mom—"

"I'm so sorry," Spencer says. "I know we've never met, but I'm Spencer. I go to school with Megan. She couldn't sleep and called to talk about stuff."

"In your pajamas?" Mom asks in disbelief.

I shrug nonchalantly following Spencer's lead. "We just drove around."

"It's my fault. I'm so sorry," Spencer says. "I told her to leave a note or something."

I give him a sideways glance.

"Megan, you didn't even take your phone. Why would you just up and leave in the middle of the night without telling anyone?"

"I'm sorry. I woke up from a bad dream, and we started talking. I just needed to get out of here."

"She wanted to sit in the car, but I really wanted to get something to eat, so we went to get some fast food."

Mom eyes Spencer and seems to believe him. Why is he lying for me? He barely knows me and I'm the nut who ran out in the middle of the road. "Well, thank you for bringing my daughter home." She turns to me. "But you cannot do that again."

"I'm sorry," I tell her.

"Have a good night, Spencer." Mom wraps her arm around me, and we make our way inside the house, not before I glance back at Spencer.

As soon as we're inside, Mom turns to me. "What's the real story?"

"What?"

"You don't expect us to believe that you wanted to talk to some guy and went to get food at two in the morning," Ron says. "Given your track record, there's no way that's the truth." His eyes bulge and I can smell alcohol on his breath. Seriously. Why is Mom still with him? She deserves so much more and doesn't see it. I didn't see how bad Vincent was for me. You never see it; only those on the outside.

Blood rushes to my cheeks. I hate him so much.

"Ron," Mom warns. "Go away so we can talk."

"I'm just as much a parent as you are."

"Ron."

He pouts and walks away.

"Mom, that is the truth." Tears well in my eyes. "I'm really sorry. I just couldn't sleep, and the dream scared me so much."

"You could've awakened me." She sounds hurt that I didn't go to her. I hate making her feel that way."

"Why haven't you told me about Spencer before?"

"I don't know. We kinda just started talking." Nothing was truer than that.

Mom lets out a sigh. "I was really worried about you. I hope you understand why I have to know where you are at all times."

"I get it." As much as I'm a scared and annoyed, it is nice to have someone care about me. Especially since my real parents turned their backs on me. Guilt rises inside like a cloud of smoke billowing. I never meant to hurt her. I love her. How can I leave her for Arvada and Casper? "I promise it won't happen again." At least, I hope it never happens again.

Thirteen

egan?"

"Hmm?" I bring myself to meet Dr. Brown's eyes.

"Is everything okay? You seem very distant today."

"Yeah. Sorry. Lack of sleep." Understatement of the year. I'm still trying to figure out what happened last night. It's left me agitated and short with everyone.

"Do you need any help with that?"

"No." Definitely don't need anything to add to my daily assortment of drugs. Especially after what happened last night.

Maybe I need to tell Dr. Brown everything. My side of the story. Whether it makes me sound like a complete lunatic or not. I have to get this off my chest, and if she's here to listen, so be it.

"Your mom told me you left in the middle of the night with your friend Spencer."

I can feel the heat creeping into my cheeks. "Yeah. He's a friend."

"She says you know him from school. Was he there that day?"

"What day?" I ask but shake my head. "Oh. Yeah. His friend Tyler died."

"I'm sorry to hear that. Did you know Tyler?"

I shake my head. Tyler's not dead. Casper's not dead. But where would the victims be from this supposed shooting? Are they really dead? I mean would everything revert back to the way it was once Vincent and I return to Arvada? I'm hoping for that. No one deserves any of this mess. I don't understand any of this and I need to find him. My head hurts from all the confusion.

"You promise that whatever I say in here won't leave the room."

"Yes," Dr. Brown says.

"You swear it will stay between us? I mean, you've already heard it from my mom. You aren't already planning on locking me away for good? Or confirm to my mom that I'm a psycho?"

"First of all, you are not a psycho and anyone in need of help isn't a psycho. I'm not going to lock you up or anything like that. I am here to help. However, in order to do that, I have to know what's on your mind. What you're thinking. You can tell me anything."

I choose my words carefully. I don't want to bring up Arvada. "Cherry says I broke up with Vincent the night of prom. She says Casper and I dated the whole summer. None of that is true. Vincent held me hostage the night of prom until I escaped. *That's* when he shot me. Casper and I have been together for a long time."

"What makes you think he shot you then?"

"Because that's when it happened. The school shooting never happened. Vincent..." I let the words trail. I can't tell her he messed up time. "He created the story in everyone's minds and that's what they believe," I tell her, though as I said it aloud, I'm not sure it makes me sound less nuts.

"Why would he create such a story?"

"Because he's got issues. He's a manipulative, egotistical, narcissist. He's spent plenty of time manipulating me and abusing me."

"I have no doubt he's left scars deep inside you."

"I have no memory of any of this. Not Casper and me during the summer or the shooting."

"Unfortunately, that can happen in traumatic situations. You develop a sort of amnesia and post-traumatic stress. It will take time for your mind to heal."

I shake my head. "I remember everything that happened."

"Tell me what you remember."

I shake my head again. "It doesn't matter anyway. I just...I miss Casper so much." Tears rush to my eyes, and I bite my lip to keep it from quivering. I want to know what happened last night.

"I know. I'm sorry."

"He makes me so happy and it's like every time we get together, Vincent's there to tear us apart. He's never happy unless he gets what he wants. But I love Casper. He's my world. It's really hard being here without him."

"Of course, it is. It won't be easy for a long time." She pauses. "I notice you still speak in present terms about Casper."

I roll my eyes.

"It's hard to come to terms. What are some things you want to work on, Megan? What do you want to get out of these sessions?"

"I don't know. My mom's the one who wants me here."

"Do you have any plans when you graduate?"

"This whole thing is ridiculous. The shooting never happened." The more I think about this, the more insane it sounds. The more I talk, the more she will put me away which means it would be harder to get back to Arvada. I have to play along with this charade. This was a mistake. I'm so stupid. They'll lock me up and I'll never get back home.

She looks back at me with no emotion. It's almost like she has no idea how to react to what I just said. Everyone gives me that look. "Do you think you're avoiding what happened?"

"Avoiding? Absolutely not. Hard to avoid the fact that my ex-boyfriend shot me and almost killed my boyfriend many times. Look, I know all this sounds crazy, I get it. One day I'll be able to prove it." I can't talk about anything with anyone. I have to go along with their story and what they want me to believe.

"Why not start from the beginning? I want to hear your story."

I cross my arms in front of my chest. "And have you judge me? I'm okay."

"It's not my place to judge, Megan. I think it will help you and me understand together. Once you talk about it and get some of this deep-rooted pain out in the open, you will start to feel freer."

"You already know my story. No sense in rehashing it."

"I understand if you aren't ready. It may take time. But I am here for you."

I chuckle a little. "Yeah, because my mom is paying you."

"That's not why I'm here. I want to help you. I want you to come back next week with a goal in mind."

Guilt overcomes me. Why do I have to be so mean? Dr. Brown is really doing her job, but I can't tell her the truth. It doesn't even matter.

Once our session is over, I meet Mom in the lobby. I slow to a stop when I see Spencer and Mom talking. Why is he here? Is he stalking me? Watching my every move like Vincent? What if he's working with Vincent, reporting back everything I do to him?

I shake my head as if getting rid of the paranoid thoughts.

"Oh honey, look who I ran into."

"Um, hi," I say.

"Hey," Spencer says. He smiles a little, and I like it. It's a sweet smile.

Mom grabs her purse and puts on her coat. "I'll go get the car and meet you out front. It was nice talking to you, Spencer."

"You too, Mrs. Potts."

She gives a smile and walks out into the blustery day.

I turn to meet Spencer's eyes. First time I met him was at night, now seeing him in full light, I can't get over how attractive he is. Even though he wears glasses, his amber eyes shine through. I've never seen anyone with such an eye color. It's like the color of dark honey. It takes me a moment to stop staring.

"Your mom told me you see Dr. Brown."

I want to crawl in a hole and hide. "Great."

"It's okay. I see her, too."

"I guess that makes us best friends now. What else did my mom tell you? That I'm crazy?"

"No, not at all. She's worried about you."

"Yeah. Everyone is. I'm fine though."

"About as fine as me I imagine. That's my go-to response, too."

I shrug. "I'm just biding my time until I can get out of here."

"Out of where? Are you moving?"

"It's nothing." When I meet his eyes again, I see sadness and it makes me feel guilty. I did this to him. I gotta find Vincent. I don't want to be stuck in this human world dealing with therapy and shootings and all of the nonsense.

"She told me you're a writer."

Everything in me freezes. Did she tell him about my 'imaginary world, too?' "What? Why would she say that?"

He shrugs. "She sounds proud of you. She also sort of asked me for my number." He grips the back of his neck.

"What? Why? Is she trying to pick you up?"

He chuckles. "No. She said since we're friends, she wanted numbers in case you decide to leave again without saying anything."

I roll my eyes. "Whatever."

"Are you feeling better?" he asks.

"Why did you do that?"

"What?"

"Why did you lie for me? To my parents. You don't even know me."

"Is that your idea of a thank you?"

"Answer the question."

"You know, I take back my comment about how you aren't mean."

"Sorry. Everything is confusing right now."

"I don't know why I did it. I just saw that you panicked in the car when you mentioned your parents. Thought I'd help you out. I'm sorry that I did."

"I didn't ask for your help."

He lifts an eyebrow and nods once. "Noted. Next time you run out into the road I'll just ignore you."

"I'm sure you're having a field day with this. Just like everyone else."

"You think I told people about it?"

I shake my head. I don't know what to think and I'm feeling so lost and defensive. My mind is all over the place. Once I see Mom pull up, I start walking toward the door.

"Have a good night," Spencer says. "Don't run out in front of cars."

I want to tell him off, but I don't. His comment hurts, but I wasn't nice to him. And now Mom has his number? What for? So she can get more information from him that she can't get from Cherry? How many people does she have spying on me?

I slide into the passenger seat and close the door. Mom's got the heat blasting and she takes off as I snap in my seatbelt.

"Spencer seems like a very nice young man."

"Yeah." At this point, she knows more about him than I do. Depending on what Mom told him, he knows more about me than I do him. How weird is that?

"He says he feels terrible about the other night and hopes you didn't get into trouble."

Well at least he knows how to lie.

"He talked a little bit of how much he's struggling and hopes you're going to get better. I told him I hope so, too."

"Guess I'm the topic of conversation nowadays. Megan Devereux. School shooting victim. Ex-boyfriend killed several and injured many. Whatever did she do to drive him to do it?"

"Megan?" she says my name, dismayed. "No one is blaming you for this."

"I wish you would stop talking about me to everyone. Cherry, too. I feel like everyone knows everything about me, except me."

Mom frowns. "I'm sorry. I never meant for it to be like that. I wanted to get to know him, especially if you're going to be sneaking out of the house late at night without a word."

I'm never going to live that down. She's going to remind me of it every chance she gets or flash it in my face. I don't want to talk anymore. I'm tired of talking and I'm tired of everyone thinking they know the truth and when I tell them, they don't believe me.

Maybe tonight I can ask people in the online forum if they've seen Vincent. It's a stretch, but the way they talk it may actually be possible.

Fourteen

ragon Shooters. That's the name of the forum. I need to create a profile, but I'm scared. Aren't the police monitoring these things? Maybe I can lie to them and say I'm looking for him. I wonder if he's somewhere out there dead.

I don't even know what to call myself or what to say once I get in there. I decide to call myself *Montresor*. Vincent always called me that. Means "my treasure." Only he knows that name. I doubt he's told anyone that.

Once I'm set up, I get a welcome message. There are so many people in here and so many different chat topics within the group. I wish Jonathan were here to guide me through this. I reply to the welcome message and start skimming through the different channels. One in particular catches my eye, called *Where's Waldo*. I don't even know how to feel about the lack of seriousness by these people.

I click on the channel and catch up to the conversation. It's about Vincent and they're calling him Rogue. I know this because earlier in the chat they praised his ability to walk into a school dressed as an executioner from the medieval days and shoot people like it was nothing. Now, they're talking about where he could be. Some suggest he's left the country. I know that isn't true.

I don't know what to say without giving myself away. I also know I'll get thrown out if I tell them what I really think of this entire channel.

I'm trying to find him. I type.

We all are. alkalinez_3 says.

purityangel: *he's probably in Canada.*

death2u: *doubt it. feds lookin for him.*

alkalinez_3: *so dumb. He should be hailed a hero. Killed all those bullies. And that girl who fucked him over. Anyone know if she's dead?*

My heart pounds as heat pours over me. They think I messed with him? They want me dead?

puritypangel: *ugh. no. she survived. last i heard she was released. rogue is so hot and if i ever see him i'll protect him.*

death2u: *lol. U would. Have ur way with him too?*

puritypangel: *definitely. that girl is a whore. the newspapers are all sayin her bf died. she left rogue for that piece of crap. like right after his mom died.*

alkalinez_3: *wow. I hadn't heard that. Where'd you hear that?*

puritypangel: *I have my sources.*

I can't stop my rising pulse. I'm trying to maintain my composure and not get emotional. How could they want me dead? How could they think these things? I want to scream at them.

Montresor: *didn't he have any friends?*

puritypangel: *yeah. he's kinda been quiet about the whole thing. doesn't want a lot of attention*

Montresor: *who is he? i need to talk to him.* I hope I don't come off as desperate or give myself away. How can I convince puritypangel to give me information?

puritypangel: *i can't just give you that lol*

Montresor: *I heard that girl is crazy. Like batshit.*

puritypangel: *we all know that*

Montresor: *u think rogue will come back to finish the job?*

puritypangel: *one would hope but it would be dumb for him to return* death2u: *unless he changed his looks. He's smart. He did get away.*

purityangel: *true. I wonder if I did something to her would he find me? We could be together.*

death2u: *lol obsessed much?*

purityangel: *u have no idea*

These people are scaring me. I don't want random people to come after me hoping to get Vincent's attention and praise. I can't show them I'm afraid. I need to find his friend. How does this purityangel know so much about the situation? Is his friend really this person? The profile says she's a female, but I know anyone can put whatever online. I'm not very good at this. Cherry was always much better at sleuthing than I ever was. Would she help me though?

Fifteen

hat happened?" Casper asks, a worried look in his eyes. "I woke up and you weren't here." We're in another dream, and while it isn't as real as the other night, it's better than nothing.

"I don't know. It was really scary. I woke up panicking and running through the woods. I was back in the mortal world. Running for my life. I have no memory of anything. I remember falling asleep next to you and that's it."

A muscle in his jaw twitches. "Did someone take you? Did Vincent find us?"

I shake my head. "I don't think so. Nothing's changed in the human world since before I left. Just my memory."

"There has to be a way for you to be able to stay here. Not in these dreams. I need you, Megan."

"I need you."

We spend time in each other's arms and eventually I wind up in his lap as he caresses my hair. I tell him about Spencer, therapy, and the online forum.

"Cherry might help you,"

"I have to be careful with her. She's been telling my mom everything."

He shakes his head. "It's almost like your life before we left."

"Kinda. It's different though. Mom and I are closer now. It's weird."

"That's good, though."

I nod.

"Have you seen my parents?"

"No." I haven't even thought about visiting his parents. I should. I don't know what to say to them.

He frowns. "I miss them and Cora."

"I wish you could return. You haven't seen any orbs to take you back?"

"No. The witch created the orb last time. It's weird. She said we had to be thinking about each other at the same time. I think about you all the time though."

"I think about you all the time. Maybe we should plan it better. Like at a certain time."

"Okay. Let's try that next time. Tomorrow night?"

I nod. "Can you believe those people want me dead?"

He kisses my head. "Don't listen to them. You didn't do this, Megan. None of this was your fault and you don't deserve to die."

I move to a sitting position out of his lap and face him. "This is every bit my fault. You, me, Vincent. We messed up everything. We messed with fate, the mortal world, and everything. We have to fix it."

"We will."

"How? Will everything be fixed once Vincent and I return to Arvada? Will everything go back to normal?" My voice rises.

He squeezes my hand. "Yes, Megan. It will. I trust the witch. She knows what she's talking about. Everything will be okay."

"How can you be so certain? How are you so calm?"

"I have to be. I can't stand the idea of you having to find Vincent. There isn't anything I can do and it kills me."

I let out a sigh. "I know. Maybe Vincent's friend can help me get to Vincent. What's happening in Arvada?"

Casper talks to me about how Belle Palais is undergoing a rebuilding process. How they're prepared for another war or if and when Vincent returns.

The familiar tug of me being pulled from the dream. I know I'm waking up. I kiss Casper and wake up, my eyes wet with tears.

Sixteen

"So, are you going to tell me what's going on?" Cherry hits her brakes hard. I grip the passenger handle, forgetting how much her driving makes me nauseous. She speeds up and continues to tail the person in front of her. "Ugh. These people can't drive. Come on! Do the speed limit."

"What do you mean?"

"Dude, seriously? Your mom calls me freaking out because you're not home and you don't have your phone. Oh, and it's like two in the morning. And you're out with some guy?"

I let out a sigh. Apparently, there are no secrets anymore between Cherry and Mom. "Nothing is going on. I...Spencer texted me and he came to pick me up."

"Spencer? Spencer who?" She slams on the brakes as a light turns yellow and the car in front stops. "Ugh! You could've made that light." If there is anything to miss about her, her driving is definitely not one of them. I grip the door hoping we make it to our destination in one piece.

"Spencer Peterson."

"That name sounds familiar. Why would he suddenly text you?"

"What's with all the questions?" I snap. Her questions irritate me. I don't want to answer them. "It's nothing."

"Geez. I was just curious. You could've called me, you know. Why didn't you?"

Because I never called him. This lie is hurting my mom and Cherry. "I don't know. Probably because you're just fishing to get information for my mom." I can feel my temper rising and I take a deep breath like Dr. Brown taught me. Anytime I'm feeling angry or flustered, take a breath. I don't mean to get upset with Cherry especially since I need her help. But now I don't know if I can ask her because she might run to my mom.

"That's not true. What is going on, Megan?" She places her hand on my arm. "Is everything okay?"

"Everything's fine."

"Why are you avoiding it? Why won't you tell me?"

"Because you've already told my parents everything," I yell.

Her jaw drops then closes it, resuming her pity look. "Megan, I had to. We all want you to get better."

I nod. "I'm fine, okay?

Things between us are so different now. I don't know how to be around her. I'm scared to say anything without her reporting it to my parents or the doctors. Just like it was with Vincent, I'm forced to pretend to be perfect so I can find my way back to Casper.

My head is starting to hurt, and I want to go back home. Being out is supposed to help me, but when Cherry turns into a cemetery, I wonder if she thinks this is truly a good idea. What is she thinking? Maybe I can use this to my advantage and convince her to help me.

The cemetery is ridiculously huge. Are there maps for it like at the mall? Rows and sections are full of gravestones of various sizes. My chest tightens once her car slows to a stop.

"Come on," she says as she opens her door.

Taking a deep breath, I join her outside. The day is cold and calculating. Wrong day to forget my beanie. I don't want to be here. As I scan the lot, I see fake flowers scattered amongst the headstones. The sun disappears behind the clouds as I follow Cherry between graves, careful not to walk on any. I hate cemeteries. I can't remember the last time I was in one. The ground sinks beneath me and I fear stepping into a hole or a hand reaching out to grab me.

Cherry stops and I almost bump into her. She takes my hand and squeezes. "Megan, you never really got to say goodbye. You weren't able. I brought you here today so you could." Her blue eyes plea almost as if I don't do this there will be no hope for me.

The ground is still freshly brown and the dead grass surrounding it just makes it look pitiful. I know Casper isn't really dead and that it's just his human self or rather everyone thinks it's him. When I look at the gravestone with this name chiseled deep into the marble, pain punches me in the chest. It's too real and I don't like it.

Casper Truitt
Born August 10, 2002
Died October 31, 2018

"I know this has been so hard for you," Cherry says. "But just try to face this. I need you, Megan. I need you here. You're stronger than you think, and you can overcome this."

I don't know what to say to her. Of course, I don't want to leave her behind, but I can't leave Casper behind either. Not after all we've been through.

Cherry pats my shoulder. "I'll give you some time alone." I watch her return to the car, and I'm left beside an empty grave.

Am I supposed to talk to it? Am I supposed to pretend Casper's spirit is just sitting on the headstone hanging out playing a video game? Drinking a coke? Tossing popcorn in his mouth?

Whatever it's worth. "Casper, I will come back. I will save you. Just hold on. For me. For us. We will end this."

"Do you feel better?" Cherry asks once I shut the car door.

Yeah, I feel tons better I want to say. "I need your help."

Her eyes widen like a Labrador retriever. Eager to please. "Absolutely. What is it?"

I tell her about the online forum and everything that was said including the part where they think I should be dead. The whole thing leaves a bitter taste in my mouth.

"Omigod! Those people are assholes! I will beat them up right now."

I smile a little, loving the old Cherry coming out.

"Isn't that considered a threat?"

"I don't know. But one of them knows Vincent's friend. I need to find him."

"Why?"

"I need to ask him questions."

"Don't you think the police already have?"

"I'm sure they have, but they won't tell me much. Please Cherry. You're so much better at this than me."

"I don't know, Megan. I mean, would he tell you anything or would he protect Vincent?"

"Protect him from what?"

"What about you? What if you keep digging and these crazy psychos come after you? I mean that one already knows you're out of the hospital. How does she even know that? Ugh. How can she crush on *him*?"

"I can learn how to fight." It's not a bad idea. I remember some things Casper taught me, but I need more training especially now that my body is weird.

"I don't know. It sounds like it would be dangerous. I mean, you've never even met his friend. What's he like? Does he support Vincent and what he did?"

"Then come with me. Two is better than one. That's if this person will give us his information."

Cherry lets out a sigh. "Okay."

"Will you promise to keep this between us?"

She hesitates.

"Cherry?"

"Your mom wants me to tell her everything. We just want you to get better."

I stare at her in shock. "Bringing me to the cemetery is supposed to help with that? Why do you have to report everything back to her? I can't even trust you anymore." I'm regretting that I told her about the online forum. Now, Mom will probably ground me from the computer or whatever. Taking it away along with my music and phone. Like she always did before.

"Because so far nothing you're saying or doing is healthy."

I cross my arms and stare out the window. Definitely telling her I saw an orb the other night is a huge no. I haven't seen since that night, so I wonder if it was a dream.

"What am I supposed to tell your mom when you end up dead or missing because you wouldn't let it go and some internet psycho found you? I don't think you realize how serious any of this is. It pisses me off that you're so nonchalant about what happened. I know you don't remember, but damn Megan, it's like you don't even care that it happened. That any of us suffered that day."

I've never heard Cherry talk like that before and it makes me feel guilty. She went through something traumatic as did so many people and I wish I could make her understand. No amount of me talking is going to prove anything though. I have to return everything to normal. Which brings me back to finding Vincent's friend.

"I'm sorry."

She sighs. "I'm really sorry. I know none of this is easy for you and I can't imagine what you're going through. I only know what I've dealt with, and I've had more time than you. I'm trying to help. Maybe I'm being too pushy. It's just...your mom was super worried that night you ran off and it worried me. I know I told your mom about that other world stuff, but I felt like they needed to know. Maybe it'll help in your recovery. I don't know. I'm not an expert."

"I know. You're my best friend, Cherry. I need to know that you aren't going to run to my parents with all the things I say. You know they'll lock me up if they keep hearing the crazy things that go through my head. Or anything that happens."

"I'm sorry. I really am. I'll help you with this online thing. We'll find Vincent's friend, but Luke is coming with us."

"Okay. You're not telling my mom, right?"

"As much as I hate keeping things from your mom, given the situation, I will this time."

I'm not sure I fully believe her. I guess I'll find out.

Seventeen

he whole thing was dumb," I tell Dr. Brown the next week. I prop my head against my hand with my elbow digging into the arm of her couch.

"Do you not like speaking to graves?" she asks.

"Does anyone? I mean, it isn't like anyone's there. You're talking to a piece of marble. Or whatever."

"Maybe Cherry thought it would help you."

I shake my head. "Maybe it helped her. I can't tell her the truth because she just looks at me like I'm nuts. It's like I have to tiptoe around her. Be a good little girl because if you show any emotion, it makes people uncomfortable and how dare you make them feel that way."

"Did she say that?"

"No, but it's implied. I did that with Vincent. Hid my feelings because I didn't want to upset him. If I ever said anything, he'd get upset and tell me my feelings weren't valid or that I was being ridiculous. Or get defensive. But after a while I couldn't do it anymore."

"No one should. That's not how people should be treated. Perhaps this is the only way Cherry knows to help."

"She told my mom everything. Even after I asked her to keep it a secret." Except so far, she seems to have kept our secret about finding Vincent's friend from my mom. Cherry was miraculously able to sign on to the forum and convince purityangel for the friend to meet up with us. I don't know how she did it. Tonight, we're planning to meet up with him.

Dr. Brown nods. "She betrayed your trust."

"Exactly. How can I talk to her about anything?"

"Perhaps, you can give her little bits of information and test her. I'm sure Cherry is just as lost and confused as you are."

I relax a little, realizing I've treated Cherry like crap. She doesn't know. I'm a terrible friend. But telling my mom everything? Why would she do that? I hope she doesn't tell Mom about tonight. I'm trusting her with this, and I hope she doesn't fail the test.

"Do you feel a little better after seeing Casper's grave?"

"Not really. He's still not here. It's all a ruse."

Dammit. I didn't mean to say that, but Dr. Brown has a bizarre way of getting me to open up.

"What is?"

"Nothing."

"No, Megan. Tell me, please."

"All of it. The school shooting. Casper's death. None of it happened."

"You've mentioned this before. Why do you feel that way?"

"Because it's the truth." I tell her, meeting her eyes. She doesn't look shocked or anything. She's hard to read. "I know you think I'm nuts."

"Megan, I do not think that. I want to know what you're thinking. Why do you feel like none of it happened?"

I let out a frustrated sigh. "We aren't humans." I know I'm treading dangerous ground. She can easily lock me up in a padded cell and I'm potentially signing my own death sentence. The words tumble out of my mouth before I can stop them. And before I know it, I've told her everything. All about Arvada. The war. The Elves. Sprites. Casper and me. And Vincent. She doesn't look at me like I've lost my mind.

She nods and asks questions, and when I'm finished, she takes a deep breath and lets it out.

By the time I'm done, I feel better, almost like a huge weight has been lifted. Though a different weight is added. What have I done? Didn't she already know all of this anyway from Cherry and Mom? Is hearing it from me going to make it worse?

"How do you plan to return to Casper?"

"I have to find Vincent and once I get the Jewel, I can return." No turning back now.

"Do you plan to find Vincent on your own?"

"No, of course not." Except that's exactly what I had in mind, but maybe it's better if I ask Cherry or someone else to come along when I finally find him.

"Perhaps we should focus on one task at a time."

"Like what?"

"While I think we need to continue therapy, I wanted to get your thoughts on returning to school."

"When?"

"When you feel up to it. I think it could help quite a bit."

Is she serious? School? Didn't she hear anything I told her? School won't matter once I'm gone. Maybe this is my chance to skip out on school in order to find Vincent. "Am I supposed to go back now?"

"It's up to you, Megan. No one is expecting you to do anything you don't want to do, just remember that.

I only brought it up to maybe help keep your mind focused on other things."

"I don't want to. At least not yet."

"I understand. Perhaps you can start back in January."

"Okay." I tell her and get up to leave. Part of me wants to tell her to forget everything I told her about Arvada. She's being too okay with it. Does she know Vincent? Has he done something to her mind to make her an enemy or something?

I leave therapy regretting that I ever said a word about it all. I hope when I return the next time, it won't be too late to tell her it was all a lie and made up. Maybe somehow, I can sneak back in her office and remove her notes about that. Last thing I need is to be locked up. The anxiety grips me. I need to take those notes out. I'm such an idiot.

The wind blasts through me and I hug myself tighter. It's freezing outside. I'm wearing a scarf, a coat, a beanie, but it feels like I'm wearing nothing. I'm still shivering, and my nerves aren't helping one bit.

I wish Cherry and I were out being normal teenagers getting hot chocolate and seeing a movie. Not meeting Vincent's friend or trying to find Vincent. Casper's words repeat in my head: *the witch doesn't want us meddling in the human world*. We don't belong here. Which means when I do find Vincent, I have to leave all of this behind, including Cherry.

Luke, Cherry, and I walk inside a frozen yogurt place. Cherry's choice. It's too cold for frozen yogurt, but she insisted. It's too bright inside and there are only two other people in here.

Cherry takes a bite of her frozen yogurt and some of it drips on her chin. Laughing, Luke wipes it with a napkin.

I'm nervous, and their cute couple stuff annoys me. I don't know why. Maybe because my boyfriend is stuck in another world. I should be happy for her. I am, I'm also jealous. Why can't the four of us be on a double date? Why can't Casper be here wiping yogurt from my chin? Why can't he be here so we can hold hands or laugh and giggle?

I blink away the tears.

The door opens and the bell rings. Looking up, my shoulders slump, and I sigh. Not Vincent's friend, but Spencer. He spots me and starts making his way toward our table.

Great. I don't need this tonight.

"Hey Megan."

"Spencer."

"Omigod." Cherry stares at him wide-eyed. Recognition washes on her face.

"What?" Luke and I exchange a confused look.

"Spencer Peterson," she says.

"That's me."

"*You're* Vincent's friend."

"Wait. What?" I ask, my heart catches in my throat.

"I was."

My heart slams into my ribcage. Nope. I definitely don't need this. "You—" He was out there the night I came back from Arvada running for my life. He was there after my therapy session.

Oh no. He's working with Vincent. He's reporting everything back to him somehow. An uneasy feeling swallows me, and I can't breathe.

"I can't believe you." I get up from the booth and rush out the door, hating the harsh way the cold hits me. I'm going to be sick. Everything swirls around me.

"Megan, wait!" Spencer calls after me.

I twist around and see him, Cherry, and Luke following me. "Why? What is this?"

"What is what?"

"What game are you playing?" Cherry demands. "You're friends with those psychos online? What do you want with Megan?" She moves in front of me, and Luke stands protectively in front of us both.

Spencer shakes his head. His hands remain in his jacket pocket. "I'm not up to anything. An old friend of mine told me someone wanted to talk to me about Vincent. She asked if I wanted to talk."

My eyes water. "They all want me dead. Is that what you want, too?"

His jaw drops. "What? No. What are you talking about?"

Cherry launches into everything they said about me. I can't believe I never noticed Spencer before. I never saw he and Vincent hang out. I never even heard Vincent mention him. Were they really friends or what?

"Damn. They said that?"

Cherry narrows her eyes. "Like you don't know. Come on, Megan."

"No, wait! I want to talk. I *need* to talk. Honestly, part of me hoped it was you asking."

"You have my mom's number now. Why didn't you call her for a meet and greet?"

"Can we talk? We can talk inside the yogurt shop."

I swallow hard. Maybe he has answers, but I don't trust him. "Fine."

Eighteen

itting across from Spencer Peterson isn't as awkward as I thought it would be. Luke sits next to him and Cherry next to me. My arms are crossed, coat still on as I wait for him to start talking.

"Look, I'm not out to get you."

"You knew exactly who I was that night. Why were you out there?"

"Out where? What are you talking about?" Cherry asks.

I curse internally. She doesn't know he found me running out in the middle of the night.

Spencer glances at Cherry.

"Wait. Is this the Spencer you hung out with on a whim? And you didn't know who he was?"

"We met at Dr. Brown's office," he says.

Good to know he can still lie. Now, to get rid of Cherry and Luke without hurting her feelings. "Cherry, can you give us a few minutes?"

"What? No. I'm not leaving you alone with him."

"I'll be fine. Please."

She lets out a sigh as she and Luke get up from the table. "We'll be over there."

"Why were you out there?" I ask again.

"Maybe one day I'll tell you."

"Avoidance. Something you learned from Vincent."

He smirks. "I don't know you well enough to start telling you about my personal problems. Isn't she your best friend though? Why haven't you told her the truth?"

"It's complicated. Are you really friends with those people online?"

"Some of them."

"How do you know purityangel?"

"I know her from alternative school. Same way I know Vincent."

"He went to an alternative school?"

He lifts an eyebrow. "Are you really surprised?"

"No. Not really. Okay, so what's her deal? Why were they saying I should've died and that they could finish the job? Are you all planning something against me?"

"No. I don't know what they said or why. I'm not in that group and I never would be. She obviously has issues."

"So do I, yet you don't see me in an online group touting what he did. I actually believed you that night in the car. You're like these people. You believe what he did was the right thing—"

"I'm gonna stop you right there." His intense gaze holds my eyes. "I do *not* condone what he did at all. I know you don't know me but it's real brazen of you to assume that of me."

Heat rushes to my cheeks. "But you're friends with people who do."

"I wouldn't say we're friends. Not that you deserve an explanation, but I haven't spoken to Vincent in over a year. We stopped talking right around the time you two started dating. I had no idea what he was going to do. I watched you in class slowly deteriorating and I knew it was him making you fall apart. I reached out to him a few times because I heard about his mom. He never responded."

"How did you know it was him doing that to me?"

"I've known him for a long time. He's always been very manipulative. I'm pretty sure he and Lacey, purityangel to you, got together and she's still obsessed with him apparently. I wanted him to change, but he never really did. He kept getting progressively worse."

"He never once mentioned you."

"I wouldn't have expected him to. We had a fight and of course, it was my fault. I couldn't really tell you what it was about."

I don't know what to say to him.

"I'm sorry they said those things about you. That's really messed up. It's really messed up that there's a forum out there about this."

I nod. "I take it you have no idea how to find him."

He furrows his eyes. "Not the slightest. He's super smart though."

"You knew I was trying to find him. Why didn't you tell me anything then?"

"Because I don't know anything. I don't know how to find him, and even if I did, I would tell the police."

"Yeah, because they're working so hard."

"You really think you're going to figure out where he is? Then what? You're actually going to go after him?"

"That's the plan."

"You've got to be joking. He's a murderer, Megan."

"He has something that I need."

"Like what?"

I cross my arms in front of my chest. "Nothing. You wouldn't understand."

"My advice to you is that you need to stay as far away from him as possible. He tried to kill you and he may not miss next time."

"He won't kill me. He still loves me, and I plan to use that to my advantage."

He shakes his head. "You're gonna get yourself killed."

"Does purityangel know anything? So many people were offering a place to him."

"He wouldn't take them up on it. He knows people are searching for him."

"What about his dad?"

"Megan, don't you think his dad has been through enough? Leave him alone."

"Where is he?"

"I'm not telling you. Didn't you date Vincent? Shouldn't you know him better than anyone?"

I blush. "There's so much about him that I never knew."

"Welcome to the club. He's a complicated guy. There were times we'd hang out and it was innocent guy stuff. Other times, he was too intense. I figured out later it was because he was using. I thought maybe he would've changed because he met you."

"I really tried. I tried to be a good girlfriend and comfort him." As I speak, tears rush to my eyes and my voice shakes. I'm not expecting this emotion. "It got hard because everything I did was wrong. Everything I said was wrong. I couldn't be myself around him. I know he was dealing with a lot, especially his mom, but I couldn't be who he wanted." I look away, grab a napkin and dab at my eyes. I hate crying in front of people, especially someone I barely know.

"I'm sorry you had to deal with that."

I look up and meet his eyes. What just happened? Why am I telling this complete stranger these things? "I can't believe I told you that."

"It's okay. I don't mind listening. I can only imagine all the shit he put you through. You don't deserve that. No one does."

For a second, Casper flashes in my head. He's said the same thing to me.

"It's okay, Megan. I'm here for you. I don't mind listening." Casper sits at the edge of his bed while I'm pacing in his room.

"I had to break up with him."

"I know."

"What is wrong with me? Why did I fall for him? How did I fall for him?"

"He's manipulative. He lured you in."

"You tried warning me so many times. I didn't listen."

"But you did. You found the strength to leave him."

"I never meant to hurt his feelings. I didn't break up with him for you, though. I mean, yes I have strong feelings for you, but I couldn't stay with him."

"I know. You don't have to validate anything. You had to do this for yourself."

"Megan?"

Blinking, I stare at Spencer wide eyed. What was that? I don't remember that happening. Was that from another life? Did I have a vision?

No, only Vincent shows me those. Is he here? Is he nearby? He can't be. There's no way he'd show me a vision of Casper and me alone.

"Um. I need to go. Thanks."

"Wait, you're leaving?"

"I have to go home." I have to find the orb again or find Casper in my dreams. Something's going on and I don't know how to explain it.

The whole way home I keep thinking about the weird vision I had while talking with Spencer and the fact that I told Dr. Brown about Arvada. I still can't believe I did that. I have to find a way to get my file from Dr. Brown.

When Luke pulls into the driveway, I get out of the car. "Hey, Cherry can I talk to you for a second?"

"Yeah. What's up?" She shuts the door.

"Cherry, I need to see my file."

She raises her eyebrows in confusion. "Your file?"

"Dr. Brown's file on me."

"Okay. Why?"

"Because I have to know what she's saying about me. What she's telling everyone." The thought that she could confirm to my family that I'm crazy doesn't sit well with me.

"Don't you know? I mean, hasn't she already told you what you have?"

"No. No one tells me anything. Wait, what I have? What do you mean?"

She hesitates. "Megan, I'm really not the person to ask. I only know what your mom has told me which isn't much."

"What has she said about me?"

"Just that you're going through a lot and that it may take some time for you to recover."

She's hiding something, and now I want to know what my file says even more. "Recover from what? The fact that I'm stuck here forever?"

She narrows her eyes. "What do you mean you're stuck here?"

"Nothing. I just need to read my file."

"Why do you need to read it so badly?"

I let out a groan. "I told her about Arvada. Now she's going to think I'm a psychotic person. I made a mistake. It just came out. I can't be locked up, Cherry." Tears well in my eyes.

She takes my hand. "Hey, it's okay. Tell her you made a mistake."

I shake my head. "I can't do that. It's already been said. I need to remove it from her file. She can't have proof that I said it."

"How are you gonna read it? Pretty sure they're kept under lock and key."

"We can break in."

She chuckles. "Good one."

"I'm serious."

Her face falls. "Come on, Megan. We can't just break in. There are probably tons of alarms and cameras."

"Then you create a diversion and I'll go in and get the file. If they all think I'm as crazy as they seem to think, they could lock me up. I can't be locked up, Cherry."

"Your parents would have to make that decision."

"And you know as well as I do, they'd do that in a heartbeat. To get rid of me."

"No, they wouldn't. Your mom has changed. I've seen it. She's almost lost you."

"Are you actually defending them?"

"Why are you so paranoid? I mean about everything. Are you scared that Vincent will find you?"

"Vincent left me here. If I get locked up, I can't make it back to Casper. Don't you get it? I'm running out of time." I close my eyes, internally kicking myself. Why can't I keep my mouth shut? I'm trying to prevent this very thing, yet the words tumble out before I can stop them. "I didn't mean that."

Recognition rests on her face. "I see."

"Will you help me?"

"Break in? No, are you joking? Besides, how is reading your file going to help anything?"

"I'll know how not to act." Aside from a few seconds ago.

"This is ridiculous. Why don't we go shopping tomorrow? We can have some much-needed girl time."

"What? No, I don't want to go shopping."

She stares at me like she wants to say something, but she shakes her head.

"What?"

"Nothing."

"No, tell me."

Cherry meets my eyes. Her chin quivers slightly. "We can't go break into some office so you can read your file."

"Why can't you help me? Do you think I need to be locked up?"

"No, I don't think that. Do you want to kill yourself?"

"What? Why would you ask that? Where is that coming from?"

"When you make comments about getting back to Casper or wanting to be with him, it scares me. It sounds like you want to die to be with him."

I let out a sigh. "It slipped. I didn't mean it."

"Yeah, you did."

I let my shoulders slump and I bite my lip knowing I have to somehow right this situation before she tells my mom. I don't need suicide watch added to my list. "Maybe you're right. I haven't been sleeping well and the dreams are messing with me."

"I can imagine. This isn't easy for anyone. It doesn't help that that psycho is still out there."

"Please don't tell my mom."

"I won't. I promise. Just tell Dr. Brown you didn't mean it. But Megan, you can't keep saying these things. You have to face it, otherwise I fear for you."

I shake my head and roll my eyes.

"I hate that you ignore what happened or can't remember. People *died*, Megan. Of course, none of us ever thought it would happen to our school. No one ever thinks that. I hated that day. Scared out of my mind, hugging myself, not knowing if I would make it out alive. Not knowing if you were okay." Her eyes begin to water. "I hate that we can't really talk about it, but it happened. And so many of us are just trying to figure it all out one day at a time. So many of us are suffering yet *he's* still walking around free."

"Then help me sneak into Dr. Brown's office. If they lock me away, there is no hope."

Cherry shakes her head. "I can't help you. Not like this."

"I thought we were friends."

"We are friends. You think we aren't because I won't help you break the law?" she asks, offended.

"Never mind."

"Megan?"

"I gotta go."

I turn toward the front door and as soon as I walk inside, I want to curl up in a ball and cry. I don't know where this will take us. Tears swell as the pain of losing my best friend overwhelms me. She's betrayed me, just like Florence did. I've never felt more alone, and I don't understand what I've done to her. We've been friends since we were kids. Why is she so against helping me? Is she jealous of Casper? Is she sad that once I return to him she won't have me?

Guilt wears on me at the thought. I've already left her once, without even saying goodbye. Not that I had a choice in that matter. It's true though. What happens to my family and Cherry when I go back to

Arvada permanently? Will they think I died? Will they think I'm just missing? Maybe once she and I have cooled off, I can talk to her again. Try to make her understand. I wish I could take her with me, but I can't.

We're almost out of high school. Surely, she'll make new friends once she goes to college, right? She won't even think about me or remember me. If only I had Vincent's power to erase memories, that's what I would do. I don't want to cause heartache to anyone, and I don't want to hurt them.

But I can't stay here.

I try to sift through my memories of past lives, trying to remember if I ever had a close friend like Cherry, and I can't. Nothing really comes to mind. It's like it's all blank.

Strange. I vividly remembered them in the immortal world.

Maybe that's what happens here. Or maybe that's a product of Vincent's magic act or whatever it's called.

I shake my head, in an attempt to free my mind of all this mess. I need to figure out a way to break into Dr. Brown's office. I briefly think maybe Spencer could help me, but I don't want to drag him in any of this. He's probably still friends with Vincent and doesn't want to say anything to anyone. I don't blame him. I already hate being associated with Vincent as it is. I can't imagine what going back to school will be like. That's if I even return. I barely made my way through the awful messages on Facebook. Now my mom and Dr. Brown want me to actually face these people? They all think it's my fault. That I drove him to kill everyone because I chose Casper.

Sadly though, it is my fault. All of it and I have to fix it. I have to start from scratch on trying to find Vincent since Spencer was no help.

I'm wound up and I can't sleep so I open my laptop and start searching and reading forums. There has to be something out there that will lead me to Vincent so we can end this altogether.

My pulse edges higher when I see an article posted in the forum.

Wrecked Car on I10 Believed to belong to Vincent Young.

I skim through the article and it's not very detailed. They found his Accord completely smashed in on the front and driver side. Blood was found; the windshield is shattered; the airbag is deployed. The car was in the middle of nowhere Arizona, near Tucson. Some people in the forum think he crossed the border into Mexico or that he escaped as far as California. Some said they think he's going to wind up in Alaska.

He never told me when he would come back. Why would he have traveled so far away? Can he not get back to Arvada? Is he misleading investigators? Given the severity of the crash, I don't know how he'll survive without help. Stranger things have happened. I know one thing is for sure: I can't go on some wild goose chase after him.

And what if he dies? I won't have the Jewel and can't ever get back. As much as I can't stand it, I'm hoping Vincent survives and comes back.

<h1 style="text-align:center">Nineteen</h1>

My leg won't stop shaking. Dr. Brown is talking, but I have no idea what she's saying. I'm looking at her, but I keep glancing at the clock. I have yet to figure out how to get her out of the office so I can read my file.

I didn't sleep at all last night and I'm sure it shows on my face. I was up late in those stupid forums and still not finding much. I feel like all my efforts are wasted. There has to be a way to find Vincent though.

And because I didn't sleep, I didn't get to see Casper. Not seeing him every day is starting to take its toll. I'm tired of everyone telling me I need to focus on something else. *Work on writing. Go shopping. Take the dogs for a walk. Go visit your brother.* I don't want to do any of those things.

Dr. Brown finally stops talking and she walks me out of her office, down the hall to where my mom waits in the lobby. They start talking, and I'm still not listening.

Now's my chance.

"Oh, I forgot my scarf," I say. "I'll be right back."

Dr. Brown nods and continues to talk to my mom.

Every time my heart beats, it feels like it's pumping heat all over me. I'm shaking. Slipping into her office, I rush to her desk. I have to know what she's written about me. Luckily, my file is still sitting on her desk. I don't have much time. I open the thick file, thumbing through page after page of notes, charts, almost everything about me. I flip through so much and I'm trying to read as much as I can.

Megan Devereux. Age 17. Date of Trauma: October 31, 2018. Megan suffers from a tragic school shooting that has led to dissociative amnesia caused by dissociative identity disorder. Megan is beginning to suffer from complicated grief. On October 31, Vincent Young shot several people at Spring Valley High School including Megan. Megan's boyfriend, Casper was shot and killed in front of her. Megan fell unconscious and went into a month-long coma.

Medication prescribed: antipsychotic, antidepressants. I believe Megan isn't taking her medication as prescribed or at all. She doesn't believe the shooting happened as her mind has completely blocked it out along with several months of her life. She suffers from derealization and identity confusion.

This is the craziest thing I've ever read. I read on.

It has been a month since she has awakened yet she seems to believe she is from another world. She has mentioned that she is not human and must return to this other world to where Casper awaits her. That she and Casper made a pact to be together in human lives and would be reincarnated in each life. She is so far not responding well to treatment. I have spoken to her mother about taking Megan to a mental institution, but I believe right now she is strong enough to overcome. She is able to handle everyday tasks and takes care of herself. Though she is inattentive at times and seems to be on autopilot.

I rip out the page about me mentioning Arvada and shove it in my pocket.

"Wow."

I gasp and look up to see Spencer leaning in the doorway. My heart jumps to my throat.

"Read anything interesting?" His arms are folded across his chest.

"I just...You wouldn't understand."

"You do realize she won't forget what you've told her, right? She types everything up, I'm sure."

Dammit. Why didn't I think of that? Have I become dumber since my coma? I close the folder.

Spencer crosses the room. "Must be pretty bad. You look like you're going to be sick."

I swallow hard. "You can't say anything."

"We keeping more secrets now?"

I stare at him. "Please."

"Okay, Spencer. Let's get—Megan, why are you still in here?"

"Um..."

"She was admiring the kids' artwork. She said the one of the little girl with her puppy is her favorite."

Dr. Brown moves behind her desk as I slink away from it. She looks from Spencer to me, and I know she doesn't believe him. She's too smart for that.

I grab my scarf. "I'll see you next time." I rush out of her office, my ears ringing, and tears about to rush forward.

She knows. She's going to tell my mom and they're going to put me away.

Why does Spencer keep lying for me? What's his deal? What's he gaining by doing that? I don't understand.

It's going to be a lot harder getting out of here and I'm running out of time. I can't mention Casper to anyone. Not about me returning to him. Nothing about Arvada. I have to act perfect. Do what they want me to do. Act how they want me to act. Sadly, I'm used to that. It's what I've had to do my entire life.

Twenty

ugging myself, I stand outside with my mom watching little flurries fall from the dark sky. I can't recall the last time I saw it snow. It's even more beautiful than I remember. The little bits of cold hits my face in a refreshing way. I breathe in the clean, crisp scent and drink in the silence of the night.

It's Christmas, and it was a good day. I spent it with my family and Cherry came over for a little bit. It's a little emotional though. Casper isn't here and there is a somberness in the air. My mom is especially emotional because she thought she lost me. I love being with them and it makes it even harder knowing

I have to leave them. But I have my own life and I feel guilty for meddling with the humans and for hurting them.

I wanted to talk to Casper's parents, but I chicken out every time I pick up the phone. I'm not sure what to say to them.

I keep looking for an orb. I want to see Casper—not in a dream. Especially today. We've been spending every night together in my dreams. I wake feeling sad and I cry for a little bit before I get up. I miss him and I feel like I've wasted so much time, but Casper says it's okay. That I need to get well. If I'm not physically okay, I can't face Vincent and he's right.

I have been pushing myself in therapy to get better. I can walk much better now and I'm hoping Mom lets me start driving soon. I have places to search clues for Vincent.

I've kept a lot from everyone, as far as my dreams, the truth and pretty much everything else. Especially my plans to find Vincent once I'm well enough. I've done everything they've asked. So far Dr. Brown hasn't mentioned the page missing from her file. Oddly enough, it wasn't long after I read my file when she told me my diagnosis. She explained a bunch of psychobabble words, and I listened like the perfect patient I am.

"Honey, why don't you spend some time with your father?"

"What?" Is she seriously suggesting that? She never wants me to go to his house.

"I think it'll do you good. Different atmosphere. You still have a couple of weeks before school."

"Are you sure?" I'm excited at the idea to see my dad. I don't know the last time I saw him.

"Of course, I'm sure. I really think it'll do you some good."

I nod. "Okay." I'm not sure this is a good idea. It'll just delay my search even more. "Actually, it might be better if I stay here."

She furrows her eyebrows. "What? Since when do you pass up time with your father?"

I never do. I'm always upset that she grounds me preventing me from seeing him. But I can't leave. "I just think I should stay home. I mean, I have therapy still."

Crossing her arms in front of her chest, she lifts an eyebrow, clearly not believing me. "Megan, you need to go. You always feel so much better when you go there."

For my mom to practically beg me to go to my dad's is strange. She never even expressed disappointment or anger that he didn't come to the hospital. Something's not right. "Why are you pushing this?"

"Why are you avoiding it? Is it because he didn't visit you?"

"No."

"Are you taking your medications?"

I roll my eyes. "Yes, Mom," I lie. My mind is already messed up. Why would I take those pills to screw it up even more? I've been taking one each from the bottle and flushing them each night.

"Then what is it? You'll go for a week."

I let out a sigh.

"This wouldn't have anything to do with you trying to find Vincent."

I curse internally. *Cherry.* Why is she doing this? She promised she wouldn't say anything to my mom. I can't trust her anymore. "No. Why do you think I'm doing that?"

She stares at me in disbelief. "You need to go, Megan. Forget about finding Vincent."

"Fine," I say, but only for now.

Mom squeezes my arm, and we turn to go inside. I never saw an orb. Defeated, I follow her then to my room.

Lying in my bed with Savannah at my side, I pull out a picture of Casper and me from my wall of pictures. It's the one of us at a concert. I still have no recollection of it but I love seeing his smile. It's rare that I see it anymore. Holding it against my chest, I try to will the tears away, but it's no use.

Unable to fall asleep, I get out of bed and twist open my blinds to gaze out at the snow. It's sticking to the ground but not the roads. Even in the darkness, the snow makes things brighter. Out of the corner of my eye, I spot a wispy blueish color.

Casper.

I follow the orb back to Arvada and frantically search for him. It's dark and the thick fog doesn't help. The cold rushes over me like I'm in an icy cave or something. I don't remember Arvada ever being this cold.

"Megan." His voice brings me to my knees.

"Casper."

"I'm here."

But I can't see him.

"Where are you? Casper!"

"I'm here, Megan. Save me."

My heart crashes into my chest. Running toward the sound of his voice, I see him at the edge of the cave, standing tall. He's beautiful. I dart into his arms and inhale his clean woodsy scent. He brushes my hair and leans down, pressing his lips to mine.

When I pull back, Vincent is staring at me as a grin spreads across his lips. His dark eyes hold mine causing a shiver over my body. He grabs my wrists preventing me from running.

"No! Why are you here? Where is Casper?"

He stands aside, revealing Casper's still body. His blood hair is matted with blood. There's a puddle beside his head. "I killed him."

I let out a scream and twist out of Vincent's grip.

"No matter how far you run, Megan, I will always find you. I will finish what I started."

Shaking, I dart away from him. The cold hits my lungs making it harder to breathe. I can't get the image of Casper's dead body out of my head. And Vincent's scary, intense look. Did I not find an orb? Did I actually find Vincent? I can't be running from him or be afraid of him.

Rolling over in bed, I grimace once I feel something cold and wet. I know it isn't Savannah's nose. When I open my eyes, I squint from the brightness. Once my vision focuses, I gasp and sit up. All around me are tombstones. I'm lying in the dewy grass in front of Casper's grave.

I found an orb, then Vincent. I was running from him. That's all I know. Did he do something to me? Did I run all night and wind up here? I look at my clothes and I'm still wearing my pajamas. I don't see my car at all. I get to my feet hugging myself and start walking back home. At least I'm wearing shoes but I'm so lost and confused. I don't remember much of anything after running from Vincent. Was it a dream? Was it real?

Casper's dead body flashes in my mind. I shake my head as if trying to shake the image away. I don't understand what happened. I found Casper then he turned into Vincent. Did Vincent find Casper? My heart hammers wildly at the thought. What if he did something to Casper? What if he returned to Arvada and killed him for good? I shake my head.

No. Vincent didn't kill him. He's still alive. How did Vincent find me though? Does he know about the orbs?

What is happening to me? Why does this keep happening? Are the orbs throwing me back into the human world?

I check my pockets, but I don't have my phone. As I walk, I try to ignore the few passing cars. What are the drivers thinking when they see some girl in her pajamas walking on the side of the road? I wish I was directionally smart so I could travel in the woods and away from onlookers, luckily, there aren't that many.

I want to cry, and I can't wait to get home. What is Mom going to say? Maybe I can sneak inside. Who am I kidding? There is no way to sneak inside a house with five dogs.

I'm exhausted by the time I reach my house. Taking a deep breath, I open the front door and it creaks a little. I carefully walk past the living room, breathing a sigh of relief to find no one in there. As soon as I get into my room, I shut the door, peel off my shoes and crawl under the covers.

My heart pound and I tremble. I breathe in and out, trying to calm myself. I'm home now but it only brings me little comfort. Not knowing what is happening to me is freaking me out. Did Vincent do something to me? Did he put a spell on me that makes me forget pieces of time?

The door to my room opens and it's Mom. Savannah levitates up on my bed with ease. Her little tail is wagging so fast, and she darts into my face, making sure I know how excited she is to see me.

"Good morning. Did you sleep okay?" She crosses the room and sits on the edge of my bed.

"Yeah." I pull myself into a sitting position and hold Savannah close to me.

"Savannah wound up in our room last night. Did you have bad dreams?"

"Um...yeah."

She caresses my face and gives a pitiful smile. "I'm sorry, honey. I wish I could make it all go away. I'll make some breakfast. Get dressed and pack your things. We'll leave by ten. Your dad is meeting us at the state line around noon." She leaves.

What's she talking about? It takes me a moment to remember the conversation we had last night. I guess Jonathan isn't going, otherwise he'd just drive us both. I don't want to ask Mom for any details. I fear she'll think I've lost it. I already feel that way.

I hate this lost feeling and I hate that I keep waking up in random places not knowing how I got there. Is the orb doing this to me? Why didn't the witch warn Casper about memory loss? Why does this keep happening? After last night, I don't want to find Vincent. What if everyone's right and he will finish what he started if he sees me?

Then I'll have no other way to return to Arvada.

The Vincent last night was completely different than the one who saw me in the hospital. He was kind and kept apologizing. He said he would come back for me. Last night, he clearly wanted to kill me.

Is it because he knows Casper and I have been seeing each other?

Holding my head between my hands, I let out a groan. I'm so frustrated and I can't stand any of this. I hate all of this. I can't tell what's real and what's a dream anymore. I don't even know if right now I'm dreaming or what.

Savannah licks my face and begs me to pet her. I hold her close to my chest, all twelve pounds of her and cry. It seems like the only thing I can do that feels good.

When I'm done, I get out of bed and pull out a suitcase and start packing. I don't know how long I'm staying with my dad. I didn't know I was going. I throw some clothes in the bag and some pictures of Casper and me.

Seeing Dad will be good though. I miss him and I've not seen him in a long time. Maybe it will be good for me to get my head in the right place.

Mom pulls into a gas station where I see Dad's car. My pulse edges higher and I'm elated. It's been a long time since I've felt this way. I almost can't wait until Mom's car comes to a stop.

Dad gets out of the car, his tall, lanky body moves with a confident gait. My stepmom stays in the car as usual with my half-sister. She's always afraid to get out of the car and face Mom. It's usually awkward between my parents. They never say a word to each other. Mom stays by her car; Dad stays near his. If they have to say anything to each other, it's through me or Jonathan. Never face to face.

Mom and I hug tightly and her chin quivers.

"Mom, what's wrong?"

She shakes her head. "You have fun, okay? I'll see you in a week. You call me if you need anything. Got it?"

"Okay. I'll be fine."

"I love you."

"I love you too, Mom."

She seems to get emotional every time we say goodbye, whether it's her going to work or me going out with Cherry. I can't imagine how it must feel to let go of your child and not know if you'll ever see them again.

I turn and make my way to Dad who gives me a big hug. He's wearing a short-sleeved button-down shirt with jeans. His hair is completely gray now, and his looks older and more tired. He smells like some cheap cologne, as always. He loves the scent, but I think they're terrible.

"It's good to see you," he tells me as he opens the trunk. He takes my bag and puts it in there. "How was the ride over?"

"It was good."

He opens the passenger door and I'm surprised to see it empty.

"Where are Kimberly and Olivia?" I slide into the passenger seat and wait for him to get inside the car.

"It's just you and me the next week kiddo."

"What? What's wrong?"

"Kimberly's staying with her sister. I wanted some time with you."

"Dad, I'm fine. Is that really why they aren't here?"

He lets out a long sigh and frowns. "Kim and I are just having issues."

"What? Why?"

"I don't even know, Megan. She says she needs time to think and didn't really give me much to go on. I probably haven't been at my best because I've been worried about you."

"Do you think she's seeing someone or talking to them?"

He shrugs. "How are you? You look great. I'm sorry I never visited you in the hospital. Work and this mess have been crazy."

I nod. "It's okay." I guess it is, at least. I don't really know how to feel. Dad's never exactly made too much of an effort to come see us or anything like that. It's easy for him to be there for Kim and Olivia. He's always broke. He doesn't have money for gas. Something's wrong with the car. He doesn't trust the car to make the trip. There are any number of excuses and it makes me wonder why he really doesn't want to see us. I wonder how he was able to meet Mom this time. I try not to let the money thing or excuses bother me, because he could be worse. I better make the best out of this week because this will probably be the last time I'll see him. The thought saddens me, as it usually does, knowing I have to say goodbye to everyone.

"No, I should've been there. Hospitals creep me out. And knowing what put you there." He shakes his head.

"What do you mean?"

He clears his throat. "It would've been hard seeing you like that after that asshole..." He stops. "I can't believe they haven't caught him yet. He's a kid. He can't be that damn smart to outrun police for this long. They must not be doing their jobs."

Because Vincent's not here, but I don't mention it to Dad. He doesn't know anything unless he does and isn't saying anything. Wouldn't surprise me if Mom blabbed it all to Dad. Honestly, they can barely talk to each other without it turning into a yelling match. Mom used to ground me and prevent me from seeing Dad because that was part of my punishment. It's dumb but that's how she is.

But she's changed now, and I know it's because of what happened to me.

"I'm really sorry for what happened to you and I'm just thankful you're okay."

"Thanks, Dad."

"And I'm sorry about Casper. He was a good man."

I hold in my irritation at Dad's use of past tense. I want to scream to everyone that he's not dead. But then I'd look like a crazy person for real. "Yeah." I hate the sentiment especially after last night. I have to meet Casper in a dream. I have to know for sure he's okay.

Dad and I spend the rest of the drive talking about things from physical therapy to his work as a grocery store manager to how Mom's been.

I used to spend time getting annoyed with Dad over how he doesn't make the effort to visit or to pick us up or how he doesn't take much time for Jonathan and me. Every time I'm with him when it's just the two of us, I feel so connected to him. Like no matter how upset I am with him, it goes away the second I see him, and we talk. Like all is forgiven. I guess that's why it hurts even more knowing he doesn't make that effort to see us. I'm not really sure if it really is that he can't afford it or if he doesn't want to see us or if he's afraid of driving. I get jealous when I see him with Olivia, wishing he were like that with Jonathan and me as kids. Maybe he was.

I shake my head. None of it matters because he's not really my dad. But he's never turned his back on me. And it's going to hurt to have to leave him behind. In all the lives I've lived, he's my favorite father. Since my parents disowned me, my human parents are the only ones I have. Once I go back to Arvada, I won't have any parents. The thought saddens me, and I truly believe this will be the last time I see my father. I know Casper's waiting for me, but I'll explain it to him once I see him in my dreams again, he'll understand. He knows how much I've been missing my family here, although I wonder how much time I have left.

Twenty-One

t takes us a little over two hours to get to his house from the state line. He lives just north of Atlanta in a quaint suburb. It's similar to a few suburbs in Birmingham but bigger. Grocery stores on every corner and across from each other. Malls and shopping centers galore. Never a shortage of churches either. Driving through the city is always fun, though. Seeing all the many tall buildings and interstates with seemingly hundreds of lanes. Makes me think of prospect and growth. Thriving. Something I haven't been doing at home.

His two-story house is quiet now that Olivia isn't here. He sets me up in the guest room upstairs where the bathroom connects to Olivia's playful room. Pastel yellow walls with an animal wallpaper that runs across each of the walls in the middle. It's weird not having her here.

The baby blue walls of the guest room are calming, and Kim's porcelain masks hang haphazardly all over the walls. Some are insanely ornate with intricate face paintings and glitter and feathers. Others are plain with a basic star around an eye. One of the masks has a purple collar around it like a royal jester. It reminds me of one of Claudette's dresses. I wonder if she's changed him or done something to him. Casper said he hasn't retaliated or attacked since Vincent and I left.

I've always liked the masks. They seem to have their own story, and I always try to think of what it is. I wish I could write something, but my mind is all over the place lately, not that I've even tried at all.

After unpacking and getting settled, I meet Dad downstairs to watch TV with him. I roll my eyes at the HGTV playing and chuckle.

"What?"

"Still watch this?"

"Heck yeah. One day I'll fix up some things in this house."

"Like what? It's fairly new and it's pretty."

He doesn't answer, which is usual of him.

"Your mom told me about Spencer." Dad swivels his recliner to the side to face me on the couch.

His comment catches me off guard. Since when does he and Mom ever talk, let alone have a civil conversation?

"You snuck out of the house to meet up with him?"

Heat pricks beneath my cheeks. I can't believe Mom told him. She probably told him about Arvada, too. *Wonderful.* "Um. Yeah. Why?"

He lets out an exasperated breath. "Megan. Why would you do that?"

"It's really not as big of a deal as Mom made it out to be. You know how she is. Exaggerates everything."

He mulls it over. "Yeah, she does."

"It really wasn't that late," I lie. "We just couldn't sleep and we hung out in the driveway for a while."

He raises an eyebrow.

"He's harmless."

"You're not gonna start dating him, are you?"

"No," I say too quickly. "I'm with—" I clear my throat. "I'm not dating anyone."

Dad nods and turns his recliner back to the TV, slowly rocking back and forth. "Good. That's good. Don't want to rush these things."

"Are you still painting?" I ask, trying to get him off the subject of my love life.

"A little. Are you still writing?"

I shake my head and lower it.

"It's okay. Just focus on getting well. That's the most important thing right now. Oh, Janet and her boys wanted to come over one day and see you if you want."

"Yeah. That's fine." Aunt Janet is Dad's younger sister. She has two boys, same age as me. I don't know the last time I saw them. Or any of my family for that matter. Dad doesn't like to be around a lot of people, and I guess that includes family. Nothing crazy happened on his side for him to want to stay away. I think it's just him and his fear of going places.

"If you ever need to talk about anything, you know I'm here."

"I know." Dad's always been a good listener, and I've talked to him plenty about things going on in my life. But I can't tell him any of this. He will for sure think I'm nuts. Especially if I tell him what happened this morning, which I myself still don't even know what that was.

"Thought about making fried squash, fried chicken, and fresh green beans for dinner."

My mouth salivates. "Sounds good."

"Remember when we stayed up late frying all that squash?"

I chuckle. When I was about ten, he had grown squash, and we stayed up late, slicing it and frying it so we could freeze it. We made so much that night and ended up eating a lot of it, too. Surprisingly, neither one of us got sick. Not like the time Jonathan ate a ton of Easter candy one night when we were playing card games and ended up puking all over the bathroom. Dad ended up cleaning that, and I felt bad for him.

He laughs.

We're quiet for a while, both engrossed in HGTV, at least he seems to be. I can barely pay attention to it and I constantly glance at my phone, wishing Casper could text me. I still text him, which is kinda pathetic, but it helps me during the day when I can't talk to him. I can't just bottle it all up until I see him in my dreams.

But there's a new number in my phone. One that I snagged from Mom's phone. Spencer Peterson. When I scroll to his name, a funny feeling rises inside my stomach, and I don't know why or what it is. It's almost like a weight floating around. Should I text him? Should I not? He wasn't exactly nice the last time we spoke. But neither was I. Though he did lie for me. Again. I only got his number in case I needed to talk to someone about my mysterious happenings. Sadly, Spencer's the only one who knows. I don't really know how to feel about that.

I turn over my phone and put it next to me.

Dad's still rocking and watching TV.

"Are you okay?" I ask him. He's quiet, which isn't necessarily unusual, but we've not seen each other in months. Usually, the first few days he's chatty; telling me random stories from work or about a neighbor who won't mow their lawn or some hooligan driving past the house with the radio blaring. I wonder if he's got so much on his mind and wants to ask me things but doesn't know how. We've always been close. Ever since he and Mom divorced, since I couldn't see him as much, we wrote each other. I wasn't allowed to call him or email him because I was grounded or whatever Mom's excuse was at the time. We've always talked to each other about things that go on in our lives. It's one of the things I appreciate about him. He's willing to listen to me and doesn't take my problems as insignificant because of my age, like Mom does. I still have all of his letters somewhere in a plastic tub. Some are long, some short. But every single one of them valuable.

Is Dad worried about me? Worried about Kimberly and him? Does he think I've changed? Am I different?

The way his forehead creases, I can tell he's thinking about something. "Yeah. Why?"

I shrug. "You're quiet."

"Just trying to figure out what to have for dinner this week."

I laugh a little at the simplicity of what he's thinking compared to what I thought he was thinking. Dad's a planner, too. He's always planned dinner, weeks at a time. It helps with his budget, but what if he's not in the mood for whatever's on the menu that particular night? I don't know if I'm just lazy and don't feel like taking the time to plan or if I just like the spontaneity of it.

"What about burritos one night?"

"Sure."

"Country fried steak?"

"Yeah." I know he's going to list everything for the week, so I wait until he's finished before I ask him a question. "So have you heard from Kim at all?"

"Not really."

"Was this sudden or what?"

"I don't know. I think she believes I'm not in the mood for a three-year-old."

"There's gotta be more to it than that. That sounds like an excuse."

"We've just gotten on different wavelengths, I guess."

I always wondered when their twenty-year age difference would cause issues. "I'm sorry."

He waves his hand dismissively. "Don't worry about me. How's it been since you've been home?"

I shrug. "Fine, I guess."

"Has your mom and Ron been okay with you?"

"Yeah. Mom's been fine. I try to avoid Ron as much as I can. He got mad at me when I didn't come to dinner one night as soon as he'd like."

"What? Doesn't he know it takes you a little longer to get around?" he asks, his voice rising. He's never liked Ron, but neither have a lot of people. His arrogance and belief that he is better than everyone tends to steer people away.

"I made Mom cry one night. We were just talking about things. Ron told me to stop upsetting her."

Dad shakes his head. "He'd better stop treating you like that, or I'll have a talk with him."

"It's okay. I'll be out of the house soon." I hope, at least.

"He shouldn't be doing that. You've been through a lot."

I nod. Talking about all of this makes me sad and a little annoyed. Sad because I'm going to miss him when I leave, annoyed because I feel like I'm wasting so much time here instead of searching for a way to return to Casper.

And what if I can't return? What if I really am stuck here for eternity?

Anxiety crawls its way inside me, twisting around my stomach and latching onto my heart. I take a deep breath. I need a distraction. I need something. I need Casper.

"I think I'm gonna take a nap," I tell Dad and retreat to my room.

Staring at the masks is a bit unnerving now. It's like having all these people watching and judging me.

Like in real life. Every move I make. Every word I say. It's all being evaluated. Making sure I pass the test or something.

I finally fall asleep and find my way inside a dream with Casper. I'm relieved that it's him and not Vincent.

"What do you mean he was there?" Casper asks, holding my hands. We're standing on the beach and I'm loving the soft way the water caresses the shore. It's a cool night and the way the stars clutter the sky in a chaotic pattern feels magical.

"I followed the orb and landed in Arvada, but it was Vincent. It wasn't you. Something is happening to me, Casper. I don't know. I'm losing time. I keep waking up in weird places without knowing how I got there. I have no memory. For several hours."

"Did Vincent do anything to you?"

"I don't know. I still haven't seen him since that first day I woke up. But what could he have done?"

Casper holds me closer. "There's no telling. I'm so sorry."

"I can't find him. I saw something that he may have been in Arizona, but why is he traveling so far away? Why hasn't he returned to Arvada?"

"Maybe he can't. It's okay, Megan. You have to get well first, remember? Spending time with your dad is fine. Spend as much time as you can with him. We'll find a way. I promise."

"You don't always have to try to convince me that things are going to be okay."

"I know. I wish I could. Maybe you should focus on your human life."

"What do you mean?"

"Instead of spending so much time and energy finding Vincent or finding your way back here, live your life. You wanted to return to this human life for a reason. You're there. Live it."

"Why does this feel like a goodbye?"

"It's not, Megan. I want you here more than anything, but you don't need to risk your life getting back to me."

"What are you saying?"

"That I don't want you to find Vincent because it's too dangerous."

"This again?"

"What's going to happen if your family locks you up? You would be miserable. You've spent too much of your life locked up. If Vincent finds you and kills you..." He shakes his head.

My eyes water as I stare at him. "You don't want me to come back?"

"You know that's not what I'm saying."

"What am I supposed to do? Live out my life without you? If I die, I'll be reborn in another life not knowing who you are, and you won't be there."

"We'll always have the dreams. I will find you there. This will give the option for Vincent to return here so I can kill him."

"I can't believe you're saying any of this." I start walking away, my heart sinks to my stomach. I don't like this feeling or this talk. "I won't be able to just pick up my human life and not have you in it."

"I'm here. It was only a suggestion. I didn't say you had to do it." He gathers me into his arms, pulling me tight against his chest.

I can't believe he would suggest a thing. Does he not love me anymore? Is spending time with Saida in Arvada making him forget about me? I've been fearing that my mind will forget him, I never stopped to think that maybe he's forgetting me all along.

Twenty-Two

ad wipes his chin and rests his elbows on the table. It's still strange that Kim and Olivia aren't here, though I am enjoying alone time with Dad.

"That was so good." I pat my stomach and try to breathe. I haven't eaten that much in a while. It feels good to be able to eat like a normal person. Waking up from a coma is probably the strangest thing ever. Having to relearn so many basic things is surreal.

"Yeah, it was." He watches me almost like he's observing.

"What?"

He shakes his head.

"What is it?"

"I know you've only been here for a few hours, but I don't know what your mom is talking about."

"What do you mean?"

He sighs and starts clearing the table.

"Dad?" I follow him into the kitchen.

He turns around, arms crossed and leans against the counter. "Your mom has told me some things. She thinks you should spend some time in a facility."

"What?" I read my file, but I had no idea she was really considering that. Have I been doing bad things? Acting bad? Okay, I'm sure all the stuff Cherry has told my mom isn't helping at all. That's my fault for trusting Cherry.

"She told me you want to find Vincent. I've wanted you to come over because I want to teach you to fight. I've read about them finding Vincent's car and he may come back for you and I'm not always going to be there."

"Dad, I'm fine."

He shakes his head. "You're still going to learn, kiddo."

"Okay. Is that why Mom was pushing me to come over here? So you could evaluate me, too?"

"No. She wanted you to get away from things for a while. Besides, I haven't seen you since the summer when you and Casper came over."

I tilt my head and look at him. "You've met Casper?"

He furrows his eyebrows. "Yes. Don't you remember?"

"Memories are still hard sometimes," I tell him.

He nods. "I'm sure they will be for a time."

When he's done cleaning the dishes, we push the table against the wall. We stand face-to-face on the large rug. It's weird. I remember some things that Casper taught me after my attack. I didn't even know my dad knew how to fight. Although for guys, doesn't it come naturally to know?

"I know if you ever see Vincent, you're already going to be on edge. Unless he comes at you from behind. If he does that, head-butt him. You'll want to hit him in the nose. You can also do this if he grabs you from the front. Use your keys or anything you have on you to strike him in the face, the eyes, whatever you need." He shows me how to put the keys in between my fingers.

"Am I going to remember all this if I am in danger?"

"I sure hope you do. Tomorrow, we'll get you some pepper spray, too."

We spend a couple of hours in the dining room. He teaches me how to get out of a bear hug, how to punch, how to kick, and a few other things. I know we'll be practicing this throughout the week, which is fine because I want to know these things. I want Casper to teach me more, but our time together is so limited, and it's never guaranteed.

When Dad and I arrive at the store, I wander off to the electronics to look around. I'm sure if Jonathan were here, he'd be drooling over all the video games. Once Dad finishes his shopping and getting me pepper spray, we check out and make our way out to the car. We load the bags into the trunk and as Dad returns the buggy, I feel someone staring at me from afar. When I look up, I gasp when I see him.

My heart lurches forward and fear grips me. Squinting in the dark, I shake my head. That can't be Vincent. Just a few feet away, he's standing under a parking lot lamp, hands in his pockets, staring. Dark hair, blue eyes. No, it's just some creepy guy staring.

Something is happening. Suddenly, I'm in Vincent's room in a prom dress and Vincent's staring at me.

"You choose him every time."

"What are you talking about? I've never chosen him."

"This whole year you've chosen him."

"*This has nothing to do with anyone but you and me. I've finally realized who you are. You're manipulative and only care about yourself.*"

He scoffs. "*Everything I do is with you in my mind. It's all for you.*"

"*Oh, really? The drugs you bought were for me? You constantly putting me down and call me names? That was all for me?*"

"*Jesus, you're still pissed about that? When are you gonna get over it?*"

My jaw drops. "*Are you serious? Nothing you do is for me.*"

"*Casper's the one who manipulated you. I can't believe you'd rather be with him. Even after everything I do to keep you two apart. I vandalized your car and framed him, yet you believed Casper. I spread the rumors about you sleeping with him. I was the one who killed Adam because he came after you and you still hail Casper as your hero.*"

Air traps in my lungs. He killed someone? His confessions boggle in my mind like dice in a cup. I feel sick and my knees are weak and I'm starting to feel sleepy. It's too much. I can't even look at him. "*Why?*" *My voice is barely audible.*

"*Because I would do anything for you. I even tried killing him. I have given you my heart, Megan. I have given you everything you can ever imagine. What more*" *do you want? Is this what you really want? You made a promise to me, Megan. Are you just giving up on us?"*

"Giving up? I've tried for several months with you. I know who you are now." I don't know why I'm still standing here. I need to get out of here away from this dangerous and obsessive man.

He narrows his eyes and moves closer to me. "You never tried. You're a fucking liar, and I fell for your lies. You told me you'd run away with me, that we'd be together forever."

"Things change. I thought you'd never hurt me, but you did. You just admitted more things. I have to go."

I try to move around him, but he snatches my arm. "You aren't going anywhere."

I hear the front door open and close, and I almost fall over. What is wrong with me? Why am I so tired? I have to stay awake. Vincent drugged me. I know he did.

"Vincent!" his dad calls from downstairs.

"One sec, Dad," Vincent calls back. He turns to me. "Might as well get comfortable. But if you don't change your mind, you'll regret it."

"Megan?" Dad calls and I blink several times and look around. I'm standing by Dad's car in the parking lot. Scanning the lot, I don't see anyone or Vincent. But he showed me a vision. I know it was him.

Fumbling with the door handle, I finally open it and climb inside the car.

"You okay?" Dad asks.

"Yeah," I lie, trying to keep my voice level and calm my breathing. My heart is thrashing inside my chest. It had to be my imagination. Vincent isn't here. He can't be.

But the vision…

That wasn't how it happened. Vincent's dad never came home that night. After he confessed everything, he drugged me and locked me in the basement. He tortured me for days. I set the house on fire almost killing him. I ran to Casper and Vincent shot me.

But even that memory is fading. What was that vision? Why is Vincent feeding me different memories? He mentioned the dreams and realized how Casper and I found each other. Didn't he? What is wrong with me? Why is everything so messed up in my head?

If I could get back to Arvada, none of this would be happening. I would be cured. My mind would be set right.

But it's taking me forever to get back or even find a way back.

By the time Dad and I return to the house, I'm tired and lie down for a bit.

Tears cloud my eyes as I curl my legs into my chest. I feel so lost and incredibly lonely. I have a text open for Cherry, but I don't know what to say. If I tell her I think I saw Vincent, she'll tell me to tell Dad.

She'll tell my mom or maybe she won't believe me at all. She thinks I'm on some suicide mission. Then the police will be involved. I don't want that because there's nothing the police can do. Not in this world. I don't even know if I really saw him. I guess it's technically possible for him to travel from Arizona to here in a matter of a few days, but he doesn't know I'm here.

I scroll over Spencer's name. Should I text him at all? My heart palpitates at the thought. He's the only one I think I can trust right now. At least so far, he hasn't blabbed everything to my mom.

I bite my lip as I type out a message.

Hey, it's Megan.

Hey what's up? he asks.

Not much. At my dad's. Is it cool that I texted?

Yeah. it's fine. You okay?

I wait a few seconds before responding, unsure of what to really say. **It happened again.**

What did?

Can I call?

Sure.

A burning sensation spreads across my chest as I click on his name. I don't know why I'm so nervous.

"You okay?" he asks, and I hear the concern.

"I don't know. I woke up yesterday in the cemetery." I keep my voice low just in case. Dad's never been one to spy on me, though he's never exactly had a reason until now and it feels like everyone is spying on me. "I have no idea how I got there."

"Jesus, Megan. Have you told anyone?"

"You're the only one who knows. Why does this keep happening?"

He lets out a breath. "I don't know. Have you told Dr. Brown?"

"No. I've told no one. They'll lock me up."

"Okay, okay. What were you dreaming? Or do you remember?"

"I was dreaming about Casper."

"Maybe you're missing him and subconsciously made your way to the cemetery."

"That doesn't explain why I came to running in the woods the other night." I stop and remember that dream. Wasn't I dreaming about Vincent? "I was dreaming about Vincent. He was after me."

"Maybe your dreams are forcing you to do things. Or you're stressed out and sleepwalking. I did that in the beginning."

"You did?"

"Yeah. Dr. Brown put me on medication, so I don't anymore. One night, I woke up behind the wheel in my car."

I gasp and try to push the tears away. "I don't want to do that."

"No one does."

We're quiet for a moment.

"Where does your dad live?" he asks.

"Outside of Atlanta."

"Nice. I've always wanted to go there. Parents divorced, too?"

We talk for a while about my parents, their divorce and his dad who abandoned them when he was six. He'd show up every couple of years until Spencer was fourteen and finally told his dad to leave for good. It's weird how much we tell each other about our lives in such a short amount of time. I realize he was trying to get my mind off things, and it worked. It's weird that he's experienced similar things as me.

"I feel like you know so much about me and I know nothing about you," I tell him.

"What do you want to know?"

"I don't know. How old are you? What do you like to do? What was your life like before…?" I like talking to him. His voice is soft, yet relaxing. It's also better than sitting in the room by myself thinking and aching for Casper. He gets my mind off things.

"You…really want to know all that?"

"Sure. Why?"

"Not many people care enough to want to know. I'm not used to it. Especially someone like you."

"Someone like me?"

Spencer clears his throat. "You're always so nice to people. You're incredibly smart and I'm not exactly top of our class. You're very with it and aware. Most girls like you don't talk to guys like me."

My cheeks feel warm. "That's so cliché."

He chuckles. "It's true. Most girls when they find out I have dad issues or that I've been in trouble most of my life, they tend to run away."

"Well, maybe I'm not the girl you think I am. What kind of trouble were you in?"

He lets out a long sigh. "Stealing, skipping class. Got caught smoking. Got into a lot of fights. Gave my mom plenty of heartaches. Once I left alternative school, I met Tyler. He was a cool guy. We did normal things like watch sports or play video games. Concerts. Didn't feel the need to fall back in my old ways."

"And now?"

"I've not really done much since that day."

"Yeah, I get that."

It's weird how Vincent has turned this place upside down, yet no one can find him. Except I swear I saw him today. How would he know where I am? But I know the answer to that. He's stalking me like some creeper. It doesn't make sense. Is he popping up whenever he feels like it and going back to Arvada? Wouldn't he continue to mess up time and events if he did that though? Either way, I hate the feeling of someone following me. What if he follows me to my dad's house? What if he breaks in and hurts my dad?

Twenty-Three

Dad and I practice fighting more and end up watching a Hallmark movie afterward. It's always funny to me that he digs those kinds of movies. I try to block the paranoid thoughts of Vincent coming after me or my dad from my mind. They're still there.

During the movie, I text Spencer. I really enjoy talking to him and learning about him. He doesn't strike me as the type of person who was always in trouble as a kid, but you never really know a person until you do.

Guilt starts pushing through, but Casper wouldn't care if I had a male friend. That was Vincent who couldn't stand me talking to anyone else. He hated that Casper and I had to partner up for an assignment, and even in Arvada, he always hated it when I talked to anyone or got close to anyone else but him. What did he expect since he was never there or that he pushed me around too much?

Do you ever think you see something or someone, but you don't? Like it's all a hallucination? I ask Spencer.

Sometimes. You mean like a ghost?

Maybe. I dunno. I thought I saw someone tonight, but I couldn't have. They couldn't have been here.

Why can't they?

They just can't. I dunno. It was weird. It felt too real.

I can't exactly type out a text to him about how I think I saw Vincent. There really is a manhunt and the police probably tapped my phone. I'll be damned if they get to him first before me.

I'm sorry. I bet your mind makes you see a lot of things. Do you have nightmares?

Yeah. Some nights, my dreams are good. Only he doesn't know that's where I meet Casper.

Oh.

Do you have nightmares? I ask.

All the time. Probably why I don't like sleeping.

☹ **I'm sorry. You can call or text anytime if you have one and need to talk.**

Thanks.

I really mean that. I'm not just saying it.

I really appreciate that. you are incredible kind. Even after everything you've been through. Not many people are.

Tell me about it.

Shit. Sorry. Of course, you know that.

It's okay. I really like talking to you. You help make me feel better.

I do?

Yeah. You have a calming effect.

Same here, Megan.

After the movie, I say goodnight to Dad and Spencer and go to bed. It takes me a while to fall asleep and when I do, I find Casper easily. Something doesn't feel right. He's angry. The grimace on his face looks like he's about to explode. This isn't like him.

"What's wrong, Casper?" I take his hand, but he jerks it away. Blood rushes to my cheeks. What have I done? Why is he being distant? Is he still upset from the last time we saw each other? Does he not want me to find him in the dreams anymore?

"Who is he?"

"What?"

"Who's the guy, Megan?" He's glaring off in the distance, and when I turn my head in the direction of his eyesight, I see Spencer leaning against a tree.

"That's my friend, Spencer."

Casper cocks an eyebrow. "Isn't that the guy who's friends with Vincent? Didn't he almost hit you with his car?"

"He didn't mean to. It was my fault, really. He's not friends with Vincent anymore."

He shakes his head in disappointment. "Do you hear yourself? You're still the same. Always falling for guys who hurt you."

"I'm not falling for him. He's the only one I can talk to about the weird things that are going on with me."

"You can talk to me."

"Not all the time. You want me to leave you so you can be with Saida."

He narrows his eyes. "She's a friend, Megan."

"Why are you being like this?" This isn't Casper. What is happening? "I fell for you, and you've never hurt me."

He leans down, his brown eyes morph to a dark blue. His hair changes to black as night. "You made me shoot those people. You made me do terrible things. It's your fault."

I freeze, unable to run. My feet are heavy like I'm wearing weights around my ankles. "Vincent? How are you here?"

"I will always find you."

"You have to take us home."

He shakes his head. "You are home." His lips spread into a chilling grimace. "It's my turn to torture you."

"No." I have to get away. I push him back, but he catches my arms.

"You did this. You made me do this."

"Stop." Tears flood my face. "You didn't have to do it. Take us back home. We can't stay here anymore."

"You're here forever. I told you no one would believe you. I told you I would punish you."

Using what Dad taught me, I slam my head into his nose, breaking free of the weights. I take off as fast and far as I can. Casper's nowhere to be found, but I keep going.

"You did this to yourself!" he screams after me.

I run as fast as I can through the night. Vincent's stalking me in real life and my dreams. I don't know how to make any of this stop.

I jolt awake. As soon as my vision comes to focus, I freeze. Tall pine trees surround me and I'm lying on a bed of damp leaves. The early morning sun peeks through the woods. My breaths come out in white puffs. I feel a tingling inside my chest and my heart palpitates.

What am I doing out here? Where am I? I get to my feet and use a tree to stabilize myself. I feel sick and while it's freezing outside, I'm sweating.

I have to get back to Dad's house, but I have no idea where I am.

Of course, I don't have my phone on me, and I'm in flannel pajamas. No shoes. I hate the feeling of wetness between my toes. I hate how I can't stop myself from trembling. I hate not knowing if I'm going to step on a snake or not. But it's winter. They're hibernating, aren't they? I hate not knowing where I am or how I got here. I keep walking and try not to think about anything except making it back to Dad's house okay.

I know I should tell someone about this, but I can't.

By some miracle, I find my way back.

"Where have you been?" Dad asks before I close the front door.

"I was just walking around." Luckily, I was only in the woods behind Dad's neighborhood, so it wasn't that far away.

His eyes rove over my attire and when our eyes meet, he's clearly in disbelief. "In your pajamas?"

I shrug.

"Megan," he presses. "You're barefoot."

I can't run away from the truth, yet I don't know what to tell him. If I tell him the truth, he'll tell Mom and they'll for sure throw me in an institution. I know he's expecting an answer, but how do I explain what I don't know?

"Okay." I roll my eyes. "I saw a mama and baby deer and I wanted to get closer, but they kept moving away. Then I got lost." I hope he believes my ridiculous story.

Wrinkling his forehead, he tries not to smile and shakes his head instead. "Get cleaned up. I'll have breakfast ready soon."

I nod and retreat up to my room. Once there, I close the door and I can't stop the tears that cascade down my face. I hate this feeling; this feeling like I have no control.

How long was I gone? I didn't find an orb this time. I was dreaming. The dream was weird. Is Vincent torturing me there now, too? Has he found the only way Casper and I can connect? He's messing with me. Always messing with me. Or am I going crazy?

I have to get back.

Seeing my cell phone on the edge of my nightstand, I crawl across the room to fetch it. It's eight-thirty in the morning, which means it's only seven-thirty in Birmingham.

Is Spencer awake? Would a text wake him? I don't want to bother him, but I need someone to talk to.

I type out a text.

It happened again. I'm really scared.

My phone starts ringing only after a few seconds. It's Spencer.

"Are you okay?" he asks.

"I don't know what to do."

"It's okay. When do you come home?"

"This Sunday."

"I think you should either call Dr. Brown and ask her to call in a prescription or wait until you see her again. If it were me, I wouldn't wait. She told me it was because of the trauma I experienced that's causing me to sleepwalk. Could be the case for you, too."

Except, I'm not exactly experiencing any trauma. Just some psychotic man who won't leave me alone. I wonder if some drug could really help prevent whatever magic Vincent has over me. What if whatever Dr. Brown gives me really messes up my mind more than it already is? Or what if it prevents me from seeing Casper in my dreams? Although maybe it could help me sleep and stay asleep and stay with Casper. I don't know what to do. I don't take the meds she's given me now.

"It's not a permanent fix but it'll help," Spencer says. "At least, it helps me."

"You don't have them anymore?"

"Mine weren't as severe as yours. At least, I wasn't waking up in random places."

"Thanks. I'm sorry I bothered you so early."

"You don't bother me. I know you're going through a lot. Where did you wake up?"

"In the woods behind my dad's house. I had a nightmare again. Vincent was chasing me."

"I'm sorry. He haunts my dreams, too."

My heart breaks at his statement, and I want to do something, anything to help him. To help everyone who's suffering. All because of Vincent's selfishness or whatever it was that caused him to create such chaos and pain. I have to end this.

If I can just hold on a little longer to get strong enough to fight Vincent.

Twenty-Four

herry and I arrive at the mall in one piece, thankfully. She stops in almost every store, and I try to play along and pretend like I'm having fun. It's harder than I thought it would be. The whole way to the mall she tried to get me to talk about my trip and chastised me for giving her one-word answers. I guess she doesn't realize how scared I am to tell her anything.

I haven't called Dr. Brown or told anyone about the sleepwalking or whatever it is that I'm doing. I swear it's something crazy that Vincent is doing.

"Hey." Cherry rests her hand on mine with a concerned look. "I'm really sorry I upset you earlier. I suck at this so much. I'm not trying to be a crappy friend."

Guilt settles over me because I know I'm not being a good friend either. I'm letting everything bother me and consume my mind. I relax and give her a reassuring smile. "No, you didn't upset me. It's just...everything. Everything Vincent has done." Which is true but I'm still afraid of how to act around her.

She frowns. "I know. The police will find him though."

I roll my eyes internally. Fat chance of that ever happening.

I don't know how my mom convinced me to come tonight. It was either this or continue to let her ask questions about my trip. How can I care about clothes or makeup when the love of my life is possibly being tortured? When *I'm* being tortured. None of this matters and none of it will matter once I leave here. If there really is a fugitive on the run, how can anyone carry on as if nothing happened? If Vincent really did shoot up a school, why is everyone acting like they don't care? Sure, it's been a couple of months but still. Kids are still hanging out, staring at their phones in large groups, laughing. There are too many people here.

I recognize some kids from school. They're all laughing and playing around. When some of them see and recognize me, their stares soon shift into glares. I look away feeling the warmth on my face. An uneasy feeling roils in my stomach. I want to leave. I haven't forgotten their messages to me on Facebook.

Cherry flips through tops as several hang on her arm, talking about school. I'm not really listening.

"Can we go?"

"What? Why?"

I nod toward some of the kids. "Because they're staring at me."

She rolls her eyes. "Just ignore them."

"They blamed me. They look pissed."

Cherry bites her lip and frowns. "I know. They know you were injured. You just have to ignore them."

Yeah, that's so easy to do. All of this is my fault. "I'm going to fix it."

Cherry looks confused. "How? This wasn't your doing. Don't you dare blame yourself."

I glance up and my hands curl into fists when I see a couple of kids walking toward me. My throat is dry, and I can't seem to keep a steady breath.

"Shouldn't you be locked up?" Casper's friend, Brad asks. His icy blonde hair has gotten a little longer and his eyes are sadder even though he's glaring at me.

Cherry moves in front of me. "Why don't you run along?"

He shakes his head. "I don't see how you're walking around free."

Looking past Brad, through crowds of people, I see him. Vincent is across the way behind the fountain dressed in all black with a hat staring at me. Anger wells inside me. How dare he show up here like this?

My pulse edges higher as I bolt toward him. Pushing Brad out of the way, I race through the crowd.

"Vincent," I cry, but he runs from me.

I hear Cherry yelling my name, but I can't stop. I won't stop. I chase him down the empty hall with maintenance rooms and out into the parking lot.

When I reach the door, I push it open and find myself alone at the loading docks. Orange lights glow in the foggy night, and I can't see Vincent anywhere.

What is he doing? Following me everywhere? Spying on me? Was he really there? Is he making me hallucinate now?

"Megan!" Cherry yells making me jump. "What are you doing?"

"I was chas—I thought I saw someone."

"Who?" She looks at me like I'm crazy.

"It's no one."

She frowns and bites her lip. "We-we should go home."

Nodding, I follow her without a word back to her car. We're quiet on the way home. I know she's judging me. I've ruined whatever friendship we could have. She shouldn't be friends with me anyway. People at school are already saying things and she shouldn't be associated.

"I'm sorry about what he said."

I stare out the window. "Guess I need to get used to it."

"No, you don't. You didn't do anything." She lets out a frustrated groan. "People suck. Do you think you saw Vincent?"

"What? No." No way am I telling her what I saw. I don't even know I really saw him.

"I heard you yell his name."

I let out a sigh. "I don't want to talk about it."

"If you saw him, we have to call the police. I didn't see anyone. You were chasing no one."

"I thought I saw him, okay? No big deal." I know I saw him. Of course, he only shows himself to me.

"Have you seen him before or thought you did?"

"No."

"Have you remembered anything about that day?"

"No."

"How can you not have a single piece of memory of the day your ex-boyfriend massacred several people then left several others for dead, including you?" She lets out a curse. "Sorry. I'm really sorry for that. It's just...it's just odd that you have zero memory of it and zero reaction to any of it. Including...you know."

"Including what?"

"Casper."

Suddenly I don't want to be in the car with her anymore. I want to be at home.

"It's almost like ever since you woke up, you've kinda shut down for weeks or something. But you have to keep fighting. You can get through this."

"What are you talking about?" I ask, feeling my anger rising. "Still think I'm suicidal?"

"This isn't funny, Megan. You and Casper were so in love. A rare kind of thing. It's just...I hate how you haven't even cried or anything for Casper. I hate that you can't even remember Vincent shooting you and Casper." Her chin quivers, then she clears her throat.

"Ugh. Just stop, okay? I'm sorry that I'm not who or what you want me to be right now. I've told you everything that happened, and you completely ignored it. Now, everyone thinks I'm crazy. Everyone believes it was my fault." Tears collect but I bat them away.

"Megan, listen to me. Please. There is no other world. There is just this one. You didn't go anywhere. Maybe inside your head, but you've physically been here the whole time."

"Stop saying that." I don't care what I sound like. I'm so angry and frustrated with everything.

"It's true and you'll only heal and get through this if you just let Casper go. He would want you to."

Let Casper go? How can she say that? That's exactly what he told me, too.

"Will you please let it go? This entire fantasy." She shakes her head. "If you keep living it, you'll lose your mind."

"I'm sorry, okay? This isn't easy for me. I've spent months being tortured and that's all I know. It doesn't matter what any of you say. It isn't going to change the way I feel or what's happened to me. I can't just wake up and forget it all."

I'm tired of arguing with her. I know I can't convince anyone. It's the worst feeling when no one believes what you have to say. What you've experienced. This is the worst. The vast feeling of loneliness. This darkness weighs heavily on me, and I don't know what to do.

On the way home, Cherry grips the steering wheel tight. She bites her lip. "I don't know what to do anymore. I don't know how to help." She's bawling and I feel terrible. Maybe hearing too much of the fantasy world is too much for humans. If only there was a way, I could bring her with me to show her.

She's quiet now.

We don't say a word the rest of the way to my house. I suspect she'll want to report what happened to my parents.

Instead, she leaves the car running in the driveway.

"I'm sorry," I tell her. "I'm sorry my mind is such a mess and it's clearly affecting everyone."

She's hurt and upset and conflicted, almost like she feels guilty for being upset with me. "I know it's not easy for you and I'm letting my own irritation and anger take over. There's so much I'm feeling and it's hard because it feels like you aren't feeling any emotion. My therapist says maybe you're still in shock. If you can't remember anything, of course you won't feel the aftermath of it. I'm not being very patient with you and I'm sorry."

"We'll get through this," I say, hopeful. "Please don't tell Mom." I feel like I say that to her every time we hang out or talk. But I know she'll tell her.

Everyone believes I'm just a human and that there is no other world. Arvada is real and I have no one to talk to about it. Except Dr. Brown. But does she really listen? Or is she just taking notes and writing reasons why I need to be locked up? I wonder if Spencer would believe me. Would he help me find Vincent?

Twenty-Five

Clutching the straps on my backpack, I stare at the brick building before me under a dark cloudy sky. It's been raining the last few days and today can't decide if it's going to rain or not. The cold January air cuts through me like I'm wearing nothing.

Students congregate in the parking lot. Some chatter in quiet laughter. Some make out. Most seem half asleep. But it's quite a somber scene. There's a huge banner across the front of the building welcoming the students and stating that we are not victims. There's a memorial of sorts nearby with piles of flowers, mementos, and pictures of all six victims.

Casper's picture is plastered all over. As I enter the building, I see his face smiling back at me.

It's too much. It feels too real. Hammers pound inside my head as I watch people. This is the most ridiculous thing. Why did I come? I don't belong here. This isn't my life. This is just my human life. Bound by some spell.

Casper isn't dead.

Making my way to class, whispers echo in the hallway.

Is that her?

He died because of her?

It was her fault.

Just ignore them, I remind myself. None of it is real. I won't be here much longer, dealing with silly high school drama. Everyone is watching me. I don't even know why I'm at school. I have my car back and I could go anywhere. Not sure how I can skip school without Mom or Cherry finding out.

Cherry meets me at my locker. "Hey." She looks at me like I'm going to fall apart any second or I'm going to become the Hulk. It's the same look she's been giving me since I woke up from the coma. "I'm not really sure how any of us are going to get through this."

I shrug. "Soon it won't matter anymore."

Her eyebrows come together. "What?"

After our last argument, I said stupid things again—not at all helping my case. It's only when I'm angry that I seem to slip up. "I just mean the world keeps spinning no matter what happens." I open my locker and take off my backpack, relieving my shoulders from the weight.

"Are you okay?" She gives me a pitying look and I wish she would stop asking me that. And stop looking at me like that. How can I possibly be okay? I'm stuck here while Casper is in Belle Palais. With Saida of all people.

"I'm fine," I snap and immediately feel ashamed. Cherry doesn't deserve my bad attitude. She's only trying to help. "Sorry." My hand is on a book and instead of pulling it out, I lean against the locker. "Why are we here? Doesn't it all seem so insignificant now? School?"

"I think it's more important than ever. Just to return to some kind of normalcy. To have that second chance. I know I wasn't in the hallway with you, but I could've been. I could've been one of the kids in the parking lot that day." She shrugs. "Makes you appreciate things more, I guess."

I grab my book and close the locker. The bell rings.

"Well, if you need anything, just let me know."

"Yeah."

Cherry makes her way further down the hallway toward her class and I walk the opposite way through the thinning crowd.

The first two classes are a joke. Teachers ask if we can have a moment of silence for those we lost, and while some people look at me like I'm a pathetic, fragile girl, others glare at me like I'm the one who walked in with a gun. Teachers try lecturing. No one is paying any attention.

Is this how it's going to be from now on? Why did Vincent do this?

I can't deal with this today. As I walk down the hallway to my next class, I slow to a stop. Something about the hallway gives me a bad feeling and I don't like it. It feels like something bad is going to happen. I start trembling and breathing hard. I clutch my chest and shut my eyes tight trying to calm down.

"Megan!" someone calls my name.

When I turn around, I'm face to face with Amber McLachlan. I haven't seen her in months. Nor have I thought about her. She cut off her long, blond locks. Her hair comes to her chin now, and she appears sadder. She doesn't seem to be engulfed in a vanilla scent. "What?"

Her eyebrows furrow. "Um, hi. How are you? We've not had a chance to talk since...well you know."

"Why are we talking now?"

She clears her throat and pink colors her cheeks. Since when does Amber blush? Definitely not when she clocked me, giving me a black eye for simply speaking to Casper.

"Do you need something?"

She looks as if she's about to start crying. "I was just seeing if you were okay."

"Why do you care?"

"Why are you being so mean? You weren't like this before."

"What are you talking about? You and I have always hated each other."

Realization washes over her face. "Y-you don't remember, do you? You...saved me that day."

"What?"

"Yeah. Um. I've been meaning to thank you or whatever. I didn't visit you in the hospital because...I just couldn't bring myself to. After the shooting," she lowers her voice. "I can't deal with hospitals or anything." She looks away, embarrassed.

"Yeah. Imagine how I feel." I don't have time to argue with Amber or deal with her. Last time we spoke, she clocked me. Why would she ever think we were friends?

"If it weren't for you, he would've shot me."

Rolling my eyes, I turn for the door and walk outside, leaving her standing alone. How on earth could I have saved Amber?

Opening my car door, I throw my backpack inside, frustrated. I hate this. I hate all of this. I don't have time to waste. Once I slide into the seat, I insert the key in the ignition.

Casper tells me a joke and I roll my eyes, laughing as we walk hand-in-hand down the hallway.

"What? It's true." He smiles my favorite smile. The one I feel so in love when I see it. Like I'm the only one who ever sees that heartwarming smile.

He leans down and kisses me. "See you after class." He goes inside his class and as I make my way toward mine, I hear a loud pop. Screams echo in the hallway. Is someone setting off fireworks?

Everything is slow motion.

The hallways soon fill with panicked, crying people.

As I round the corner, I gasp in time to see Vincent pointing a gun at Amber. My heart stops.

"Vincent, no!" I yell, pushing myself in between him and Amber McLachlan. We've definitely had our differences, but I don't want her dead. I don't want anyone dead.

Vincent gasps and withdraws his gun. "You're defending her? After all the things she's done to you. Why? Because Casper made you be friends with her?

I maintain a shield to Amber as I move her to the nearest door with my back. "You don't want to do this."

As my chin quivers, I try to keep myself steady. Once Amber reaches the door, she flees, leaving Vincent and me staring at each other.

I blink realizing I'm still sitting behind the steering wheel. My car is still running. The vision leaves me almost paralyzed. I look around the parking lot knowing Vincent is here. He's the only one who can make me see visions. Why would he show me that? Why would he create a vision for me to see?

To torment me, obviously.

Where is he? I have to find him.

I know you're nearby.

But I don't see him anywhere. I lock the car doors just in case.

Vincent surely did a number on these poor people and me. I've been wanting to go to Vincent's old house in hopes of finding something. I doubt it'll help.

If Vincent's back, where could he be staying? I rub my face trying to get my head to stop aching.

Vincent lived in the east side of town. Maybe the remains of the house are still there. Unless they rebuilt it from the fire.

Putting the car in reverse, I head to Vincent's old house.

I pull into his old neighborhood twenty minutes later, surprised I can remember exactly where it is when I have no memory of the last several months. Go figure. Once I spot the house, I pull over to the curb. The home doesn't look burned at all. It doesn't look new either. It looks...untouched. Except for the graffiti all over.

Killer.

You deserve to die.

Psycho.

Murderer.

The words overlap multiple times. Overgrown shrubbery covers most of the bottom level of the house. The front door and windows are boarded up. Police tape once wrapped around the property, now lies on the dead, brown grass. The whole scene creeps me out. Everything has changed in this world. The yard had always been perfectly manicured as Vincent's dad took care of it, probably to get his mind off his sick wife.

Cutting the engine, I get out and make my way toward the house in the freezing cold. I grip my car keys, hoping somehow it will settle the parade going off in my stomach.

The board isn't securely on the door and I'm able to open it with ease. Inside, I take out my cell phone and use the flashlight. Everything appears the same as I remember. I need to find information. Charging up to Vincent's room, I push open the door. It's just as I recall.

There are no pictures on his desk or posters on the wall. Drawers hang open haphazardly, and when I look, I find that they're empty. The bed sheets torn from the bed. It's almost as if the place has been ransacked. Any piece of evidence that could lead me to him in some way is gone. Did Vincent do this? Was it really the police?

Something catches my eye on the floor. Bending over, I grab what ends up being a picture. My heart lunges to my throat. It's a picture of Cherry and Vincent. What is going on?

Cherry? Does she and Vincent have something going on, too? Is she helping him like Florence did? Can I trust no one? Is this why she refuses to help me? I feel so betrayed. What if this whole time, she's been a spy for Vincent? She's helping him by keeping me here. She's in on this giant secret. How can she do this to me?

My pulse edges higher. I don't even know how to bring this up. She's already told my parents. She wants me to be locked up so I can't go back to Arvada. She actually believes me but has to fake it. She's working with Vincent. I can't believe this. It makes sense now. It's why she lied to everyone. It's why no one believes me. I put a few pictures in my pocket and search for more. Cherry will never tell me where to find the witch.

I can't concentrate on anything anymore and I'm getting dizzy. My phone buzzes and I see that it's a text from Cherry.

Are you okay?

I take a deep breath. I have to play my cards right. **I'm taking a sick day.**

Still not up for it?

No.

I'm sorry. Anything I can do?

No. I'm just going to sleep.

Okay. Feel better.

As I walk outside, I come to a halt once I see a police officer parked behind my car. Just my luck. I can't get caught up with them. I have to run.

Turning away, I bolt to the back of the house. The officer chirps his siren, but I ignore it.

"Hey! Come back here!"

Somehow, he's right behind me. He snatches my hand forcing me to face him. He must be one of Vincent's men. He's tall and burly. His muscles look like they're going to bust through the tight uniform. His reddish-gray hair blows in the wind and his dark eyes stare into mine.

"What are you doing here?" His voice is stern, and I glance at his gold name badge. *Ozark.*

"I was looking for something."

Officer Ozark lifts an eyebrow. "In a crime scene? There is no trespassing on a crime scene."

"Crime scene? The crime didn't happen here."

"It's evidence. Plus, neighbors have been told to call police anytime they see someone show up here. We've been hoping that Vincent will return to the house."

Not if he knows police are stalking the place. Is this all they're doing? "He's too smart for that."

"Do you know where he is, Megan?"

"No. If I did, I wouldn't be here. I'm sorry. I've learned my lesson. I need to get home now." I stop. "How do you know my name?"

"I know you're a victim in the shooting. Why are you out here?"

"I just wanted answers. It won't happen again." I turn around and start walking away, but he stops me again.

"You don't listen very well." He grabs handcuffs from his belt and slaps them around my wrists. "You're under arrest."

"For what?"

"Trespassing. Come on. I really don't have time to deal with teens messing around with this place. For the past two months, we've had to watch it because of you teens. You can't take the law in your own hands."

He tosses me in the backseat of his patrol car. My heart's beating fast. I can't breathe.

No, this can't be happening. Why is he doing this? How am I going to explain this? Who can I call? Am I seriously getting arrested?

"I've learned my lesson."

"Yeah. I'm sure you have. You can't take it upon yourself to break into a crime scene."

"Please, don't do this. I just want to find him. That's all. After what he did to me."

"Well, maybe you can come to the station and answer some questions. If you know where he is, I suggest you speak up."

"I don't know where he is," I yell.

"Hey, calm down."

This officer is impossible. I don't know what to say or how to get myself out of this situation. Panic heightens inside me the further from my car we drive.

Twenty-Six

An officer presses my finger into black ink, then on a card leaving my fingerprint. I'm trying so hard not to lose it. I never thought in a million years I would be arrested. Although, King Jacques and his men arrested me and were going to hang me.

"You seem like you know something about Vincent that we don't," Officer Ozark says as he and Officer Freeman sit across from me. Pretty sure they aren't allowed to question me.

Yeah, definitely not telling police about Arvada. "I don't. I wish I did. Last I heard, he was in a crash somewhere in Arizona."

Officer Freeman nods. "It wasn't him."

"What? Then where is he? Why haven't you found him?"

He frowns. "We are trying. If you have any information, you should tell us."

"No. Some people in forums think he may have gone to Mexico or Canada."

"I'm not going to charge you, Megan," Officer Freeman says. "I assure you we'll find him."

I roll my eyes internally. I can't believe I was arrested. They let me make a phone call, and by some miracle, I remember Jonathan's number. His is the only one I remember for some reason. I wouldn't mind calling Spencer because I know he'd come get me without issues. Unfortunately, I don't know his number by memory.

It seems like forever by the time he gets there or maybe it's waiting in a police station. Watching people in and out of this place. Never realized so many people committed crimes every day.

When he arrives, he looks at me, disappointment written all over his face. Jonathan signs me out and he's incredibly quiet when we get into his car. He doesn't start the engine right away. He just sits and stares out into the cloudy day. Still, no rain.

"You're very lucky they didn't charge you. Trespassing? What were you doing?"

"I was looking for something."

"What could you be looking for at a crime scene? Why were you even near that place?"

"You won't understand."

"Why *that* place? You realize this means the police are going to be watching you now. Megan, it's bad enough I had to pick you up at a police station. I almost lost you. I can't lose you. I hate what happened to you and I wish I had been there to protect you. I can't always be there. You have to stop seeking whatever it is and live your life."

"How can I live my life? I have to find Vincent. I'm not doing this to get into trouble or danger. I just...needed answers."

"Megan, you can't go looking for him."

"Why? No one else seems to be."

"They'll find him."

I let out a frustrated groan. "No one's found him, Jonathan. They won't. The cop even asked me if I knew where he was."

"And you go to *his* place. Who knows what could have happened had that cop not found you? That sicko is running around. He could've found you. And..." He shakes his head. "Why weren't you at school?"

"School doesn't matter. None of this does. All of this is ridiculous."

"What are you saying?"

I let out a sigh. "Nothing."

"Are you talking about suicide?"

"What? No." Why does everyone think that?

"Dr. Brown mentioned to look for signs."

I roll my eyes. "I'm fine. I promise."

"I'm worried is all. Mom told me about the whole fantasy world. It sounds like a complicated way of wanting to die."

Great. Everyone knows. Just one more added to the list of people who think I'm crazy. "I don't want to die, okay? I know there isn't another world. It was something I said to Cherry who took it too seriously," I lie and turn my gaze out the window. I don't know what to say and I'm not sure there is anything to say to make any of this better.

"You were dead for one minute, Megan. I can't lose you," Jonathan says. Even though he doesn't look at me, I can see the pain in his eyes, hear it in his voice. "That asshole is out there, and I can't stand the thought of him or anyone hurting you again. I have a hard-enough time with this Spencer guy that you snuck out of the house with." He shakes his head. "Promise me you'll stop this erratic behavior. I know you're dealing with a lot and you're getting help. But you have to try."

Instead of arguing, I concede. "I promise."

He takes me back to my car and follows me home. Much to my luck, he doesn't say a word to Mom or Ron.

Twenty-Seven

migod, it was so funny," Cherry laughs. I smile, trying to act like the normal girl I am. A normal girl who got arrested yesterday and who also found proof that her best friend and ex-boyfriend are working together. I didn't sleep at all last night and it kills me how much I miss Casper and that I haven't seen him in a while.

"Not hungry?" she asks as I move my fork around my salad.

I shrug. "Just don't wanna be here."

Loud voices echo in the cafeteria and I'm trying to ignore all the stares and the horrible feeling in my stomach as I watch Cherry.

"I wish we could hang out tonight, but I have to work. Oh, do you have notes from anatomy yesterday? Apparently, I completely spaced."

The bell rings and as we make our way out to the hallway, I grab her hand.

"What is it?" she asks with a little crease forming between her eyes.

"You're helping him, aren't you?"

"What? Helping who?"

"Vincent."

Her jaw drops. "Are you kidding me? Why would you even think that?"

"It's happened before. I found a picture of you and him."

There's a long pause. "What are you talking about? Why would I ever even be with him?"

"You always liked him. You always wanted me to be with him instead of Casper."

"Only because I thought Casper was a dick, but he wasn't at all. I was completely wrong about him. I know that. What picture are you talking about?"

"I even told you how Vincent treated me, and you ignored it."

"I'm sorry, Megan. I really am, but I would never help Vincent. Ever."

"Do you remember when I got attacked at that party?"

"Yes."

"It was one of Vincent's men. He brought them from our world to find me."

"What? No. It was some douche from another school."

"He wound up dead. Vincent killed him."

She gasps. "He did? Do the police know any of that?"

"You know where he is, don't you?"

"No, I don't. Did you have a bad dream or something? What's going on?"

"You. I know you're only talking to me because you want to make sure I end up in an institution. Why else would you be telling my mom everything? I can't believe you."

Her eyes narrow and she presses her lips together. "I am not helping Vincent. I would never do that. I'm only telling your mom things because you need help, Megan. I can't believe you would even accuse me of something like this."

"Because it's true." I pull out the picture from my back pocket. "I found this. How could you do this to me?"

"You're unbelievable. Why don't you look at the picture?"

I turn it around in my hand. It's different. It's not Cherry at all. It's me with Vincent. What is he doing? Is he messing with my head? I swear this picture earlier wasn't me. It was Cherry. "No. It was you and him. What are you doing?"

She shakes her head. "You know what? I can't do this anymore. I can't be your friend. You need help and you refuse to get it."

I cross my arms in front of my chest. "Fine. One less person watching my every move."

Tears fill her eyes, and she turns to walk away leaving me in an empty hallway.

Then I see a figure at the end of the hall. He's wearing a hat, jeans, leather jacket, all in black. His hair is blonde. My heart throws itself against my ribcage. It can't be Vincent. Has he made himself visible to only me?

He starts moving toward me and I dart into the nearest bathroom and hide in a stall. I shouldn't be running from him, but every time I've seen him in my dreams, he terrifies me.

Twenty-Eight

ow can I ask someone I barely know to help me find a killer? I'm biting my lip when the phone rings. I haven't spoken to Spencer since I was at my dad's almost two weeks ago. I haven't even seen him in school either and I hope he's okay. I'm not even sure what I'm going to say.

"Hello," he answers.

"Hey, are you okay?"

"Yeah, why? Are you? Still waking up in weird places?"

"No. I haven't seen you at school."

"I've been there."

"Oh."

"Miss me?"

I clear my throat, hating how awkward this is. I don't know what to say or how to bring up anything. "Um…"

"I'm kidding. I've been wanting to call you, but I didn't know if you'd want me to."

"Why?" I ask.

"I just…didn't know if you'd ever want to talk to me."

"Why wouldn't I? You've been really kind to me, and you've gotten me through a lot of things."

"Do you want to grab some dinner?" he asks.

It takes me off guard for a moment. "Sure. Come by at seven?"

After I hang up, I wait. I feel like that's all I've done lately. I guess it's better than running. While I wait, I start researching online about Vincent and the shooting some more. Looking for any leads I may find but there's nothing. Part of me thinks he's found a way to return to Arvada and that's why I haven't seen Casper in my dreams or any orbs. I've been trying hard not to think that that could be the case. I have to have faith that Casper is okay.

I want out of here. I don't want to be tortured any longer.

Spencer shows up on time, and Mom greets him with a cautious smile. If I told her the truth, I know she would love Spencer immediately, but I can't let her know that I unknowingly ran out into the woods and almost got hit.

He's dressed in jeans and a polo shirt that accentuates his broad shoulders. His brown hair is cut short, and he looks good. I hate that I have that thought. It almost makes me feel guilty. Mom sternly reminds me that I be home by ten and I follow Spencer outside.

"I was thinking we could go have some pizza," he says once I slide into the passenger seat. He shuts my door and comes around to the driver's side.

"Okay. Can we go to somewhere other than Cosmo's Pizza?"

"Don't like that place?"

I look down at my hands. "Vincent took me there."

"Noted."

As soon as he cranks the car, I turn to him wanting to know if this is a date. I never know with these things. Why should it matter? I'm with Casper. My mind is a jumbled mess right now, so much that I don't even know if what's happening is real.

"You look great," he says. "How's your back?"

"Ugh. It constantly aches. Sleeping sucks. It's like I can't find a comfortable enough position. Were you injured?"

"Me? Other than PTSD, no."

I don't know why but I laugh. He chuckles. "Sorry. I don't know why I did that. This is weird, right?"

"What? Us having dinner?"

"Yeah. I mean, you and Vincent used to be friends and you almost ran me over because I was running in the middle of the woods."

He shrugs. "I don't really have experience in this."

"Oh. It's not your normal way of meeting girls?"

He smiles and it's sexy. Sweet and innocent. I briefly wonder what it would be like to kiss him. I look away. Why do I keep having these thoughts? I shouldn't. Guilt punches me as I think of Casper. Sadness begins to creep over me. I have to keep telling myself I'll get back to him.

"Are you okay?" he asks.

"I'm fine."

"We don't have to do this if you don't want to."

When I turn back to him, I realize my arms are crossed in front of my chest, my fingers digging into my arms. I relax. "No, sorry. I want to."

"You can talk to me about anything. I promise, I'm a good listener."

I nod but I can't tell him what's going on in my head. He'll think I'm a nutso like everyone else does.

Spencer pulls into a parking space. "It's a little weird. I keep feeling...like we were meant to meet that night. I keep asking myself why you're even giving me the time of day. But I—" He shakes his head. "Never mind."

"No, tell me." I touch his hand. My heart skips a beat as he rotates it to intertwine his fingers with mine. I don't pull away even though I should. This isn't right. It's not fair to Casper. But the softness of his skin and the gentle way his thumb rubs my hand feels good.

"I feel connected to you, Megan. I don't know if it's because of what happened and talking to you lately. I like you. I know you've been through hell, and I guess I want you to know that I'm here for you."

"Why?"

"I like talking to you and I'm starting to care about you. You never make me feel bad about myself and trust me there's plenty there."

"I like you, too. I feel calm around you." The words escape my mouth before I can stop them. I have a weird feeling inside me. Part of me wants to let go of Casper and move on. The other part is hanging onto him for dear life. I don't know if I'll ever make it back to Casper, but I have to try. For a second, I want to desperately tell Spencer everything. The truth. The way I feel like none of this isn't real.

But I don't. I've already scared off one person and I don't want to do that with Spencer. Plus, I don't need more proof that I need to be locked away.

He squeezes my hand as we go inside the restaurant. The food is so good, and I can't remember the last time I ate so much. I haven't really been eating much since being released from the hospital. Being around Spencer relaxes me and any anxiety I have been feeling vanishes. We talk all through dinner. We laugh.

"Savannah can't figure out how to get out from underneath the covers. She burrows her way in, but if she gets too hot, I hear her and feel her panting. And I have to pull her out. Like, come on dog."

Spencer laughs. "Bruno ran away one time. Or so we thought. We called his name, yelled, screamed. Nothing. Turns out, he was hiding underneath my car."

"I've missed Savannah. I feel like I've been gone for so long."

He frowns. "You kinda have."

I nod. We're quiet for a moment. "Maybe there is something you can help me with."

"Sure. What is it?"

"Just...hear me out before you make up your mind."

He crumples his napkin and pushes his plate away. Resting his elbows on the table, he waits.

"Vincent's been on the run. Police aren't going to find him. I need to find him. I need answers from him.

I went to his old house and ended up getting arrested."

His eyebrows lift. "Gotta criminal over here."

"I need help finding him and I'll understand if you say no."

"Megan—"

"I know it's dangerous. I know it's crazy to even contemplate this. No one's found him and they aren't going to."

"What will he do if he sees you?"

"He won't hurt me. He's had numerous opportunities to do that if he really wanted to."

Spencer slowly nods.

"I know this is a lot to ask and I'm not asking you this because of our situation. First and foremost, you don't owe me anything, Spencer. I assure you of that. I just can't do this alone."

He lets out a breath, and we're quiet for what seems like a long time. "I was there that day. I've always felt guilty. Like, I go to this school and something traumatic happens and I didn't help. I did nothing. Six people died. Others were injured."

"You wouldn't have been able to stop him."

He shakes his head. "You don't know that. Tyler and I heard the shots in the hallway. He went into hero mode. I really tried to stop him. But that's who Tyler was. A hero. He ran toward the sound, and I couldn't stop him. Vincent..." He shakes his head and pauses. "There was so much blood. His body was crumpled in an impossible position. I can't ever get that image out of my head."

Chills run up my spine. I want to cry at his words. His agony that I caused. I take his hand. No one should ever experience such a thing.

He draws in a shaky breath. "When it was over, we were outside, and I saw them wheel you out. I thought you were dead. I saw so much blood and death and pain. I wish I could've done more."

"What would you have done?"

"I don't know. I would've tried stopping him. I would've helped people escape."

"You can't beat yourself up over that. I know it's a lot harder than it sounds. I'm really sorry, Spencer."

"No one knew the guy. He had no friends. He hung out with no one. Except you."

Heat rushes to my cheeks and I look down. I feel like I've done something bad. Like I chose to date such a monster. How on earth could I do that? The loud chatter of the restaurant seems to return, or maybe I blocked it out.

"Can I ask what attracted you to him?"

"He wasn't always bad. I don't know. He's very manipulative. I began seeing that early on, but it was like I couldn't escape him. I've tried so many times. He absolutely hates Casper. Hates that we fell in love. He's tried to make me forget Casper, but it hasn't worked. I need to reach Vincent so that I can save Casper." I blush again as the words spill out of my mouth.

"What?"

I clear my throat. "Um, are you ready to go?" Looking around at the crowded restaurant, unease creeps over me. I don't want to be here anymore. What if Vincent is watching us right now? I feel like Spencer is judging me.

"Yeah."

We walk out into the cool night toward his car. He opens my door and then gets in on his side.

"Sorry about that," I tell him.

"It's okay."

"I just...I can't tell you the truth because you'll tell my parents. You'll believe them and everyone else that I'm crazy."

"You know I don't think that."

I shake my head. "You will. It's just...I asked Cherry for help. She thinks I need to let the police handle it. Obviously, they aren't doing anything. So, I thought I'd ask you, but it's okay. Forget I asked."

"What time do you have to be home?"

"Ten. Why?"

"I want to show you something."

He starts driving until we're in the middle of nowhere. It's dark and there's nothing around us except woods and fields. I feel like I should be scared, but I'm not. There's so much about Spencer that I don't know. He's a mystery, just like Vincent was. While Spencer has a darkness inside him, it isn't at all like Vincent. But don't we all have a darkness inside us?

Spencer slows the car and pulls over on the side of the road. Vast fields surround us with trees interspersed. No houses. No buildings. Nothing. The crescent moon is the only light.

He lets me out of the car.

"Why are we here?"

"This is where we collided."

His words take the breath out of me.

"You were like a deer darting out into the road. I slammed on my brakes, and you looked so terrified. So lost. Then you told me what happened. You were shaking, and I had to help you. Vincent messed with you, and I could see the stark fear in your eyes. I still can."

I look away.

"I was driving around. Thinking, as usual. Thinking about that fucking day because it never goes away. I—I was." He struggles with his words. I move closer to him and take his hand. "I was out here because I wanted to kill myself."

My heart drops.

"I don't know. I...wanted it to end. I've been to therapy. On medication. Going to school sucked.

Everyone else walked around like zombies. Teachers tried teaching but no one was ready. I was meant to find you. Even in the small amount of time that we've known each other, my days don't seem so bad after all. It's almost like you saved me in a way."

I squeeze his hand.

He takes a deep breath and clears his throat. I reach to wipe a tear from his cheek, and he catches my hand. He meets my gaze with an expression that makes my heart flutter. "You're not crazy, Megan. No matter what you tell me, I won't think that. Trauma fucks you up and that's okay. After that day, I've dealt with a lot of things. I'm still dealing with it."

I nod. "Aren't we all?"

"My point is Vincent has screwed up so many of our lives and he's been on the run for months with no reprieve in sight. He has to pay for what he's done. I want to help you find him."

"What?"

"We need to find him. He's caused enough harm on you. Me. And a lot of other people."

"Really? You'll help me?"

"Of course."

I hug him and when I feel his arms around me, encapsulating me, I feel safe. I love the warm feeling. I breathe him in. A tangy scent of lemongrass.

Again, Casper crosses my mind making me pull away.

"Are you only hanging out with me because you feel bad for me?" I whisper.

He shakes his head. "I've liked you for a long time, I just never did anything about it."

"Even after all that happened, I still never reached out to you. I'm a firm believer in that everything happens for a reason. There's a reason you and I collided. I keep thinking what if I had talked to you? Would you have been running out here by yourself?"

"We can't focus on the what ifs of life."

"I know. I'm just letting you know, it's okay. There's a lot that goes on my head that I'm sure people think I'm crazy or that I have no reason to feel the way I do."

"Thank you for telling me that. D-do you still feel like...killing yourself?"

"It's...complicated. I never *wanted* to kill myself. I got tired of feeling that way. I'm getting better. Therapist and meds. You."

Blood rushes to my cheeks. I'm not sure he would really feel that way if he knew the truth. That I'm the one who caused this. If I hadn't tried to kill Vincent, he wouldn't have returned us here messing up everything.

"What about you? Do you remember anything from that day?"

"No," I say for his benefit. "I remember getting shot and Casper telling me it'll be okay. But all I can remember is the pain. Then it went away."

Spencer slides his hand in mine, and we stand in silence on the side of some dark country road. I don't want to let go. I want to comfort him. Resting my head on his shoulder, I relax more. I hate that Spencer has experienced so much pain over something that never happened. If Vincent dies, will his spell over everyone lift? Will Spencer's pain be gone? He doesn't deserve this. No one does.

If anyone should feel guilty, it's me. But can I tell Spencer the truth? Will he think I'm insane?

After a while, Spencer drives me home where we sit in the driveway.

"I know I should tell you the truth, but I can't," I tell him. "At least, not yet."

He nods. "I understand."

"Um. Thank you for dinner. I had a good time."

He sighs and shakes his head. "You don't have to lie."

"I'm not."

"It was intense and sad."

I shrug. "What about our lives isn't, right now?"

He chuckles. "You."

"What?"

"You are not intense or sad for me."

I smile and shift my gaze to the window. "I feel that way about you. You've really helped me the last few weeks." I feel safe with him, and I've only ever felt that way once before.

Spencer gets out of the car and opens my door. He helps me out and his eyes hold mine. I can't tear away from the intense look in his eyes. The pounding in my chest vibrates my entire body. He leans down softly pressing his warm lips to mine. He moves slow, but I'm on fire. He takes my face in his hands and my body continues to hum.

Casper. He's waiting for me.

I draw back from Spencer, breathless.

He curses. "I'm sorry. I—"

"It's okay. Um. I'll talk to you later." I step around him, heading to my door, my fingers touching my lips.

"Megan?"

I twist around, and he moves closer. "We'll find Vincent."

"Thanks. Yeah. Um. I'll talk to you tomorrow."

"Have a good night."

As soon as I close the door to my room, the tears overwhelm me. How could I let Spencer kiss me? Why would I do such a thing? My heart breaks. I don't know what I've done. Each day without Casper feels like I'm losing my connection to him more and more.

Spencer's going to help me find Vincent and then I can return to Casper. His face is becoming a distant memory. I hope to find him in my dream, so I can tell him everything.

Twenty-Nine

$\mathscr{I}$ did a bad thing. I'm so ashamed of myself. Here I am kissing another guy while Casper's stuck in Arvada waiting for me. I've finally found him in a dream, but I need to make sure it's really him and not Vincent.

"Casper?" I see him by our tree as I cry. More like sob. Will he forgive me?

He rushes up to me, but I put my hand up stopping him. "Is it really you?"

"Of course, it is. Why what's happened? He wraps his arms around me. "Megan, why are you crying?"

"I haven't seen you in weeks. Every time I dream you-you turn into Vincent."

He strokes my hair as he lets me cry.

"I can't get back to you. Spencer...he agreed to help me find Vincent, but he-he kissed me."

Casper stiffens.

"I didn't want him to." Except I did. "I'm so sorry."

He draws back a little. "What is going on? I mean, are you serious about returning here? I told you to live out your life, but you keep telling me you want to come back. Then you kiss someone else?"

"It was an accident. I-I didn't mean it and it means nothing."

"What do you want, Megan?"

"I want you."

"Have you even tried to find your way back?"

"Yes, every lead turns dead. I can't find Vincent. I keep thinking I'm seeing him in places, but I think it's my mind or him playing tricks. Please don't give up on me."

He cups my chin lifting my eyes to meet his. "Megan, if that's the life you want, stay there. I love you and I miss you, but so much is happening to you. I don't want you going after Vincent. He's too dangerous."

"No, I can do this. My dad taught me how to fight. Let me prove it to you. I can do this."

I feel the dream tugging away, and I try so hard to hold on. I wake up alone in my bed. It's a relief that I'm not in some field or the cemetery.

I hate these feelings. I hate missing Casper so much. I hate how much my heart aches.

My phone vibrates and it's Spencer.

I'm sorry for kissing you. I don't know what you think of me or if you think of me that way. If you need time, I will understand.

My phone buzzes again.

We'll find Vincent. I promise.

I want to tell him I enjoyed the kiss and that I'm still thinking about it. I want to tell him that Casper and I are together, but he won't understand. I start typing.

I have to make this right. And I don't want you to hate me.

Hate you? Why would I hate you?

My phone is vibrating with his name across the top. I swipe to answer.

"Are you okay?" he asks, his smooth voice sending butterflies to my stomach.

"Yeah. Just tired of the dreams."

"Me, too."

"Sleep is overrated," I say, and he laughs.

"I don't know. I do like to sleep. I just haven't been able to lately because I keep seeing all this crap in my head and it tends to stay with me, you know? Makes me feel like such a broken person."

"Maybe I can help. For what it's worth, you aren't broken. Bent maybe but not broken. We can mend this."

"We?"

"I mean, you and me. Once we find Vincent, he can give us answers."

"Where do you think he's hiding?"

"I don't know. He's smart and he's good at eluding people. Do you think your friend purityangel may know some people?"

"I don't know. I can ask, but I'm sure she's already gone down that road, especially if she's been praising him for what he's done."

Makes me wonder if any of these people are from Arvada posing as humans. What about Adam? He was from Arvada. "There was a guy from." I stop myself. I can't tell him he's from the immortal world. What was the school Cherry said he was from? "He's from Eldridge High School that Vincent knew. He..." I pause. "He attacked me. Maybe purityangel knew him."

"Damn, seriously? I'm so sorry."

"It's okay. Casper was there and saved me."

"Sounds like he's saved you more than once."

"He's always saving me."

"What's his name?"

"Adam Norton."

"Oh damn. I remember Adam. He attacked you? He had serious issues. Clearly. I haven't heard about him in a while. I guess I could track him down, but would you really want to face him?"

"Um. He's...dead."

"Wait, what?"

"Yeah. Vincent killed him."

"What? Why?"

"He said it was because he attacked me."

"Did you tell anyone this?"

"No."

"Why?"

"I didn't know he killed him until he…" Drugged me and held me hostage in his basement. "I only found out right before."

"Let me talk to her and see what all I can find out."

"You can tell her not to wish my death either."

"I'll talk to her."

"Maybe we can go undercover at the school and ask around."

"Okay Nancy Drew."

I roll my eyes. "Let's try to get some sleep. We have quite a lot of sleuthing to do."

He laughs and I love the sound. "You got it."

Thirty

pencer meets me in the parking lot at school the next day. The early morning sun casts a glow around him. It's a cold day. One of the coldest of the year so far. I miss the warm weather. Being at the beach or pool like a normal teenager.

"Morning, sunshine," he says and hands me a coffee. It reminds me of when Casper brought me one. I don't drink it, but I take it anyway.

"Hi."

"Not a morning person, are you?"

I smile. "No. Are you?"

He shrugs. "I used to be."

"Find out anything?"

"Lacey, or purityangel to you, told me about Adam and Vincent. I didn't mention the attack, but she said it was probably a drug deal gone bad or Adam being stupid. I don't know. She's very protective of Vincent which is weird to me and makes me wonder if she knows more than she's leading on. Anyway, she did mention this trailer park where Adam lived."

"Okay."

"I wouldn't get your hopes up, but it could be a starting point. Personally, I don't think Vincent is still here in this state."

"Where is the trailer park?"

"It's about an hour north of here."

"Let's go."

"We'll go after school."

I lean against his car trying to ignore the immense dread building inside me. "I don't want to go inside." I told Mom and Dr. Brown that I would really try today.

"I know. Pretty sure no one really does."

"They all think it's my fault."

"Because they're looking to blame someone and unfortunately, you're the closest thing they have. You had nothing to do with it. None of this is your fault."

I look away and bite my lip. He's wrong, though. None of this would have happened if it weren't for me.

"Megan, you don't actually believe that."

I don't answer.

"Look at me."

I don't.

"Look at me." He lifts my chin, and my eyes meet his. "You did nothing. How could you even think that?"

I move back. "Because it is. It wouldn't have happened if I. If I—"

"If you what? You couldn't have prevented this. Don't let them get inside your head. They just want someone to blame and the one person to blame isn't around."

"If Casper and I hadn't gotten together, I could've saved so many lives. I could've—."

Spencer takes me in his arms, and I breathe in the lemongrass. "Megan, stop. You have every right to do what you want. You're not wrong for living your life."

Except everything I've ever done is wrong. Everything I've ever wanted is wrong.

"Come on. Let's go to class. We'll go look around Adam's neighborhood later."

Nodding, I walk beside him as we make our way inside and once the inevitable bell rings, he turns one way and I go the other. The strangest feeling overcomes me. Emptiness? Longing? I don't know, but I don't like watching Spencer and me going in opposite directions.

Taking a deep breath, I amble down toward my locker. It sucks not seeing Cherry waiting for me. But I can't be friends with someone who could potentially be helping Vincent. Although, what if Spencer's friend, Lacey is steering us into a trap? Dad taught me how to fight, but am I ready?

Grabbing my books for class, I keep my head down through the hallway. Memories of Casper flash through my mind. The first time he gazed at me in this lifetime; the time he brought me ice after Amber punched me; or the many times he made my heart jump into overdrive.

It hurts. Thinking about him brings a pain to my chest that feels like something squeezing my heart. We've been fighting in our dreams, and I hate it. He suggested that I carry out this life and try finding him in another, but the way people stare at me like I'm the one who shot them scares me too much. Will they harass me? Come after me? Vandalize my house like they did Vincent's?

I sit in the back of the classroom hoping to remain as invisible as possible. Even Cherry ignores me throughout the class. Why would she want to be associated with me anyway?

A crumpled piece of paper lands on my desk. I slowly open it.

Written in dark, bold letters are words that send the guilt flaring inside me.

You did this.

Tears spring to my eyes, and I push them away.

No matter what, being with Casper has always caused issues. Wadding the paper up in my fist, I clench my teeth.

The bell rings and I gather my things. Walking out of the room, someone trips me, and I crash hard to the cement floor. Books spill around me as people laugh.

I refuse to be pushed around. Anger wells inside and I stand facing the group.

"Why are you doing this?" I yell, but I'm only met with laughter.

A girl with brown hair pushes her way through the group with a coy smile on her face. "Everyone knows it's your fault this happened. He was looking for you. You're the only one who should've died. Not the six that did. Especially not Casper."

I can't hold back the tears as my chin quivers. Anger consumes me and I launch my fist in the girl's face. A chorus of gasps sounds.

Then I'm held back by several teachers as we're all told to go back to our next classes. Except me, who is directed to the principal's office. I have no doubt someone filmed that and now it's going to be all over the internet. Shooter's ex-girlfriend punches innocent girl.

But I don't care.

Humans are cruel individuals. They are selfish and always want someone to blame. I hate Vincent even more for what he did.

"We have a no tolerance for fighting," the principal says to me.

"She deserved it." Probably the wrong thing to say, but I'm at my breaking point. There comes a time when being the bigger person isn't enough anymore and all you can do is fight back.

"Megan, you've never been in here." He sits on the edge of his desk, his hands folded in front of him. Feeling his dark eyes on me, I don't look up. I've always liked Principal Pearson. He's always been nice and seemingly caring of the students and it seems more so now. "I know you've been through a lot but hitting students isn't the answer."

I can't stop the tears that well in my eyes. "They all think it's my fault."

"What?" He kneels down forcing me to look at him. He wears thick rimmed glasses, and his black hair is short.

Pulling out the note from my pocket, I show him.

Principal Pearson looks at it and I can see the shock and appall on his face. "Who wrote this?"

"I don't know. Kids in class. It doesn't matter. They say it to me in the halls."

"This has to stop."

"It never will. This will always happen."

He stands tossing the note on his desk. "Megan, I won't suspend you and while this is unacceptable, so is hitting."

But it's okay that Amber hit me.

I nod. "I'm sorry. I overreacted. I don't want to come back. I don't belong here."

"What do you mean?"

"Can I please go?"

"Megan, you aren't having any certain thoughts, are you?"

"Certain thoughts? What like suicide?"

He nods.

I groan. "I wish everyone would stop asking me that. No, I'm not thinking about killing myself. I just...I just want to go home right now."

"Promise me you'll talk to a counselor when you need it."

Holding my books, I stand and head out the door. Thankfully, the halls are empty as I rush outside. I text Spencer to meet me out in the parking lot. My hand is red, and I know a bruise is forming.

A few minutes later, he comes out. "What's wrong? What happened? I heard you hit some girl."

"I'm leaving. If you want to help me, you should come with me now."

"Leaving? Megan, it's not even ten in the morning. What happened?"

I can't stop the tears that flood my cheeks. "They all think it's my fault. I hit that girl. I don't even know who she is. What's the point of being here if I'm not going to learn anything? I can't spend any more time here. It's a waste and I don't have a lot of time, okay?"

He places a hand on my arm. "What are you talking about?"

I let out a sigh. "I have to find Vincent. The sooner I do that the sooner all this will end. Are you coming or not?"

"Can't you wait until school is out?"

"No, I can't. Why do you want to stay?"

"Because I have to complete my senior year if I want to try to go to college. Don't you?"

"I'm not even going to college."

"Why should your plans stop because of all of this? Don't let him take that away from you. He's already taken so much. I don't pretend to know how difficult this is for you. Don't give up everything you've worked so hard to achieve."

"I gotta go." I turn to open my car door.

He grabs my arm again. "Wait. Take a breath. You're too wound up to drive. Plus, you don't even know where to go. You shouldn't be looking for him alone."

"I don't need a babysitter, okay?"

"I didn't say you did, Megan." He takes me by my shoulders forcing me to look into his eyes. He's worried and I know I need to calm down. I take a couple of deep breaths. When I see the sincerity in his eyes, it fills me with hope. There is something familiar and homelike about him and in that moment, I want to expel all of my secrets.

"Can we please go? Just for today. I can't be here right now."

"Okay."

The trailer park is larger than I thought it would be. Spencer turns onto the gravel road and parks his car at the entrance near the community mailboxes. The homes are in close proximity to one another in a weird, haphazard fashion. There doesn't seem to be any rhyme or reason to the pattern.

We get out of the car and start walking. It's colder here. Clouds block the sun and the only heat source. It's freezing out here, but I can't let that stop me. The general atmosphere creeps me out. The homes are in poor shape with piles of debris everywhere. Broken and rusted washing machines and dryers are in some of the yards. Mildew stains on the trailer siding and water damage on some roofs. Satellite dishes on top of the trailers. It all reminds me of the poor shape Village Féerique is in.

The further we walk the more I wonder if people are watching us through their windows. It's quiet here, though I bet at night it may not be. Especially when I see empty beer cans and bottles on some of the porches. Some people have couches and chairs outside like lawn furniture. I can imagine how moldy that smells.

We reach a mobile home toward the end, a little secluded from the others. It looks like storm debris has fallen on top and a window on the end is broken. The porch is leaning and sinking into the ground. Several of the boards are rotted. When Spencer opens the door, it screeches. A cat meows in the distance.

The house is dark, and everything is old and dusty. It's cold, and I can smell the mustiness and who knows what else. Stale cigarettes; rotten carpet. Bags of clothes and other articles are piled up in a corner. It's awful. If anyone does live here, I feel sorry for them. No one should have to live in such conditions.

There is still furniture inside and I make may toward the kitchen, careful where I step. The floors are completely covered in broken tables and chairs and old things. The table in the kitchen has a bare spot like someone moved everything aside to eat.

Something catches my eye. It's a piece of newspaper with handwritten words. It's an article about Vincent with the words *don't hate me* scrawled all over. Repeated multiple times like someone does in detention on a sheet of paper. It's his handwriting. He's here.

"What is that?" Spencer asks.

"It's him."

A door slams toward the back making me jump. I drop the newspaper and dart toward the sound, pushing Spencer aside.

"Wait, Megan," he whispers.

The floor beneath me sinks a little but I make it outside. I breathe in fresh air as I chase a dark figure. He runs through the woods and the bare trees offer no hiding places.

"Vincent!" I scream. Why is he running from me? "Come back."

I hear Spencer calling my name. He catches up to me as we chase Vincent.

He's so much faster than both of us and picks up his pace.

Then, he's gone. I slow down, scanning the forest for him and panting. I don't see him anywhere. Did he just use the Nuummite to escape? Is that what he's doing?

"You're a coward," I shout.

"Are you okay?" Spencer asks.

"He was right there. We had him!"

"It's okay, we'll find him again."

Clenching my teeth, I pick up a rock and hurl it. I hear it hitting a tree.

Spencer eases toward me, placing his hands on my shoulders. "Megan, it's okay."

"He left me here to torture me. All because I'd rather be with Casper."

He pulls me into him, but I don't return the embrace. He holds me until my breathing calms. We walk back to the house and search inside but find nothing but a sleeping bag and empty food packages.

After a few minutes, unable to handle the smells or cold, we walk back to his car. I dig through my purse for a pen and piece of paper.

"I'll be right back." I hurry back to the trailer and leave a note on the table. *I don't hate you. Meet me tonight next door to where we met for the second time.* I hope he remembers it was Sloss Furnace for the haunted house. I can't leave specifics in case anyone else reads this.

"What was that?" Spencer asks when I'm back in the car.

"I told him I don't hate him. Maybe he'll stay next time we come."

"Pretty sure he's going to find another place now."

"Well, maybe he won't."

Spencer starts the car, and we head back to school. I bite my lip wanting to tell him everything. I trust him and he's been helping me with so much.

"There's so much I have to tell you and I want to tell you because I trust you. But I'm scared because every time I've talked to Cherry, she tells my family, and they tell the doctor. They all think I'm insane. I'm probably about two seconds from being locked up in a mental institution."

"You know I don't think you're crazy. You can tell me anything."

I take a deep, shaky breath. "Vincent, Casper, and I aren't from here."

"What do you mean?"

"Just let me explain. Then you can ask questions."

"Okay."

It takes me a minute to figure out where to start. "Vincent, Casper, and I come from a different world. We aren't like you. We aren't human."

His eyes maintain on the road ahead as I explain everything. The war, the witch, potions, the betrayals, King Jacques. All of it. The more I talk the more I tear up because I'm terrified of what he'll think of me.

"Vincent brought me back here and left me. I thought he had returned to the immortal world to kill Casper, but he hasn't. When we returned, it messed up time and events. It created this whole school shooting. Spencer there never was a shooting. It never happened and it's my fault because I trusted the wrong people and he's still out there terrorizing. That's why I have to find him, so he can return us. Once we return, everything will go back to the way it was. I can be with Casper. Lately, the only way we've been able to be together is through dreams. This will all go away, and you won't be in this pain."

A heavy silence falls over us for the longest time. I'm not sure what he's thinking. I know it's a lot for someone to hear.

"So...you think this school shooting is just something that happened because you messed with some sort of time-space continuum?"

"It's not what I think. It's the truth."

"That's fucked up, Megan." He shakes his head and grips the steering wheel. "You can't sit here and tell me that all my messed-up mind is from some sort of time travel something or another and that it never happened."

"It's the truth." I touch his arm. "Please, you have to believe me. I know it sounds insane and far-fetched. But it's true."

He shakes his head.

"If I kill Vincent, he can't do this again. We'll be safe."

"What?" His eyes widen. "You're planning on *killing* him?"

"I have to. It's the only way that any of us can survive."

Spencer shakes his head. "Killing him will never make this go away. That's a naïve way of thinking. Even for you."

That stings. "You don't believe me. You think I'm crazy like everyone else does."

"I never said that. I don't know what to think."

"Vincent tortured me for months. I went through hell. I saw things that I can't unsee." Tears blur my vision. I wipe them and stare out the window. "It's constantly there. He's the only one who can make me see visions. Lately he's showing me bits and pieces of memories. But they're different. It's not how they happened."

"Megan..." The way he glances at me breaks my heart because it's the same way Cherry looks at me. Pity. Pity because they don't believe me. It's all made up. Pity because they think I'm nuts. I knew I shouldn't have told him. I don't like feeling vulnerable. I just spilled all my secrets to Spencer, and he doesn't believe me.

He pulls into the parking spot next to my car. "Megan..."

I wave my hand dismissively. "No, it's okay."

"I can't help you kill someone. You can't be serious about this."

"I'm not," I lie. "I'm just hurt and angry. I'm sorry I said anything at all."

I've offended him or hurt his feelings or both. I never meant to and now I regret telling him anything. He's been my only friend lately; I'm scared I've lost him.

As he drives away, I start thinking of ways to approach Vincent tonight. He has to show up. This is it. This is my chance to fix everything. I just have to wait. I want to tell Spencer, but I can't. He wouldn't understand.

What am I going to say to Vincent? What am I going to do?

Thirty-One

The warm, savory scent of lasagna wafts throughout the house making my stomach growl. Mom, Ron, Jonathan, and I sit down at the table. Mom's trying to get us to eat as a family more, but the whole time I keep glancing at the clock. I don't know what I'll say to Vincent.

Mom sets down the dish. I've always loved her lasagna. She doesn't cook often, though she's been cooking a lot more since I've been back.

I try to eat as much as I can and engage in the conversations, but I'm too distracted. How am I going to sneak out? I can't take my car. It's halfway across town. Maybe I can catch an Uber.

The minutes drag on. I can't distract myself enough to make it go faster.

My heart beats faster as 11:30 approaches. Gripping my phone, I sneak out of my room. I creep down the hall to the front door. I inhale a deep breath and open it.

Cold air greets me as I begin walking down the street to my ride. It's some middle-aged woman who has the heat blasting.

"Aren't you a little young to be out this late?"

"No. I'm older than I look," I lie.

She nods. "This address is an abandoned warehouse. Do you know where you're headed?"

"Yes." I know exactly what it is and part of me wishes I told Spencer and for a split second I almost text him.

But I don't.

When the lady pulls up beside the building under an orange streetlamp, she turns to me. "Are you sure you'll be okay? I can wait for you if you want."

"It's okay. I promise." I smile and get out of the car. She doesn't drive away at first, then after a few seconds, she does.

I slink through the side entrance, careful not to let the door slam shut. Slipping my phone in my back pocket, my heart leaps to my throat. The anger returns and I curl my fingers into fists. Everything he's ever done to me surfaces, pushing me forward up the stairs.

When I reach the second floor, I stop when I see his shadow by the window.

Vincent turns around and smiles. His dark blue eyes stare into mine. He looks disheveled like he's been homeless for a long time. Which, I guess he has. He removes his black hat revealing his blonde hair. Black roots begin to show. I still can't get used to the new hair color. I'm surprised he hasn't changed it again.

"Megan." Relief washes over his face as his lips part slightly. "I'm so glad you're okay. You look well. So much better than before."

"What did you do, Vincent?"

"I'm so sorry. I never meant for you to get hurt."

"You messed up everything. What happened when we returned from Arvada? Did it change events and time? How did I end up in the hospital? Was it the potion?"

"Calm down, will you? I don't know. It's...fuzzy."

"Why are you back here? The police and everyone are looking for you. They all think you shot kids at school."

He studies me. "You shouldn't be hanging out with Spencer. He's no good."

That takes me off guard. "How long have you been watching me?"

"It doesn't matter. You need to get rid of him."

"He was your friend. Besides, once we return to Arvada, it will undo this whole thing. You have to bring us back."

"I know that, and I will."

"Well, what are we waiting for? I'm here now so let's go back." I move closer to him.

"Megan." He hesitates.

"What? What is it? I'm sorry for what I did but you have to take us back. I can't take it any longer."

"I can't take us back."

Blood drains from my face. "Why? Where is the Jewel?"

"I don't know."

"What do you mean you don't know?"

"I don't know what happened to it."

There's a pounding in my ears. I see nothing but his face. Clenching my teeth, I charge toward him. "Stop it! Take us back now." I scream, shoving him against the window, searching around his neck. There's nothing. "Where is the Jewel? What did you do with it?"

He pushes me back and I stumble slightly. "Damn, Megan. What the hell is wrong with you?"

I'm breathing hard. My hand is curled into a tight fist, and I drive it into his face.

He curses. "What the hell! What is wrong with you?"

"Stop playing games, Vincent. Take us back, now."

He touches his lip where it bleeds a little. "You've got issues."

"Because of you! You can't keep me here."

Vincent frowns. "I'm so sorry. I never meant for any of this to happen."

"Stop saying that! Did someone steal the Jewel?"

"What part of I don't know don't you understand? All I know is that I woke up in some field and you were nowhere near me. It wasn't long that I realized there was a damn manhunt going on for me. I changed my looks and stole a badge so I could see you in the hospital. The whole time I've been dodging police and trying to find the Jewel."

No, no, no. This can't be it. "We have to find it. It's the only thing that can bring us back. I have to return to Cas—" I stop and curse internally.

Fury slithers its way across his eyes as he lunges for me. We fall to the ground, wrestling with each other. He gets the upper hand and pins me down.

"I never did anything to you but love you. You ruined my life when you left me for him. That's why I killed him. He deserved to die."

"No! Stop saying that. He's still alive. You never went back to kill him."

Glaring into my eyes, he holds my wrists tighter and lowers himself closer to my face. I turn my head hating his hot breath against my ear. "I shot Casper," he whispers. "And when I saw his lifeless body, it gave me such satisfaction. Watching him die has been the greatest event of my life aside from meeting you. If you had only listened to me, Megan he would still be alive. But you left me. For what? For nothing."

I struggle against him, but he's too strong. "I left you because you're a psycho."

The muscle in his jaw twitches. "I'm willing to forgive you. Come with me to find the witch. She can help us find the Jewel or return us to Arvada. We'll live happily ever after, just like you promised we would. As long as you never do that again."

"Get off me," I scream and knee him in the groin.

He moans, rolling over and curling himself into a ball.

I get to my feet. "I will never love you. I will never go with you. The more time you spend here the more Casper will have built an army against you."

Vincent laughs. As I turn to leave, he snatches my ankle. I fall to the ground hitting my arm hard. I kick him in the face and crawl to my feet. I run out of there as fast as I can. When I bolt out the side door, I keep running.

After a while, I stop. The adrenaline leaves my body causing me to collapse to my knees. Tears stream down my face as I tremble. He's just as crazy as when we left Arvada. I'm not strong enough to kill him.

Where is the Jewel though? Why wasn't he wearing it? I know he has it. He has to. He's just adding to my insanity. His manipulation is taking over once again. Vincent and his ridiculous games.

I reach into my back pocket and grab my cell phone to call for another ride. It buzzes with a message from Spencer.

I didn't mean to go off on you. You told me some pretty interesting things. I don't know if this is because of your coma.

Warm tears roll down my cheek as I get to my feet. I don't know how to answer him. I have to get out of here. Vincent could catch me. He knows where I live. Should I call the police? They'll catch him and throw him in jail. They won't kill him, but at least he'll be detained.

If he's in jail, can I still get the answers I need without him? Can I still get the Jewel from him? Did he hide it or did he really lose it?

I walk to a nearby gas station and wait for my ride. As I do, I text Spencer.

I'm sorry I said anything about it. I didn't mean to freak you out.

Can I call?

I look around and decide no. I don't want him hearing my voice shake or know that I'm not at home.

My arm is throbbing, and I see the blood that's seeped through my sweater. I'm no stranger to blood. I feel like something is crushing my head and that stupid nagging pain in my lower back is at it again.

No. I'm just not feeling well. I'll see you tomorrow.

Are you okay?

I'll be fine.

I hop into the Uber ride and hold myself as it takes me near my house. When I get out, my phone buzzes again, and my heart jumps thinking it's Spencer.

I'm so sorry, Megan. I didn't mean to hurt you. I've missed you so much, mon trésor.

How are you even texting me?

Burner phone.

Where is the Jewel?

I may have an idea, but you'll have to come with me.

Where?

Many miles from here.

Why would I go with you? Can't you bring the Jewel back here?

You want to go back to Arvada, don't you? Do what's right, Megan. Ditch Spencer and come with me. Destroying the phone. You'll hear from me soon.

I can't stand seeing the horrible messages on my phone, so I delete them. I feel sick like I'm going to pass out. I don't sleep that night and it saddens me since I don't get to see Casper. All night I contemplate if I made the right decision by not alerting the police. Will he really hurt Spencer? Sadly, I know the answer to that, and I have to tell him to leave me alone now.

I need Vincent to take us back, yet he doesn't even know where the Jewel is. What happened? Unless this is another one of his tricks and he really does have it.

Maybe I can find a way to drug him like I did before. It was the only way to escape him and steal the Jewel.

How would I even come in contact with anything that could drug a person? Would I go back to the trailer park or find some place downtown? I shake my head. I can't believe I'm thinking of buying drugs. What has gotten into me? I'm so desperate to get back to Casper that I'm willing to do anything. Am I so desperate to trust Vincent to go with him though?

Thirty-Two

Sneaking into the shower, I wash all the blood from me. Tears fall as I watch the blood and dirt circle the drain. I'm reminded of when Adam attacked me. I dress for school feeling awful. I'm sore and bruised. Driving to school has me on edge. Now I know for sure that Vincent is stalking me. He's watching everything I do. An uneasy feeling washes over me. I have to watch myself. I should turn him in, but I can't, and I can't possibly go with him to find the witch. But it may be my only choice. Vincent can't stop me from going back home. I refuse to let that happen.

I park my car and get out, glancing at the picnic tables by the entrance of the school. It's where Casper and I met often before school to talk about the dreams or whatever was going on in our lives. The familiar pull of a vision comes to me, and I steady myself against my car.

"How are you feeling?" Casper asks.

"I'm okay I guess." My now ex-boyfriend tried to drug me Saturday after prom. I haven't seen him yet today and I'm anxious. What if he shows up?

"Are you sure you don't want to tell the police?"

"I don't know."

He reaches across the table and takes my hand in his. "Maybe we'll both go after school and tell them everything he confessed to."

I nod. "Did I do this?" Feeling the onslaught of tears, I turn my head.

"What?" Casper moves to my side of the table and pulls me to his chest. "Don't you dare blame yourself for this. He's a messed-up guy and you had nothing to do with his actions."

"Was I good to him? Was I fair to him? He was going through so much and I wasn't there for him."

"Hey." He lifts my chin, and I meet his eyes. "You did everything you could've done. Yeah, he was dealing with a lot, but so were you. I mean, after you were attacked, he kept pressuring you. He made you feel

guilty and nothing you did was ever good enough for him."

I nod. "I never thought I would be caught up in something like this. I've lost focus of so much. School, writing, friends, family."

"Controlling people will do that. You did the right thing. If you stayed, it would've continued to get worse."

"He kept talking about running away together. Like our lives would be perfect if we ran away. I guess I got caught up in it because I've been wanting to get out of this place for so long."

"He knew that and took advantage of it."

"I know."

"I know you have never wished ill-will toward anyone and you have a heart of gold, but we have to tell the police."

"I'm scared. What if he finds out and does something else to us? What if he still comes after you because we're...whatever we are."

"Maybe the police can help. Restraining orders or maybe his parents will take him somewhere."

I take a deep breath, trying to have hope that everything will be okay. Will Casper and I be okay?

The vision leaves me more on edge than before. Why is Vincent showing this? Was he watching us? I shake my head. That never happened. What is he trying to do? Trying to prove he still has power over me? That if I go to the police, it'll only get worse? Is he trying to rub it in my face that no matter what, Casper and I will never be okay? I hate this feeling and there isn't anything I can do.

"Megan?"

I look up and see Spencer. Even behind his glasses, I can see the redness that surrounds his amber eyes and the puffy bags underneath them. Guilt washes over me. I know it's my fault for his exhaustion. I freaked him out yesterday.

"I'm sorry," I say.

"Are you okay? You look like you're going to be sick."

I nod and look around. If Vincent is watching us, he sees that I'm still talking to Spencer. I don't want anything to happen to him. "Look, I'm sorry about yesterday. It's just my crazy mind and that's all."

He shakes his head. "Don't do that. Don't pretend like it didn't happen. It's just...it's a lot to take in."

"I know."

"I have questions."

"Okay."

"Let's talk about it after school. I don't really know how to formulate anything yet."

"Okay."

He walks me to my locker in an awkward silence. I feel a little safer inside. My phone buzzes and when

I look down at the random number, I feel the blood drain from my face. I brace myself against my locker.

I'd hate for Spencer to end up dead like Casper. Do the right thing, Megan.

"What is it?" Spencer asks.

"Nothing." I give a fake smile and the bell rings.

"Are you sure?"

"Yeah. Gotta get to class."

The second he's gone, a pain in my stomach overwhelms me. Gripping my books as I stand outside the classroom, I lean against the wall. I have to heed Vincent's warning. I have to tell Spencer to leave me alone.

This has to stop.

I have to find that Jewel. I feel like my life has been nothing but that: looking for the stupid Jewel that actually doesn't mean anything. Once I find it and return to Arvada, Casper and I will destroy it.

I stare at the white cement floor of the hallway remembering Casper and me walking hand-in-hand before. I see the smile on my face. I can feel the happiness.

Then I'm face-to-face with Vincent. A gun in my face. My heart beating so hard.

"Vincent, don't do this."

"You don't get to tell me what to do. You broke up with me."

"Vincent, please. We can talk about this."

"Megan, run!"

I look over to see Casper running toward us. He's going to tackle Vincent.

The gun fires.

The noise dissipates. Everything stops.

Casper falls to his knees.

"Casper!" A girl screams. Maybe it was me. I rush toward him.

As soon as my arms wrap around him, another shot echoes in the hall, and we fall to the ground.

Blinding white pain suddenly rips through me swallowing me whole.

Burning.

Searing.

Throbbing.

I can't breathe. A wave of dizziness washes over me. It's cold. Numbness takes over and the world goes dark.

Thirty-Three

rembling as I try to catch my breath, my ears ring. Tears cloud my eyes. I'm on my knees, books spread all around me. What was that? Why is Vincent showing me this? I'm shaking and my heart won't settle. Cold sweat breaks out over me as I grip my arm, waiting for the feeling to end.

I ran to Casper and Vincent shot me. Why does he keep showing me these fake visions? Have I entered a new human life with different memories? Is that what happened when we came back, and he lost the Jewel? What if someone stole it and is messing up everything even more?

"Megan, are you okay?" Spencer kneels next to me and grabs my arms. He helps me to my feet. "Whoa, do you need to go to the nurse's office?"

I shake my head.

"Have you been out here the whole time?"

I look at him confused.

Lockers are slamming. Voices keep amplifying. There are too many people. I have to get out of here.

He takes me by the arm and leads me to an empty lab classroom. It's quiet and neither one of us turn on the lights.

"It's okay. You're safe."

Once my breathing resumes to normal, he let's go of me.

"What happened? I went to class and when I got out, you were still standing there."

"What?" Are the visions making me lose time now? I can't deal with this much longer, between the orbs and the visions and the lost time. It's making me crazy. I'm so ready to give in. Vincent wins.

"Are you okay?"

Spencer shouldn't be here with me, especially since Vincent is so close by. "I need to go."

"Wait, you said we could talk."

"Yeah, I did, but you should forget everything I mentioned. I'm not even sure what made me say all that and I'm sorry." I move around him, but he softly takes my arm.

"Megan, you freaked me out. I mean, you told me that the shooting never happened."

"I know. Just ignore it."

"Why are you hesitating? What's wrong? Did something happen?"

"No. Look, hanging out with you was fun but I really need to focus on school right now."

He furrows his eyebrows. "Why are you lying?"

"What?" How can he know that? Am I that bad of a liar?

"I've picked up on some of your quirks. What are you not telling me?"

"You don't know me, okay? You don't know anything that happened to me and as far as I'm concerned, we aren't friends."

Spencer removes his hand from my arm and backs up. "So, you were using me in order to find Vincent?"

"You should leave me alone."

His eyebrows wrinkle. "Did you find him? Has he contacted you?"

I can feel blood rush to my cheeks giving me away. I'm terrible at this. "No, I haven't found him and no he hasn't contacted me. I can't go on some wild goose chase to find him."

"And that suddenly changed since yesterday? Something's got you spooked."

I roll my eyes gaining my strength back. "You don't know what you're talking about. Look, back off, okay? I don't need you."

"It's Vincent. What did he say?"

Clenching my teeth, I push him back, hard. "Get away from me." Anger sets in and I'm almost in tears. I swing open the door, but Spencer takes my arm.

"Megan, what is wrong? Did he contact you last night? You can tell me anything. Please."

When I turn around, the concern in his eyes makes me close the door. I take a deep breath. "I never meant for this to happen. We can't be seen together. He's watching me. Spencer, he's threatened you."

His face turns white. "What?"

"I need you to be safe."

"Little late for that. How did he contact you?"

"He's been watching me. He was there the night I ran out into the road. He came to see me in the hospital."

He raises his eyebrow. "No way he could've gotten past security. How long has he been contacting you?"

I bite my lip. "I left him a note at the trailer park asking him to meet me. He did."

Spencer's eyes widen. "Are you asking for a death wish?"

"He won't kill me. He thinks I'm going to run away with him."

"Why haven't you called the police? Or told me?"

"I needed information from him."

"And you think he's just going to give it to you?"

"I have to try."

"Megan, why didn't you tell me?"

"You wouldn't understand."

"How can you say that? I agreed to help you find him, and now that you did you go rogue on me?"

"You would've wanted to turn him in."

"And you don't?"

"I do but I can't." I lean against the table, and he mirrors me.

"What do you mean you can't? Don't tell me you believe anything he said to you."

I let out a breath. "You wouldn't understand, Spencer. No one does. I don't want to get into it."

"Does it have to do with what you told me the other day?"

"It's fine. I assure you. I shouldn't have brought it up."

"But you did."

"It was a mistake."

"Megan, what's going on? Do you really believe that?"

"You know it's probably something I dreamed about. Um. Class is about to start."

"I don't care. I really don't feel like being here if some psycho is after me. You know we have to tell the police."

"No! We can't."

"Why? What did he threaten you with?"

"Spencer, let me handle him."

"You're joking, right?"

"No. I have to keep you safe. He's already hurt so many people and I can't have him hurt you."

"And how do you suggest that?"

"I'm thinking." When I was in Arvada, the only way to get Vincent and his attention was to pretend I died. Then Florence told him all about it. If Vincent has lost his memories, maybe he doesn't remember what I tried to do.

"What is it?"

"I could fake my death."

"What?"

"Think about it. If all Vincent wants is me and for us to be together, what will stop him from turning himself in if I died?"

"How do you think that's going to work? Do you have any idea what all would have to happen?"

"I know but it could work."

"You wouldn't be able to tell your family. Vincent would know they're lying."

"Have you got a better idea?"

He shakes his head, more out of frustration. "Why are you so set on vengeance? You know it won't solve anything. That's exactly what Vincent did and continues to do because you chose someone else. This bitterness will eat at you until you're so angry and that's all you have. Trust me, I started to go down this road and it's not pretty."

"Why are you suddenly changing your mind?"

"Megan, if Vincent is after me, this is worse. It was stupid to seek him out. We all know what he's capable of doing. We have to tell the police."

"Spencer, no. They won't do anything. Besides, he's watching our every move."

"Why are you protecting him?"

"I'm not. He threatened your life, Spencer. I have to do what he says and more than that he has something that I need. Everything will be fine once I find it."

"What is it?"

I shake my head. "The less you know, the better. I promise."

"This is ridiculous. I'm going to the police."

I nod, giving in. He's right. I care too much about Spencer for him to get hurt. Maybe once Vincent is locked up, he'll tell me where the Jewel is so I can return to Casper. It's a long shot but it's all I have to believe in right now.

Spencer takes my hand, and I'm once again taken aback by how safe and comforting it feels. "Are you going to be okay?"

I nod, suddenly overcome with emotions. "I'm really sorry for how I've treated you. And for causing all of this."

"Megan don't apologize. None of this is your fault."

My chin quivers. Vincent wants to kill Spencer because of me. Because I befriended him and asked for his help. Now he's in danger.

Spencer tugs on me. "Megan don't spiral down that rabbit hole. Stop believing this is your fault. He's making you think that. Sounds like he's always been good at making you believe certain things. He's manipulative."

We sit quietly for a few minutes and when the bell rings we leave the classroom. As I turn the corner, I see Vincent and gasp.

Thirty-Four

Staring at Vincent, I clutch onto Spencer's hand frozen in place. The hairs on the back of my neck stand straight up. It feels as if something is gripping the back of my neck relentless to let go.

"What are you doing here?" I ask but it's all wrong. He's not really there. Am I starting to see things? Then I see myself talking to him like I'm watching a movie or something.

"Mom died."

"I'm so sorry."

"The police came to see me, too." His voice sends chills down my spine. "Asked me if I actually killed someone or ran Casper off the road or drugged you. I can't believe you would make up so many lies." His eyes water, and he shakes his head.

"I didn't lie. You admitted those things."

He smirks. "I never said anything. I would never hurt you. I've been dealing with so much and you left me for Casper. He's been turning you against me from day one. I guess he's finally convinced you."

"He didn't have to turn me against you. I saw it for myself."

"What is it about him? I gave you everything. What could he possibly have to offer you?"

"He treats me better than you ever did."

"My mom was sick, Megan. Then she died. You never cared about me. You were so busy with Casper blaming me for everything that ever happened to you."

"I'm sorry about your mom, Vincent. I really am. But the less you and I see each other the better. You and I are no good for each other. You treated me like crap even before your mom was sick. I was your punching bag and you never let up. You made it impossible to be with you. Everything was my fault. I never said or did the right thing. You're controlling. You're always the victim. You were never there and even when you were, it was just physically. You always cared more about yourself than me and made me feel guilty. I had to

constantly watch what I said or did or else I would unleash the beast."

His dark eyes snap to mine as he clenches his fists. "That is not true."

"It is. Being around you is like constantly walking on eggshells. Vincent, you need to move on. I have, why can't you?"

"I'm sure that's another thing Casper told you. I swear you'll listen to everything he says. I wish you believed me. Since you don't, I'll give you time. If it's time you need, I'll give it. You promised me we'd be together forever. You promised to love me forever."

"Things change."

"Am I not good enough?"

I let out a sigh. "I'm not going through this again." I turn away from him, but he grabs my arm. We're alone and my pulse edges higher.

"I just want to let you know that I'm leaving. Dad thinks it'll be good for me for a while."

"Okay. I hope you get better. I have to go."

"Yeah. Just leave. Leave like you always do. Make me out to be the bad guy."

"I can't do this."

"Have fun being alone for the rest of your life. Better make the best of the time you have with Casper while you still have it."

I jump.

"Are you okay?" Spencer asks.

It's cold and I realize we're outside in the parking lot. "How did we get out here?"

"We...walked. What's the matter?"

I'm breathing hard as I keep picturing the vision. I don't remember that conversation.

"What's wrong? What were you thinking about?"

I shake my head.

"Please talk to me."

"I really don't want to freak you out."

"You won't."

"What like the other day I didn't?"

"You have to admit that was hard to hear."

"Exactly."

"Come on. Tell me."

I let out a breath. "Vincent has the ability to make me see visions and he just showed me one. He always says he has no control over what I see. But it means he's nearby."

"Okay. Does it always work in close proximity?"

"I always thought he had to be touching me, but lately I've been having them."

"What was the vision you just had?"

"It was...at school. Vincent had pulled me away to talk. Said I needed to spend as much time with Casper as I needed to. It doesn't make sense."

"What do you mean?"

"I don't remember it. He's just filling my head with nonsense. Making me see things that never happened."

There's a long bout of silence.

Spencer clears his throat. "Do you ever wonder if that world is your mind's way of coping with what happened?"

My eyes snap to his. "The shooting never happened, Spencer. I told you what happened. No one believes me. You need to leave me alone. I gotta go." I storm toward my car. Every time I let my guard down, it ends up biting me. Why doesn't anyone believe me? Is Vincent really the only one who knows the truth? Of course, he is.

My phone buzzes as soon as I reach my car.

Come to the trailer now.

Why?

It's time to leave, Megan. If you don't, Spencer dies.

Fine.

I know I have to do this. It's the only way I can return to Arvada. As I drive toward the trailer park, I try to push the tears away. This is to keep Spencer safe. This to keep everyone safe and to return things back to normal.

Thirty-Five

ulling into the trailer park an hour later, I grip the steering wheel. It's motionless here, like there is no life. My tires crunch over the gravel as I worm my way through the park to the very end. I turn off the ignition and emerge from the car. Cold air wraps itself around me, rustling through the bare limbs of the trees. I hug myself tight, hoping this isn't another way for Vincent to mess with me.

It's quiet. Too quiet. Lonely. Every single sound I hear startles me. With the blanket of gray clouds above me, I carefully make my way to the front door of the trailer and open it. The loud creaking gives me away. "Vincent?"

"You came." Vincent's voice sends ice over me as he appears from the shadows of the kitchen. Dark circles show under his eyes. His cheeks are hollowed, and he looks more emaciated. I wonder when the last time he's eaten. Or showered. He almost doesn't look recognizable. "Why have you been crying?" He reaches out to touch my face, but I move back.

"What do you want?"

"Did Spencer hurt you?"

"No."

"How are you friends with him?"

"He helped me find you."

"Didn't he almost hit you?" Disgust fills his eyes and twists his face. "You've become sick and twisted. What is wrong with you?"

"Least he never shot me."

Vincent winces and his shoulders curl over his chest. "I'm so sorry, Megan. I will do anything to make it up to you."

"You know what I want. I want to go home."

"That's why I wanted you to come. We can go now."

"Did you find the Jewel?"

"No, I'm ready for you to come with me."

"I'm not going anywhere with you. Bring the Jewel to me."

He smirks. "It's cute to see how brave you're trying to be. You don't have to be afraid of me. I made a mistake, but I won't ever hurt you again. I promise."

"Why are you showing me all these visions? Things that never happened."

"I told you. I have no control over what you see."

"You're showing me things about the school shooting. Why would you show me if it never happened?"

He lets out a breath. "It's probably all in your head, Megan. Everyone has been feeding you so many lies. It's being here and I know I messed up. I need your help finding the witch, okay? Can you please do that?"

"Why do you need my help?"

"Because it's really hard to do anything when the police are looking for you. We can get out of here once we find it, okay? I promise we'll return to Arvada. We'll be safe again."

I look at him like he's crazy and cross my arms. "No. You find the Jewel. I'll come with you when you have it. Until then, don't text me." I turn around but he seizes my arm. I clench my hands into fists ready to punch him. "Let me go."

He loosens his grip. "Please, Megan. I need your help." His eyes plead with me. "Just hear me out. I don't know what happened when we returned. Obviously, I'm aware of how much it has messed up everything. I don't need everyone thinking I killed all these people. I never did."

"You're not hiding the Jewel somewhere?"

"No."

"I don't believe you. It's the only way to get back to Arvada, and you never part with that thing. You just want to torture me because you couldn't find Casper." I smile. "He's safely hidden away. You'll never find him. Once we return, I'm going to destroy the Jewel and I'm going to kill you for good, Vincent."

The muscle in his jaw twitches and he shakes his head. He closes his eyes and takes a deep breath. When he opens his eyes, he's calmer but calm doesn't mean good with Vincent. "I'm going to kill Spencer for doing this to you. He has seriously messed up your mind into believing I'm the bad guy. I was never the bad guy, but you always seem to think I am."

"Because you are."

He slams me against the wall, pressing his hands into my shoulders. I can't prevent my body from trembling. "I am not a bad guy. Everything I've ever done is with you in mind. You can't leave me, Megan. Casper is dead. And if Spencer gets in my way, I'll kill him, too. Don't you get it, Megan? We can be together. Just like we've always wanted. Now, if I let you go, are you going to run?"

I shake my head.

"Good girl." He slowly removes his hands. "I'm going to forgive you this time, Megan. But don't ever threaten to kill me again. I know you don't mean it. I know you would never hurt me because you love me. Once we get you fixed up, you'll be back to normal."

"I don't need fixing. Why did you even bring us here?"

"I was angry when I brought you back and I shouldn't have. I need you to come with me."

"You know I can't do that."

"Yes, you can." He moves closer to me. "I have no one to trust in this place. You're the only one who knows the truth. Everyone is looking for me and I can't do this without getting caught."

"I'm not going anywhere with you."

"You want to get out of here? The witch is here, Megan. I know she is. If we find her, she can help us return to Arvada. Or at least point us in the direction of the Jewel. She's the only way."

"I thought you were going to leave me here. To suffer. To live each human life without Casper."

"I was upset when I said that. You did try to have me killed."

"I'm not going to apologize for that."

"I'm not asking you to. But you have to know I would never have left you here. I need you. I always need you."

A car comes down the gravel road and I tense.

Vincent peers through a small crack of the window. "Are you kidding me? You brought him here?"

I glance out the window and curse. Spencer.

Thirty-Six

Through the window, I watch Spencer get out of his car. My heart drops to my stomach. I have to somehow tell him not to come inside. Why did he follow me? Did I know where I was going?

"What's he doing here, Megan?"

"I don't know. I told him nothing. Don't hurt him. I'll tell him to leave."

"Why? So he can call the police? No thanks." He hides behind the door as we wait for Spencer to enter.

Once he does, his eyes find mine. "Megan, are you okay?" He moves toward me.

"Watch out," I yell, but Vincent grabs him holding a gun to his temple.

My heart slams into my chest. Tremors take over my body and I can't move. The whole room starts spinning and my ears ring. Where did he get the gun?

"Why are you here?" Vincent demands.

I grab my chest. "Vincent, no."

Spencer holds up his hands. "Look man, whatever you want to do, it's not worth it."

"Give me your phone. Both of you."

I hand over mine. "We-we aren't going to call anyone. Please don't hurt him."

Spencer gives him his and Vincent smashes both phones with his boot.

"I swear I won't tell anybody you're here," Spencer says with a shaky voice.

"Vincent, stop it. Let him go."

"Now, Megan, are you going to come with me or not."

"Don't do it, Megan," Spencer says, and Vincent cocks the gun.

Tears rush down my face and I can barely think. "No, please!"

"What's it going to be?"

"Fine. Fine. I'll go with you."

"Good girl."

With a gun digging into Spencer's back, Vincent forces him outside and I follow. I have to do whatever he says. He can't hurt Spencer.

He pushes him hard and Spencer stumbles to the dirt on his knees. He raises the gun and I tackle him to the ground.

"Run!" I tell Spencer.

Vincent gets to his feet and shakes his head as Spencer runs away into the woods. "Coward." He points the gun at one of Spencer's car tires and fires.

I jump.

"Come on. We have a long drive ahead of us."

He forces me into my car as he gets in the driver side. Vincent tears out of the trailer park kicking up dust and dirt.

I release a sigh of relief knowing Spencer is okay.

Thirty-Seven

Was that really necessary? Why were you going to shoot him?"

"He's going to call the cops now."

"Maybe if you didn't point a gun at him."

"I have been living out on my own hiding from police for months. I'm tired of it and given everything you've gone through, I know you're tired, too. I'm trying to get us out of this place, and I can't have any loose ends."

"Were you going to kill him?" My voice cracks. "He only came to see if I was okay."

"You lead him right to me. What if he had already called the cops?" He starts peering up through the windshield for helicopters."

"He didn't. Stop being so paranoid."

"Stop being so naïve."

"Naïve? I'm being completely stupid right now for trusting you."

"What do I have to do for you to trust me? I'm so sorry I shot you and brought you back here. I know what I did was wrong. We need to return back to our world. Just you and me. We can repair everything."

"Repair everything? Vincent, you left the Elves in ruins. All of it is gone."

"Then you and I will rebuild it. You were right when you told me that I could be better. I want to prove that to you. We are meant to be together. We vowed that to each other. Don't you remember?"

That vow was a long time ago. I know I have to play along. I've done it before, and he believed me then. I can finally kill him. Plus, the witch helped me before. She wants to end all of this. She wants Vincent dead, so maybe she'll help me. I'm not exactly keen on having to go on a road trip with Vincent, but it's all I've got right now.

"I remember." I swallow hard. I have to do this. For Casper. For us. I have to do this in order for our kind to survive.

"Megan, I know I'm not a perfect man by any means. I love you and I can be better. I will make this right. We'll be on our own forever, just like we always talked about."

Forever is a long time, and I plan to kill him before that.

"Please trust me."

"You know I can't magically hand over my trust."

He nods. "I know and I haven't done much to earn it. I will prove it to you. Let's just get out of this place, okay?"

"Fine." The thought of leaving trumps anything. Dad taught me how to fight but not with someone who has a gun. It never occurred to me that he'd have one.

Vincent presses on the gas and speeds away. "When we find a store, you'll need to get hair dye and other essentials. We don't have much time before Spencer calls someone."

"Where are we going?"

"Vermont."

"Vermont?"

He shrugs. "It's a lead."

I let out a breath. It's about twenty hours from here to Vermont. Twenty hours to convince Vincent we can be together. Twenty hours to concoct a plan to kill him. Twenty hours until I return to Casper. I can do this. "Okay."

"You look tired. Why don't you take a nap?"

"Why? What are you going to do to me?"

A muscle in his jaw twitches. "Nothing, Megan. I'm not going to hurt you."

I don't respond. Best not to upset him. I have to pretend to trust him.

We drive through the city and it's beautiful. The LED lights under the interstate light up and even in the middle of winter, the city seems to be thriving. Sadness fills me. I know it's good that I'm going back home. Home to where we belong. I will miss my family. I will miss Spencer and Cherry. We never made up before I left. Maybe it's for the best. I wish I could say goodbye to everyone, but it will only make things worse. I know they'll all be safe. All of them. My heart pounds against my chest. I keep picturing Casper. I have to return to him. Soon I will find him.

I still find it strange that no one came out of their trailer to see what the commotion was. Where was everyone? Were they at work?

Then a feeling overcomes me. Dread. It sits in the pit of my stomach. Did Vincent kill them all? Would he have done that? I shut my eyes tight. *No.* He's not like that.

Except, he's exactly like that. And I'm so desperate to go back home that I'm being completely naïve to trust him to take us.

Glancing sideways at him, I think of how easy it seems for him to want to kill. Like it's second nature. Was he always like that or did I make him like that? Is it my fault that he's a killer?

I take Vincent's advice and close my eyes. I hope to see Casper in my dreams so that I can tell him I'm coming home.

Fireflies surround me as I walk through a garden of beautiful roses and lilies. I catch a hint of gardenia once the wind rustles the massive trees awake.

"It's so beautiful here," I tell Casper. "I'm coming home. We'll be together." I pull his lips to mine and kiss him.

"Does he have the Jewel?"

"No, he lost it when we returned. But we're going to find the witch."

"Megan, she isn't in the mortal world. I don't trust him."

"What? She has to be."

He shakes his head. "He has to have the Jewel. It's the only way you're going to return. He knows exactly where it is, or he has it on him."

"How am I going to get it?"

"I don't know." He touches my cheek. "I hate this so much for you. I wish I could help you. You can do this, Megan. Find the Jewel and come home to me."

"I don't know if I can. He has a gun, Casper."

"You're stronger than you think. You've always been stronger than you believe. You have to believe in yourself."

There never is an easy way out of this. "I'll find a way. I promise."

"Be careful, Megan. I love you."

Thirty-Eight

It's dark outside when I wake up. Exhaustion wears on me and I feel like I'm getting sick. I sit up and massage my neck. I glance at the clock. 7:46pm. I didn't want the dream to end. Was Casper telling the truth about the witch not being here? I peek sideways at Vincent. It wouldn't be the first time he lied about not having the Jewel.

There is absolutely nothing out here. We're not on the interstate anymore but on some country road. There aren't any streetlamps. This doesn't seem like it's the way to Vermont.

"Where are we?"

"Almost to Tennessee. I need to stop for gas soon and hair dye." Vincent looks exhausted. How has he survived this long?

"Where have you been this whole time?"

"Pretty much all over."

"They found your car crashed in the middle of a desert in Arizona."

"Wasn't me. I abandoned my car months ago. I spent some time in the mountains."

He pulls the car up to a gas station that looks old and dated. The lights over the pumps flicker and I wonder if it's still operational. I see a light on inside the tiny store. The thick grime on the glass makes the light dim.

Pulling his hood over his hat, he gets out and pumps the gas. He hands me cash to go inside and pay.

The thought of going inside freaks me out. How was he able to do this before? Can he change his appearance like me? Though I can't because I'm in the mortal world.

"It's okay. I'm watching. You'll be okay. Pull your hood up and don't make eye contact."

I swallow hard. Taking my steps slowly, I walk inside and place the bill on the counter then quickly turn around.

Vincent holds the door open for me and after I ease in, he gets in on the driver's side.

"*Are you ready for an adventure of a lifetime?*" *Casper smiles like he's on cloud nine.*

I return the smile. "*You're a dork.*"

"*But I'm your dork.*"

I can't believe Mom actually allowed me to go to the beach with Casper. Granted, Cherry, Luke and Cherry's parents are going too. We have a few weeks before school starts and it's a great time to get away.

Casper turns up the radio.

"*Oh not this song.*" *I groan.*

"*This song is awesome.*" *He starts singing way off key.*

I shake my head and laugh.

Casper smirks and takes my hand. "*I love seeing you laugh.*"

"*Because I'm going to the beach. You know how long it's been?*"

"*Is that the only reason?*"

"*Hmm. Yeah, pretty much.*" *I tease.* "*Can't really think of anything else.*" *I look away and tilt my head pretending to think.*

He tickles my waist.

"*Of course, I'm happy to be here with you.*"

His brown eyes deepen with lust. "*I love you, Megan.*"

"*I love you.*"

He kisses me and in that moment it's like we're in our own cocoon of passion. I'm reminded of Elizabeth Barret Browning's Sonnet 43, How Do I Love Thee. In this kiss, I understand the love she had for her husband; the absolute unending passion and how she needed him as much as she needed basic necessities of life. Her love was as deep and wide as it could possibly go. It was so grand she saw no end at all. I realize that is how I feel about Casper. I see a future with him. In his kiss, I am home.

"Megan?"

I blink several times and I'm back in the car with Vincent on our way to Vermont to find the witch. I touch my tingling lips, still able to feel that kiss. There is no way Vincent is showing me these visions. Am I remembering things from another life of mine and Casper's?

"Are you okay?" Vincent asks.

"Yeah. Fine."

"What just happened? You were out of it for a while."

"I don't know. It's been happening ever since we came back. I've been waking up in different places with no memory of how I got there."

"What? Why?"

"I don't know. It hasn't been easy, Vincent. What made you attack the Elves? Did your father make you do it?"

"Why can't you leave my father out of it?" he says with an edge.

"Are you kidding? He convinced you to do that. As soon as he became king, it was like you would both kill anyone that went against you. There was so much death, Vincent. I still can't get the smell of blood out of my head. You didn't care." I can't help the tears that well in my eyes when I think of all those innocent people who died.

"I care, Megan. I live with this daily. I never meant for any of it to happen. We are meant to be together. You promised and you broke that. You broke my heart, and I couldn't take it."

"So you lashed out? No one deserved to die, even if they are your enemy."

"Is that why you were going to kill me? You always think you're better but you're not. You cheated on me when I needed you the most."

My chin quivers and I shut my eyes letting the tears fall down my cheeks. "Vincent, you can't help who you love."

"Exactly. I mean, did you ever love me? Were you just stringing me along because I was vulnerable? Were you and I only a joke to you?"

I never thought of Vincent as vulnerable. "No. Do you remember that night at the ruins and you told me I loved you once? It's true Vincent. I did fall in love with you."

He lets out a sigh. "It wasn't the ruins. I should've never done that."

"Done what?"

Vincent shakes his head and rubs his face. "We need to find food. I'll stop at a gas station, and you can go inside, okay? I can't be seen."

"You should've never done what?"

"Nothing. I don't have a lot of cash on me so don't buy the whole store." He drives a little further until we see a Dollar General pop up in the middle of nowhere. Of course, there's a DG out here. Why wouldn't there be?

He puts the car in park as we sit at the edge of the parking lot and hands me a wad of cash.

"Tell me what you were going to say. What do you mean it wasn't the ruins?"

"When we had that conversation, it was after we started school. I saw you and Casper in the hallway together and when he left, you and I talked in the woods beside school. You were relentless. Kept talking about how I manipulated you and all this crap. How it was all my fault you cheated on me." He shakes his head.

"No. We had that conversation at some ruins in Arvada. You're not remembering it right."

"Are you sure it's not you? You've always had a terrible memory and you've been through some things. Either way. You still ripped out my heart and you don't care. You're always the victim, Megan. Never take responsibility for your actions."

"Then why do you want to be with me? If I'm such a terrible person and I treat you so bad."

"Because I love you. I'm willing to forgive you for everything you've done. You have to forgive me, too. You're the only one for me."

"You're unbelievable."

"You said so yourself that we've both done and said things we didn't mean. That it was just how we are and it's what makes us who we are as a couple."

I also said that as a way to trick him and of course he uses it against me. He's right though. We've both done things to each other and that should only enhance the fact that we don't belong together. With my hand on the door handle, I take a deep breath. Just a little longer with him then it'll be over. That is, if we find the witch in Vermont or if I find the Jewel on him faster than that.

"Just get some hair dye and some snacks and drinks. I'll be waiting."

Taking the cash, I make my way to the inside of the store. I open the door and I'm back at school.

"You okay?" Casper asks as I meet him by my locker. It's the first day of school since the summer and I'm dreading it. We had an amazing summer. One full of laughs and love. I never thought I could be so happy. I know I made the right decision when I broke up with Vincent.

I smile. "I'm better now."

He chuckles. "I don't wanna be here either."

"It's okay. We're here together."

When Casper kisses me, I still get the fuzzy feeling that I did when we first kissed. The same heat that runs over my body and makes my toes curl.

He draws back slightly and tenses.

"What is it?" Following his eyes, I twist around and see him. The dark look in his eyes sends chills down my spine. I turn back to Casper. "When did he get back?"

"I don't know."

Vincent had been gone most of the summer to get well or something. He wasn't very forthcoming with the details.

"Are we going to be okay?" I ask.

Casper locks eyes with me. "Of course, we will."

"You promise? I mean, he ran you off the road. Gave me a date-rape drug. What's to say he won't try anything again? The police did nothing."

"I know." Casper wraps his arms around me. "It's okay. He's left us alone for two months. Maybe he's moved on. Look, I don't want you living in fear because of me. No matter what, I'm here. I will keep you safe at all costs."

"I'm not living in fear because of you, Casper. I choose to be with you because I love you. You're the one I want."

He smiles. "I love you, Megan."

He walks me to class and within minutes of the bell ringing, Vincent strolls into the classroom and hands the teacher a note.

"Megan, you need to go to the office."

Butterflies attack my stomach. I know I'm not needed in the office and it's one of Vincent's tricks. I make my way out to the hallway and sure enough Vincent is waiting right outside the room.

"What are you doing? Don't you have class?"

He shrugs. "It's a bit overrated don't you think?"

"Vincent, what do you want? We broke up."

"I need to talk to you."

"About what?"

"We just need to talk, okay? Can you at least give me that?"

I let out a sigh. "Fine. What do you need to say?"

"Not here."

"Where? I'm not going anywhere with you."

Vincent rolls his eyes. "I'm not going to do anything. Besides, we're at school. Let's go outside, okay?"

Crossing my arms in front of my chest, I follow him reluctantly. We make our way to the edge of the woods, but I refuse to walk any further.

"This is far enough. Now, what do you want?"

He sighs and shakes his head. "I don't understand what happened. You used to love me."

"Yeah, I know. Then I learned who you really are. It made me question my choices when it came to you. I would've done anything for you. I loved you but it was all a lie. You never loved me. You wanted me as a possession. Someone you could use to your advantage."

He shakes his head. "I have always loved you, Megan. You don't know what love is. You live in this fantasy where your ideas of love are so fantastical. To think you gave up real love for something so incredibly fake baffles me. I'm trying to protect you."

"Protect me? You drugged me. Who knows what you were planning on doing to me. If you're so worried about my safety, you wouldn't have left me all the time. What about the party you declined to accompany me? The one where I was attacked."

"And if you hadn't gone to that party, you wouldn't have been attacked. God knows what you were wearing that night. I've told you numerous times, I'm planning our escape so we can be happy. We've talked about this. You and me, running away to be free."

"I'm not running away with you, Vincent. Can't you get that?"

The vein in his neck protrudes as his face reddens with anger. "My mom was sick and died and this is what I get from you?" He takes a deep breath. "I don't want to fight with you. I spent the summer really trying to work on things. I'm a better person now and I want to show you that."

He takes my hand in his. "I love you so much. You swore yourself to me. We made promises. I'm better now. You don't have to break those promises."

I look up at him and freeze. His ocean blue eyes pin to mine with desire that I once craved. "What?" He's sounding crazy and I need to calm him down before he does something drastic. "I have to get back to class."

"Fine. This is how you want to play this game. I'll make you see, Megan. I'll make you understand that you belong to me."

Thirty-Nine

hat the hell took you so long?"

"I wasn't in there that long," I tell Vincent as I close the door. After I snapped out of it, I got hair dye and some food. My head is still spinning. The visions have gotten longer. I shake my head. Vincent's changing my memory of things. Is that why my memories of Casper are slowly fading? He's made me forget Casper so many times before. Is he doing it again?

Is there really a witch? Does he really know where she is or is he going to make me forget Casper? Will we return to Arvada or is he tricking me again?

"Megan, you were in there for an hour."

My mouth drops. "What?"

He shakes his head. "Dammit. This is all my fault."

"Why are you changing my memories?"

"What?"

"You keep changing everything I remember with your visions."

Vincent plops his head against the headrest frustrated. "I thought for sure you'd see a doctor by now. This is getting way out of hand."

"What do you mean?"

"Nothing."

The interstate lights leave dark shadows on his rugged face. He used to make me smile. Make me feel good. Take all my worries away. When we first met, he'd say things to me that made my heart skip a beat, like I was the most beautiful girl he'd ever met. Or how he couldn't wait to see me again or that he'd do anything for me. Within a few months, he became angry a lot. Anytime I declined him or anytime he didn't get his way, he would definitely let me know. Whether by giving me the silent treatment or yelling at me. I learned to walk on eggshells around him because I didn't know what I would say or do that would set him off. Anything does. But that wasn't why I fell for Casper.

Casper really cared for me. He loved me. He showed me what real love is.

Staring out at the beautiful scenery of mountains, I try to think of everything Vincent's said or not said rather. It's crowding inside my head, and I can't stand it. Just for once, I want to clear my mind. I want to stop worrying about everything and thinking about everything. It's too much and it's overwhelming.

At some point through the muddled thoughts and craziness, I doze off.

The rhythmic sound of the ocean waves calms me. I can't remember the last time I saw the ocean. I don't exactly have good memories of it. Every time I think of the ocean, Vincent's there trying to kill me or fight with Casper.

But tonight, it's just me, the sand, and the water. As I stare across the great expanse of the ocean with no end in sight, it scares me a little. The sheer size of it is overwhelmingly existential. It's too big for me to comprehend. It's like life. Life is dangerous. Overwhelming. Scary. Deep. Why does anyone want to stay?

"Megan?" I hear him from behind me. His soothing voice always brings comfort.

I turn around and emotions overcome me. "Casper." I let out a breath of relief. "I've missed you."

He wraps his arms around me holding me tight. Almost like he doesn't want to let me go. "I've missed you, too."

"What's wrong?" I ask. "I know it's been a while and I'm sorry for that. It's...complicated."

"Megan, you have to stop."

"Stop what?" I draw back to meet his eyes. It's too dark out here to see anything and I wish there was a light or something so I could see his beautiful face.

His reluctance to answer worries me. "Megan, you have to open your eyes."

"What?"

"Open your eyes. Put the pieces together. You know the truth."

"What are you saying?"

"Trust yourself and open your eyes."

"I don't understand."

"You have to wake up from all of this. You have to say goodbye to me."

His words knock the breath out of me. My heart drops to my stomach. "What?"

"I'm stuck here forever. You're not."

"I know. I'm trying to come back. What's going on?"

"Open your eyes. Everything's going to okay. I promise. But you have to go now."

"Why are you trying to get rid of me?"

He caresses my face. "Megan, I'm not. You can't keep coming back here. You have to open your eyes for good. I love you so much."

"Why are you saying your goodbyes to me? Why are you doing this?"

"Because it's the right thing to do. There isn't a witch. You have to leave. You need to let go."

Tears stream down my face. My heart is breaking into a million pieces. Is he breaking up with me? After everything we've been through? Why is he doing this? "What do you mean it's the right thing to do?"

"You have to wake up. You have done more for me than anyone I've ever known. You've given me life. You've made me immortal. Now it's time for you to move on. Wake up, Megan. Open your eyes."

"Stop saying that!" I yell.

"I will when you finally do it. You have to." He takes my hand in his and places it to his heart. "I love you so much. I always will."

"Don't do this. I promise, I'll return soon, and we can be together. Don't give up on me."

"I'm not giving up on you. I would never do that to you. Megan, you're the only one I love, and I will always love you. Forever. It's okay to let go. I'll be fine."

I shake my head. "No, Casper. I can't leave you."

"You can. You are stronger than you think. You have a whole life ahead of you. Don't waste it on these dreams, Megan."

His words aren't making sense. "What?"

"It's time."

"Time for what? Please don't leave me."

Casper caresses my cheek, calming me if only for a minute. He leans down pressing his lips to mine, moving in an eager yet sad way. It's his goodbye kiss, and I can't stop it. When he pulls back, he rests his forehead against mine.

"We'll always have this. Our memories. It will always be here. It's time to be brave. Be fearless. And open your eyes."

Forty

ight from the sun barely breaks the horizon. The dark blue fades into a deep orange and red. The forest speeds past us on the two-lane highway. Grogginess and sadness settle over me as I remember where I am. I move my neck and wince. Must have slept in a bad position. My cheeks are wet from tears. Crying in my sleep. There's a terrible taste in my mouth and I long to brush my teeth. Or take a shower. Anything.

Rubbing my eyes, the dream comes back to me. It was cryptic, yet heartbreaking. Was that even Casper? Or was it someone portraying him? It didn't look like him. Or maybe it did. I can't even remember what he looked like in it. It was dark. There was sand and the ocean. The more I think about it, the more it just seemed like a blob.

Open my eyes. What did he mean? Why was he saying goodbye to me? Maybe it was just a fluke. It's been a while since I'd seen him. He couldn't have been saying goodbye to me for good. I'm so close I can feel it. I can't lose him.

Peering at Vincent, he looks drowsy. Circles darken around his eyes. As much as I don't want to, we need a hotel room. Or something.

"Are you okay?" I ask.

He takes a deep breath. "Yeah. Are you? You were completely passed out and you were crying."

I massage my neck still trying to work out the kink. "What time is it?"

"It's about five-thirty."

"Where are we?"

"North Carolina. Smoky Mountains."

The only time I've ever been to the Smokies was when I was a kid with my grandparents. In the early morning light, the fog is heavy, but I can still see the beautiful snow through the forest. It's almost like it glows. Tall snow-dusted trees pass by us and every so often there are spaces to be able to see the views. The fog is so dense, it's hard to see much. Large piles of snow have been pushed to the side of the road and insanely tall icicles hang from cliffs. The windy road is empty as we climb higher. My ears pop every so often.

Vincent pulls into a parking lot and turns off the engine. The road has been cleared of some ice and snow, and it's dark. Dreading to get out of the warm car, I brace myself when I open the door. The intense cold hits me like a baseball. The wind is brutal. I take a deep breath inhaling evergreens, snow, and crisp air. It smells heavenly.

"Come on," he says, and we start walking toward a trail.

"Where are we going?" My shoes sink into the snow and my jeans are getting wetter. It's too cold to be hiking in the mountains at six in the morning. Plus, I'm not even dressed for this.

"We have to dye our hair. There's a bathroom up here we can use. Not many people come up here in the winter."

"Vincent, it's cold. There's snow everywhere."

"I know. Just a little further."

Pulling my sleeves over my hands and my hood covers as much of my face as possible. We pass a brown sign with Tennessee State Line and North Carolina State Line carved in white. I remember seeing that as a kid. "Why couldn't we have done this somewhere warmer?" By the time I say that I realize we've reached the restroom.

I've never dyed my hair before and I'm a little scared. "Do we really have to do this?"

"It'll be okay. I promise."

Staring into the mirror, Vincent grabs the scissors. With every strand of hair he cuts, a tear falls. I know it'll grow back but that doesn't matter. He cuts it just below my chin. All my long, black hair is gone. It's choppy and looks strange. If this is what it takes to get back to Casper, so be it.

He dyes my hair, and when I look in the mirror, it makes me even more sad. The blonde color I picked out turned my hair into an orangish color. I don't even look like myself. I hate it. I hate him for making me do this.

But it isn't his fault. I chose this. I chose to do this so I can return. It's only temporary.

If Cherry could see this. Thinking of her makes me sad and I feel guilty for leaving them, but I had to. I hate that my mom is left to freak out and worry. We have to get to the witch as soon as possible.

Vincent doesn't cut his hair but dyes it a dark red. It looks so weird and different.

Once we're done, we leave the restroom, and the scenery overwhelms me. Sunrise in the snow-covered mountains is unlike anything I've ever seen. The orange and red and gold colors from the sun mold into the background of the incredible mountain ranges and is masked by blue smoke.

It's breathtaking.

"I always wanted to take you here," Vincent says. "It's so calm and peaceful and you always needed something like that. You've always been on edge."

Because of you. "Let me drive."

"No. I'm good."

"Vincent, come on. You've been driving all night. It's fine. I don't mind. We need to find a hotel room or a cabin."

"Are you serious?"

"Yes, I am. We both need to rest and freshen up."

"Maybe we can find a river or something."

"You're joking, right?"

He smirks. "Never been camping a day in your life, I see."

"It isn't like you have camping gear anyway. We don't even need to stay the night. I just want a shower and you need rest."

He moves toward me. "I love that you still care. There should be a cabin at the bottom of the mountain. There's an Indian reservation."

"Thank you." I make my way toward the car, but he stops.

"Megan, you're not doing all this to turn me in, are you?"

"Why would you think that?"

"Why else would you be doing all this with me? You keep talking about going home and you even mentioned you wanted to kill me."

"I was upset, okay? I would never hurt you," I tell him, playing the same game he does with me. "You're right about us being together. We can deal with all of this once we return and live our lives." I hesitate but I need him to trust me. I reach for his hand and take it in mine, loathing myself and hating the clammy way his hand feels in mine.

He squeezes my hand and gives a small smile.

Miles later, we reach the bottom of the mountain and I see a sign for lodging at the edge of Cherokee, a small Indian reservation in North Carolina. I've never been there though. I pull the car into the gravel parking lot.

"Be quick," he says. "Here's some money. Buy some toiletries and whatever, too."

I go inside and smile at the clerk behind the counter. The office is warm and cozy. Everything smells like pine and there's some odd smelling incense burning nearby. I've always loved incense, but Mom hates it so I'm never able to burn any at home.

"Can I help you?" A man, clothed in a plaid jacket, stares at me. His dark hair reaches his elbows and deep wrinkles are embedded into his brown skin.

"Um, hi. I'd like to rent a cabin."

"Lucky. We just had a cancellation. It's unusual for someone to come up and rent one."

"Oh. Yeah, we thought we could go without. Do you have any shampoo?"

He points to the corner where a wall of toiletries hangs. Not many options but it's okay. I grab some various toiletries and see a heavier coat on the rack and some gloves. It's cold here and I'm going to need something if we're going to make it to Vermont.

"How many nights?"

"Oh, just tonight."

"Just one night? In this beautiful country?"

"Yeah."

"One hundred fourteen, please."

Counting the money Vincent gave me, I hand him a hundred and fifty. The clerk gives me change and hands me a key with a large keychain that reads "8."

After I park in front of the cabin, I get out of the car shivering. I'm grateful I bought a coat and gloves. It's freezing here and it wasn't like I could've packed anything since Vincent decided to pull a gun on Spencer forcing me to come with him.

Once again, the scenery takes my breath away. Even though the smoke hovers low, I can still make out the snowcapped mountains in the distance. I hate that I'm in one of the most beautiful places with the worst person. It would be so easy to turn him in, but I can't. I need him. Just for a little while longer though.

The room is small with two full size beds. The walls are a dingy white with pictures of the mountains above each bed. There's a small round table with two chairs and a TV on top of a small dresser. The curtains are green with pink flowers that match the bedspreads. Clearly, something from the nineties.

Vincent drops his bag by the table and plops down on the edge of the bed. He lets out a sigh and runs his hand through his hair. "I had to get back to you."

"What?"

"It's all a blur. I remember waking up and seeing myself plastered on newspapers and TV and everywhere else. You were in the hospital. I hated it." His voice cracks. "I had to get back to you to make sure you were okay. I changed my hair and wore different contacts. It was surprisingly easy to get in that place. And once I saw you..." He shakes his head. A tear slides down his cheek as he meets my eyes. "I will never forgive myself, Megan. I am so sorry."

More tears come and he covers his face. I have never seen him cry like this and I don't know how to react.

I sit beside him on the bed. How do I comfort someone who's tried everything possible to make my life hell? Is it his fault? Did he know what he was doing? I've always excused his behavior as a product of his father.

Vincent clears his throat and wipes his tears. "You take a shower first. I'll be a lookout."

"Okay."

Eager to shower and to leave this uncomfortable scene, I head to the bathroom and lock the door. It's small but I don't care.

Hot water beats down on my shoulders. It feels amazing. I think about Casper and all the times we've showered together. My dream returns to me. Casper's goodbye. Him telling me over and over to open my eyes and to wake up. What was he trying to tell me? He said the witch wasn't here. That couldn't have been his goodbye. He can't give up on me yet. I let myself weep. I have to get back to him. Soon.

After I dress, I see Vincent passed out on the bed with the TV on. I wonder when the last time he actually slept. He looks so peaceful. I hate what happened to him and what he has become.

Glancing at the table in between the beds, I stare at the phone and itch to call Spencer to see if he's okay. I don't know his number though. The only number I know by heart is Jonathan's. I miss them so much and I'm risking everything to leave them and return to Arvada.

This is for the best. I messed everything up and once I return everything will be fixed.

I want to go to the store and get food, however, my instincts are screaming at me.

Look for the jewel.

There's a pounding in my ears as I kneel in front of Vincent's bag. Not much is in there. A notebook. Pictures. Toothbrush and toothpaste. A couple of shirts. Energy bars. Water. A knife.

I sift through the pictures. Some are of his mom, and it makes me sad. Some are of me from a time when we were together.

I put everything back after checking again. No jewel.

Sitting on my knees, I look around. Vincent has always slept like the dead. What if he has it on him? Rising to my feet, I watch him, remembering the time I poisoned him with the lily of the valley berries. I snatched the Jewel from his neck and ran away only for it to possess me.

Will it do that here in the mortal world?

The heavy thump of my heartbeat reverberates through me. I creep close to him wondering how I'm going to find it without him waking.

I inhale a breath and slowly release it.

I can do this.

With a shaky hand, I softly press down on his pockets feeling for the Nuummite. I freeze when I feel something hard in his left pocket.

Reaching inside, I pull out the black, speckled jewel attached to a thin black rope. I'm not shocked that he lied to me. Does that mean he doesn't want to go back to Arvada? He knows Casper is there.

I ease away from him. I want to lash out. Cry. Scream. Hit something.

I have been a stupid, stupid girl.

Forty-One

ripping the Jewel in my hand, I watch him open his eyes and slowly rise to a sitting position.

"Megan—"

"You lied to me *again*."

"I can explain. I can—" His eyes divert toward the TV and when I hear my name, I turn to watch. "Shit. You're on the news."

My stomach drops and I gasp. My picture is next to his on the screen. It's surreal seeing myself on the television.

"After he held a gun to a man, Vincent Young kidnapped Megan Devereux. If you see her, please call local authorities. Megan's family has told police she

337

has been in touch with Vincent for weeks before he kidnapped her. Megan is a victim of the Spring Valley School Shooting last October."

"You told your family you talked to me?" Vincent grabs my arm, forcing me to meet his eyes.

I shake my head. "No. I never said a word. They-they must have gotten my cell phone records."

"Are you lying to me?"

I push him off me. "You're one to talk about lying." I hold up the Jewel.

He narrows his eyes and snatches it from me. "That's the least of our problems. We have to go. You're all over the damn news."

"You knew that would happen. Especially when you pulled a gun on Spencer. We're fine here. We're in the middle of nowhere."

He shakes his head. "We have to keep moving. We have to abandon your car."

"What? No. It's freezing out there. It's snowing for crying out loud."

"Megan, everyone is looking for us and your car. We have to be smart about this."

"We look different though. Where are we going? Are you sure we can't stay here tonight?"

"No. If the police come, we won't have any time to escape. Right now, we've gotta stay on foot and hide."

"If they spotted me here, they're going to start a manhunt here. Shouldn't we get a car?"

"We will. You'd better hope and pray no one paid any attention to you."

"Take us back to Arvada now, Vincent. You have the Jewel. What are you not telling me?"

"Megan, not now. We have to go. I'll explain everything but right now we have to get out of here."

"The witch isn't here in the mortal world, is she?"

He picks up his backpack and slides it on his shoulder. "I swear I will explain everything. We *have* to go."

I shake my head. "I'm not going anywhere with you until you tell me what's going on."

He lets out a frustrated groan and walks out the door with the car keys.

Anxiety grips me and I can't stop trembling. Something isn't right. I fell for his lies again, and I hate myself for it. Why did I decide it would be a good idea to join a suspect on the most wanted list?

The door bursts open and Vincent tosses hiking boots onto the bed. "Put those on. You're going to need them."

I don't want to know where he got those from. I cross my arms in front of my chest and glare at him.

"The Jewel doesn't work, Megan. I don't know why. Once we find the witch, she can help us. And yes, she is here."

"How do you know?"

"I just do. Please, Megan. We have to go."

Removing my tennis shoes, I change into the hiking boots.

It's late afternoon by the time we leave the cabin. I've never camped a day in my life and I'm about to find out what it's like. Vincent drives a few miles then parks at one of the overlooks.

He gets out of the car and starts walking away. Once I open the door, a gust of wind hits me. Catching up to him, we start hiking in the mountains. The deeper off path we go, the more I hope Vincent knows where he's going. Thankfully, it's winter and bears and snakes are hibernating. The moment the sun dips behind the mountains, fear wracks me. Dusk in the mountains is very dark.

"Is this where you've stayed this whole time?"

"Yes and no. I know these woods very well. But we can't stay long."

The wind picks up sending an icy wave over me. I hug myself tighter and wrap the hood around my head. Luckily, I bought gloves, but my hands are still cold. Trudging through the snow quickly tires me. I can't see anything, and I'm scared that there's a ledge somewhere and I'm going to fall to my death.

Where are we going to sleep? Am I going to have to sleep close to him like that night in Arvada in order to keep warm? Why do I do this to myself? We reach a point of the hike, and I'm out of breath. The cold hits my lungs, burning them. I can't catch my breath, a clear sign that I'm out of shape. Leaning against a tree, I slowly inhale and exhale. My legs shake and I don't think I can take another step. The pain in my back throbs, and I feel like I'm about to pass out. The only thing I've had to eat in the last few hours was a bag of chips.

"What are you doing?" Vincent asks.

"I can't. Just. Need a minute." My lungs burn for air and the cold makes it worse.

"Megan, we don't have a minute. Come on."

I inhale a deep breath. "We need a car."

"Do you see any around?"

I'm too busy trying to breathe to notice anything around me. The higher we climb, the colder it gets and the more frozen the ground becomes.

"We can't stay up here. It's too cold."

"We'll be fine."

"No. Let's find a car."

I push forward, ignoring the ache in my lungs or the numbness in my extremities. I keep imagining being warm inside a cabin. It works for a second, then the wind blows reminding me that I'm hiking inside a dark, cold mountain. I keep thinking and praying that I'm not going to die in the middle of nowhere with this crazed psychotic.

We reach a level part and cross the road. I've never stolen a car before and the thought of doing it scares me, but we don't have much of a choice.

We slither through the small overlook lot scanning the cars that people left to go hiking. I find an old car that's covered in snow. Who knows how long it's been there. Vincent clears some snow and opens the door. While he works to get the engine started, I clear the rest of the snow from the windshield.

The car starts and when I open the door, it gives a sad groan. I slide into the old car, and it smells like it had been sitting for a little while. It has a bench seat and I wonder how long the car will make it.

He shrugs. "Don't think anyone will be missing this."

It's only temporary, I remind myself.

Vincent drives away in the night. He turns the heat on, and it takes a long time for it to work. I wish it wasn't cloudy so I could see the beautiful stars. Something to keep my mind off how cold I am.

Exhaustion begins to settle over me. I feel guilty that I'm putting my family through this. I know it was Spencer who told my parents I had been talking to Vincent. Am I now considered a fugitive? What does Spencer think? I wonder if he even misses me.

Vincent stays to back roads and never goes anywhere near cities. I wonder if we've evaded the police. How long can we run from them? Every few minutes, I keep thinking a helicopter is going to hover. All we have to do is make it to the witch. We have to. I'll do whatever I have to in order to get back.

police. How long can we run from them? Every few minutes I keep thinking a helicopter is going to hover. All we have to do is make it to the witch. I have to. I'll do whatever I have to in order to get back

Forty-Two

awn is minutes away when I wake. Vincent's got the radio on, listening to the news report. "Police got a lead on Vincent Young and Megan Devereux in the Smoky Mountains. Search teams are scouring the woods as they found an abandoned car at one of the lookouts in the park."

That was fast. "I'm sorry," I say.

"I know you're not used to living this way, but you have to listen to me." He squeezes my hand. At least Vincent never deserted me.

I can't think that way. Casper hasn't deserted me. Maybe it's too hard for him to see me since it's been months. Casper would never do that to me. Is Vincent messing with my dreams now, too?

"Where are we?"

"West Virginia."

As I look out the window, the beautiful snowy mountains once again take my breath away. It's like nothing I've ever seen before. It's incredible. We reach a tunnel that literally goes through the mountain.

"Have you ever seen anything like this?" I ask.

"No, I've never been here," Vincent says. "It's beautiful, isn't it?"

I nod, my eyes glued to the window as we finish the tunnel.

"We can see things like this, you know. Forever."

"What?"

"If we don't go to the witch."

Settling back in my chair, I turn to him. "What are you talking about? You want to live on the run?"

"With you. Think of how amazing it would be. We'd travel anywhere we wanted to go. We'd see the world."

"Vincent, you forget that we wouldn't be able to do any of that. You're on the FBI's most wanted list. Unless you erase their memories of all this, we'd be stuck. We wouldn't be free at all and that's not living." Plus, I don't want to live with a psychotic man.

"Give it a few years. They'll forget who I am and what I did. The world will move on."

"How many years do you think it takes for people to forget? People don't forget things like that."

"Apparently, *some* people do."

"What's that supposed to mean? Did you erase my memories again?"

He sighs. "No, Megan. I've never done that to you."

"Are you kidding? You've done it countless times."

"Why do you want to go to Arvada? Are you going to try to kill me again? I've been thinking about this all night. You're only doing this to get back to Casper, but he's dead, Megan. He's been dead and you've been living in this imaginary world where he lives. I gotta say, it's quite an imagination."

"He's not dead," I say through clenched teeth. "How can you say you've never erased my mind? You've tried to kill me. You've tortured me."

He turns to me, his eyes full of darkness and hatred but the corner of lips turn up into a smirk. "I never once held you captive, Megan. You've concocted this whole story in your head."

"Stop it. Stop trying to make me sound crazy."

"What if we don't go to the witch? Why can't you and I live the rest of our lives together?"

"Because neither of us would ever be happy."

He sighs. "It's your fault. I gave you everything. Now you've gone crazy."

"I can't imagine why."

Vincent shakes his head. "Your craziness is not because of me. You've always been a little crazy but that's one of the reasons I fell in love with you. You never cared what people thought, and we were happy. You are my best friend, Megan. You are the only one for me. Then Casper changed all of that."

"You really believe all of it. Every single bit."

"Believe what?"

"Witches. Elves. Sprites. Dragons. None of it is real. There is no witch. The Jewel has no special power."

My heart stops. Of course, I should've known he would try to tell me something like this. He doesn't want to go back. He's scared of Casper. "Whatever."

"She doesn't exist. None of it exists."

"Just shut up, okay?"

He lets out a frustrated groan. "The whole immortal world thing. I made it all up and in your fucked-up state, you believed me. Don't even try to escape the car. We're in the middle of nowhere."

"Why are you saying this?"

"Because I'm tired of the charade. It's too difficult and you've taken it way out of proportion."

"Stop messing with me."

He shakes his head. "Not this time, mon trésor. It's my fault though. I did this to you to convince you to leave with me. But you're so set on getting back, all so you can see is *him*. I was a blind fool who believed that maybe you would see how much I've changed. How much you need me."

Open your eyes.

"Do you know how easy it would be to just crash into another car?" he asks. "Or let the car veer off a bridge?" He lets go of the steering wheel. "All of our problems would go away."

The car veers into the opposite lane.

"Vincent!"

"It would solve everything."

I know he's bluffing. He has to be. "You know we'd come back in another life," I say.

My heart thunders beneath my chest, but I have to remain calm.

"No, we wouldn't. Once you're dead, you're dead."

"We aren't humans. We're immortal."

"I struggle with that." Vincent steps on the gas. We're driving on the wrong side of the road.

"Vincent, slow down."

The car careens to the right, then left, then right. The turns are too sharp to handle this speed. Patches of ice on the winding, mountainous road are everywhere.

"What if there is an afterlife and somehow you and Casper would find each other. The thought sickens me."

"Vincent, I made a mistake, okay?" Tears stream down my face. A car honks as it moves into the other lane. "Please stop. I'm sorry for that. Once we get back to Arvada, we can live together. Happy. Just like we planned. Slow down!"

He meets my eyes, and I hope he believes me. "You're lying."

Damn. "No, I'm not. Please." I can hear the panic in my voice.

Vincent remains eerily calm. "You're only saying this because you think you're going to die. Don't you think you'd be a little calmer if you actually were immortal?"

The car remains in the wrong lane and we're going fast. Too fast. My heart jumps to my throat. A car is headed toward us.

"Vincent!" I scream.

"I need you to promise me, Megan. Promise me you'll always be with me this time. You broke that promise before."

The car lays on the horn.

"Vincent, I promise you we'll be together. Just you and me."

He releases another sigh and jerks the car toward the right lane. "You're better off here with me. There is no Casper. Just you and me. Forever."

"Yeah. You and me. Forever."

My hand cramps from gripping the door handle but I can't ease my grasp. I'm going to be sick.

"So much for immortal life." He takes my hand in his and kisses the back of mine. "It's going to be a good life. I promise you, Megan. I will always take care of you."

A siren sounds behind us, and I twist around. A police officer is right on Vincent's tail.

"Could this day get any worse?" he asks.

"You have to pull over."

"I can't."

"He's going to chase you. He's going to call this in."

He keeps driving for several minutes ignoring my pleas for him to pull over. "I can't pull over because they'll recognize me."

"No, he won't. But you're raising red flags if you don't."

Rolling his eyes, he pulls off on the side of the road. The car skids a little on ice. It's completely deserted. Vincent sneaks the gun into his hands, and I gasp.

"Whatever happens, just know this one's on you."

"Don't Vincent." Images of me telling Vincent to stop shooting flash in my head.

"The second he recognizes me, it's over."

"Don't do this."

"Shut up."

Clenching my teeth, I wait as the police officer writes any information or whatever he's doing. He's yet to get out of his car. I don't understand any of this.

"Why can't you take us back now?"

"Shut up."

"No. Stop avoiding my questions. That's all you ever do."

"I can't take us back."

"Vincent, these people will never stop hunting you. They think you killed kids at a school."

"Because I did, Megan!" he yells.

The officer taps on the driver side window.

Vincent rolls down the window. "Afternoon, Officer."

"Sir, is there a reason for the reckless driving?"

"Wanted to see what this baby could do."

"License and registration please."

"Sorry. I don't have either."

"You know it's illegal to drive without a license."

"Yeah, but I don't care."

I keep my head down, clasping my hands in my lap, scared out of my mind.

"What's your name, son?"

"Bobby McGee."

"Sir, what is your real name?"

"Dave Grohl."

"Step out of the car."

"I really don't think that's a good idea."

Recognition crosses the officer's face. It all happens in slow motion. He reaches for his gun, but Vincent's quicker. Vincent fires the gun. The officer falls back onto the pavement. Slamming on the gas, Vincent speeds away.

Forty-Three

his has to be a dream. I can't stop picturing the way blood spurted from the officer's head. My stomach is crawling with nausea, and I can't breathe. I've seen too much blood.

None of this is real. I wish Spencer was here, or least I could talk to him. Spencer? No. I mean Casper.

I can't think. I can't breathe. Vincent just shot a man. In cold blood. He could've been someone's father. Brother. Son. And I'm with him. Which makes me an accomplice. I can't stop the tears that cloud my eyes.

"Jesus, get a grip, Megan."

"You just shot a man!"

"Yeah. He's not the first one. Definitely not my favorite kill either. Are you going to throw up?" He lets out a frustrated groan and pulls over several miles down the road.

Opening the door, I collapse into the snow and hurl. I haven't eaten much but my stomach is trying to get rid of everything I've ever consumed. The cold actually feels good against my flushed face.

"You're gonna have to get used to that, you know?"

"How could you? What is wrong with you?"

A muscle in his jaw twitches and he snatches me up by my arm. "*Nothing* is wrong with me. Got it?" he says through clenched teeth. "Get back inside the damn car before someone sees us and I have to go on a damn killing spree." He pushes me inside the car and slams the door.

I'm a mess. There's a terrible taste in my mouth. I ache. I'm exhausted. I can't get that image out of my head.

As soon as Vincent closes his door, we're off again.

What did he say before the officer appeared?

I'm sifting through my mind. He said the shooting happened. That makes no sense. Does he believe it happened?

I shake my head, trying to return to normal breathing and coherent thoughts.

Open your eyes.

What was Casper trying to tell me?

"Sorry you had to see that. It was rather anticlimactic though."

"Is this all a joke to you? You killed an innocent man. These are humans. Don't you care about anything?"

"Of course, I do. I care about you."

"You can't keep doing this. You're not invincible."

"I've been on the run for months now. If they haven't caught me by now, they aren't going to."

"What did you mean about the shooting? What do you mean it happened?" I ask, but somewhere deep down inside I know the answer. Deep down, I think I've always known.

"I mean I went into the school and shot people. Including Casper."

Shutting my eyes tight, I shake my head. "No. You didn't." Even as I say the words, something feels wrong. Memories of Arvada have been fading, but not because of how long it's been since I've seen it. It's more like it was a dream I had. The way Vincent's been acting has been...different. My recent dream of Casper telling me to open my eyes comes to mind.

Open my eyes. Wake up.

What could he possibly be telling me?

You and I should live like the characters in your book. Vincent told me once. We could be so happy. Immortal. Forever. We could run away together.

Vincent actually shot up the school.

No. That can't be it.

The shooting really happened.

Vincent shot Casper.

And I'm not immortal.

They were all dreams.

Forty-Four

My heart shatters. I feel the pieces lift like dust in the wind. This can't be happening. This isn't true. The immortal world, the only place I can be with Casper isn't real?

I shake my head. *No, it exists.* But even as I think it, something is off.

"There's no Arvada, is there?"

He doesn't answer right away. He exhales. "You told me you were a writer. I wanted to create something that was just you and me. I never once thought you'd actually believe it existed."

"No. Casper and I shared dreams. He's an Elf and you and I are Sprites. You're half because of the whole dragon thing. I was there. We both were. You brought us back."

"That was probably your coma. You came up with the story though."

"What? What are you talking about?"

"Megan, we started talking about how shitty our lives are and how much we wanted to run away. You and I made up this world. A perfect world for us to live. One where there were no issues."

"No. How could you make me believe in something like that? You're lying. You always lie. You're just messing with my head like you always do. It exists."

"I have never messed with your head. Everyone else has."

"If it's not real, why did you go along with it?"

"Isn't that obvious? It was the only way to convince you to come with me and you fell for it."

"How did you know what I was talking about?"

"You told me everything. Right when you woke up. I didn't know what you were talking about at first. Then when we saw each other at that warehouse, you were still talking about it. I figured it out. I couldn't believe it.

Nausea rolls through me. "And you used this against me?" I've never felt so vulnerable in my life.

"You're so easy, but I know it's because deep down you really love me and you want to be with me. And you have to tell yourself some lie because you don't want to believe the truth."

"No! I don't love you. Stop messing with me."

"It's the truth."

"You've never told the truth a day in your life."

"You really are fucked up, Megan. You need therapy. You don't know how to love and if you keep up this mindset, everyone you meet will hate you and you will be miserable forever."

Tears cloud my eyes and I'm too stunned to move. Or react. Maybe I've become numb to his words or the way he speaks to me. He wasn't always like this.

"Why did you kill those people?"

"I should think Casper is obvious. The others...they tried to stop me. They bullied me relentlessly. Spencer didn't want to be my friend anymore because of Tyler. Everyone always abandons me. You. My mom. Dad has always hated me. Am I really that unlovable? Those people at school deserved it. They made my life miserable. I hate myself for hurting you, but you shouldn't have run to *him*."

I shut my eyes tight. The man sitting next to me created an entire imaginary world, and I believed him. Every single bit of it. He murdered people. Innocent people.

It sounded like fireworks which was a strange sound to hear inside of school. I saved Amber from being shot. I tried so hard to talk him out of it. I didn't know how many people he had shot at that point.

Then Casper yelled my name.

Tears roll down my cheeks as that day rushes over me.

Seeing blood explode from Casper haunts me. I couldn't save him. He's not here to protect me.

But now is the time to save myself.

Forty-Five

The silence in the car is deafening. It's been hours since I said anything. What can I say? Every so often, warm tears tumble down my face and my stomach clenches. Unrelenting pain stabs my heart.

We've reached Pennsylvania. I'm too distracted to take note of the winter scenery surrounding us. It starts to rain, and it sounds like rocks battering the car.

All this time.

Have I really been living in a fantasy world? How is that even possible? Am I really that messed up? Is this a real thing?

Cherry warned me. Spencer warned me. They all told me it wasn't real, and I didn't believe them.

I glance at Vincent, hating how scraggly his beard has gotten, hating how little he cares about anyone or anything except himself, hating how he manipulated me for so long, hating that I believed him. Hating that I could ever love a person like him. I feel ashamed. How could I be involved with someone like him? What about him made me fall for him? Disgust rolls over me like waves over sand.

No matter the truth, I have to get away from him. Why did I think he would take us back? Why do I believe him time and time again? What is wrong with me? Why me? Why did he do this to me? Why did I let him? Was I so desperate for a boyfriend that I just accepted it? Thought maybe he wouldn't be like that forever?

I have to get him to stop at a gas station. I can tell the cashier who I'm with and to send police.

"I have to use the bathroom."

"Talking to me again?"

"I just have to go to the bathroom."

"I'm sorry, Megan. I had no idea what all that would do to you."

"Do you feel any remorse at all for the people you've killed and injured?"

"Every day. I fucked up and it haunts me, but I have to keep going. You're here with me now and it helps."

A few miles later, Vincent pulls into a gas station. He gets out and stretches while I head toward the front door. The rain has slacked a little. It's freezing outside, but my hands sweat, and my throat feels like I swallowed sand.

"Megan!" he calls, startling me.

I twist around.

"Get some Doritos."

Nodding, I rush inside. I need to tell someone without him seeing. Lingering by the chips, I see the black man behind the counter. He's young, tall, and built. Almost like a basketball player. He jokes with his current customer. His smile is friendly. There's a woman by the beer, looking drugged out of her mind. Very thin and wearing blue jeans that could barely pass as jeans with all the tears and holes in them and a crop top that is definitely too small. How is she not freezing in that?

I have to tell someone. Fast.

The cashier finishes his transaction and I grab a bag of Doritos. Heading to the counter, the cracked-out lady reaches the counter first.

"A pack of cigarettes, too," she says with a thick northern accent as she places a six pack of cheap beer on the counter.

I grip the bag of chips in my hand. They crinkle so loudly I swear they're going to pop open and the clerk, Andre, will have to clean them up.

The lady walks away.

"Hey, good evening," Andre says to me.

I open my mouth and out of the corner of my eye, I see Vincent by the car. He's watching me. He'll know I told the clerk.

"Um, where's the restroom?"

Andre points behind me. "Last door on the right."

I swallow hard. As I head toward the back, I spot the emergency door. My heart slams against my chest. If I open the door, will the alarm sound? Can I run away fast enough? Every time I've tried, he's caught me.

I have to try. I have to get away from him. For good. Placing my hand on the door to the ladies' room, I turn and bolt out the emergency door.

The alarm doesn't sound thankfully. I breathe in the cold air. It's dark and rainy, but I don't care.

Run. Run faster. I have to get away.

I have no idea where I am, and I enter more woods. Is Vincent familiar with these woods, too? He's had several months to learn every corner of the eastern United States. That's enough time, right?

"Megan!" His voice encourages me to pick up my pace.

Focus, Megan.

My body trembles. I keep my hands in front of me.

I must find shelter.

Just keep running.

My boots keep getting lodged in snowy mud slowing me down. The hiking boots aren't good for running.

"Megan!" It sounds closer.

I have to get away.

Faster.

It feels like my legs are stuck. I'm shaking so much.

Feeling arms around me, I let out a scream as he shoves me to the ground, my face scraping against the cold snow and dirt.

"Get off me!" I yell and flip to my back.

He grabs my head and smashes it to the ground. Stars cloud my vision. I blindly reach for anything as I struggle to get him away. When I touch something cold, I seize his gun.

Blindly pointing, I shoot. And again.

He groans and grabs his stomach. I kick him. He takes my arm and snatches the gun away from me.

Vincent yanks me to my feet by my hair. He points the gun at me. "We're even now." He drags me back through the forest toward the car. Once we break the woods, I frantically scan the area for anyone to see us, but there's no one. Maybe Andre heard the gunshot. Maybe he can save me.

Vincent opens his trunk.

"No, please."

"I really have nothing to say to you right now." He grits his teeth as he holds his stomach. He pushes me inside and slams the trunk shut. I blindly search for the lever that opens it from the inside, but I don't feel or see anything.

The car begins to move and I'm once again at his mercy.

Forty-Six

I'm soaking wet, freezing. My teeth chatter as I sit in the dark trunk of an old car. I don't know how much time passes. When I hear sirens, my heart jumps to my throat. The car seems to speed up and I have nothing to hold onto. I feel it slowing down suddenly, but not because of brakes. It's like Vincent let his foot off the gas.

The car is coasting. Bracing myself, I know Vincent is going to kill us both. I don't want to die.

The car hits something and I hurl against the trunk, hitting my head on something.

There is no movement. No sound. I'm nauseous and I want out of here so bad. As soon as I hear voices,

I start kicking and screaming against the hood of the trunk.

Finally, the trunk opens and there's a bright light in my face.

"Megan Devereux?"

I nod. "Yes."

"It's her," the man calls out. "Come on, it's okay." He helps me out of the trunk, and I hurl as soon as I touch pavement. He holds my hair. "It's okay. You're safe."

Flashes of red and blue dance along the pavement. Several people stand around whispering amongst themselves. Traffic is backed up. We're on a two-lane highway. The car is completely smashed into a concrete bridge.

"What happened?"

"Had a tip called in that Vincent was here and had a female with him. He tried fleeing from us and crashed into the bridge."

A man and a woman rush up to me rolling a stretcher.

"They're part of the medical team. They're going to help you, okay?"

When I glance up, I see a woman wheeling a covered body on another stretcher. "Is that..."

"Vincent. He died from loss of blood from a gunshot wound."

I stand up and make my way toward the body.

"Ma'am, you don't want to do that."

"No, I need to." Lifting the sheet back, waves of emotion overwhelm me. Vincent is dead.

Closing my eyes, the weight loosens, and I let myself cry.

Forty-Seven

As soon as the police cruiser rolls into the driveway of my house, Mom screams as she runs toward it. The officer opens the back door and Mom collides with me. Her arms wrap around me so tight and she's weeping.

"Megan. Oh my god I'm so glad you're okay." She checks my face then presses my head against her. We stand there both holding each other crying. I barely notice Ron nearby. Jonathan walks over and caresses my hair.

"Glad to have you home, Sis."

Home. All this time I've been trying to get home.

Mom barely let's go of me all night, which is fine by me. She stays with me in bed, even as Savannah burrows under the blankets with us.

One week. In one week, I witnessed an innocent man die. I *killed* a man. I realized all along that what everyone has been telling me is the truth. I learned Vincent is even worse than I ever could have imagined.

Now he's dead.

I realized that I really am a human and that the visions I've been having are actual memories pushing their way to the forefront of my mind. I really did break up with Vincent on prom night, and he did give me a date rape drug. I remember now. Vincent's father had come home to tell him that his mother had passed. His mother was dying, and he was drugging me. I ran from Vincent's, trying to fight off the drug.

I run as fast as I can. I don't know how far Casper's house is, but I know the way and I won't stop running until I get there.

It seems like days that I run.

I finally arrive at his house and it's dark inside and out. It looks like no one is there. I ring the doorbell and try to turn the knob but this time it's locked.

"Casper," I scream and I'm sure the neighbors welcome the sounds I'm making but I have to find him. I have to tell him everything. I hold myself as my body

is shaking but I know it's not only from the unusually cold night.

Headlights blind me as they sweep across the driveway and the car halts. The door opens and I see a man running toward me.

"Megan." I immediately relax when I hear his voice.

I collide with him; my arms wrap around him as he catches me. He holds me so tight and I breathe him in.

"Megan, what is it? What happened?"

"He drugged me. I broke up with him. He's the one who tried to kill you."

"What?" He holds me at arm's length and looks at me.

"You were right. I wanted to tell you tonight that I'm falling for you. But I couldn't. He was watching and I—."

Casper pulls me to him. "It's okay. You're safe."

"What are we going to do?"

"I don't know," he says as he exhales. I feel the air travel over my head.

"I want to be with you. I want to be happy."

He holds my face in his hands. "I want to be with you, too."

"I'm sorry I came here. I didn't know where—." His lips cut me off. Soft, warm and eager. I lose myself in his kiss, forgetting, if only for a moment, knowing Vincent's confessions.

He rests his forehead against mine. His hands rake through my hair, which feels matted. He takes a deep breath and kisses my forehead. He tilts my chin up. "I love you." He fans my hair out from my shoulders and his fingers brush against my neck, sending a hot shiver up my spine. I can't tear myself away from his brown eyes and I inhale as he leans down, pressing his warm lips to mine. The same rush fills me like in my dreams. There is nothing else but us. I press my body to his, wanting him closer as our mouths slip over each other's. My heart can't be tamed. It's like a wild horse who has escaped, freely running.

For five months, we were happy. Completely and utterly happy.

Then a seventeen-year-old boy came into the school shooting several people, killing six. Casper being one of them. He warned me, and I did nothing. I never thought Vincent was really capable of anything like that.

The more I piece together the puzzle, the more it all makes sense. Somewhat, at least. And the more I regret not doing anything about it.

Now I know Casper and I never actually shared dreams or that we lived in some far away world. We never had to fight in an actual war, but we fought alongside each other. There were no dragons. I never saw any orbs. Dr. Brown explained I was sleepwalking and in a fugue type state.

But the happy memories...the love Casper and I had for each other...That was real. I refused to believe he was gone. Somewhere deep down inside I wanted the fantasy world to be real because the thought of losing someone like that was too much.

Funny the things your mind does to you when you're suffering and in pain.

In the days after I returned home, I slept a lot. I cried a lot. Never once dreamed about Casper. I told Mom and Jonathan everything. I haven't seen or talked to Cherry and Spencer. I'm not ready yet.

We always choose our path whether we realize it. Every choice we make puts us toward our way in life. Everything happens for a reason.

What was the reason for all of this? I lost Casper. I lost my friends. I lost my mind. What did I gain from it? How can I even move on from this? What do I do now?

"You can do anything you want, Megan," Dr. Brown says. I ask her these questions because maybe she can shed some light.

"It's been five months since the shooting, and I've missed five months of my life."

"Unfortunately, things like this happen to those of us grieving. It comes in forms and waves that are different to each of us. And it's okay. There is no proper way to grieve. Everyone has their own way, their own pace. However, I can tell you something that you've gained. You've grown stronger. You've not lost your friends. Those who are true to you will remain your friends. As for reasons? Death is such a strange occurrence for us to find reason. It's unfortunate, but it happens. It's a part of life. There is no excuse for what happened and it's a tragedy that we continue to try to make sense of."

"Maybe if Vincent had been serious about getting help, it wouldn't have happened. Or something."

"Maybe. But we cannot focus on the what-ifs in life."

"I know. I believed Vincent. I really felt like I was there in that world."

"During your coma, you may have truly dreamed it. And after experiencing something so traumatic, your mind latched onto something, anything it could in order to survive."

I nod.

"Are you still keeping up with your journal?"

"Every night. No matter how tired I am, I write in it."

"Good. It will help you. How about the story? Do you feel like continuing it?"

I shrug. "I don't know. I really don't want to write it, especially since I "lived" it."

"Are you afraid that you'll get lost in it once more?"

"Yes."

"That's understandable. Maybe add a happy ending to it and put it away. Just don't give up on your writing, Megan. Don't let him take that away from you."

"I know. He took enough away from me. I won't let him win. Maybe I'll start a new story."

"Good idea."

I clear my throat. "I talked to my mom about this, and I think I need to stay in the hospital for a few days." I don't want to, but I really need to. A safe place to clear my mind. Or something.

Dr. Brown nods. "It's okay. I'll have your mom fill out some paperwork. Everything will be okay."

"I know."

When our session ends, I make a mental list of the things I need to do before my hospital stay.

Ringing Cherry's doorbell, I bite my lip. Will she even talk to me? Will she forgive me?

The door opens and Cherry gives a heartwarming smile when she sees me. Tears fill her blue eyes as she pulls me into a hug.

"Omigod. I'm so glad you're okay." She holds me tight. "I can't even imagine what he put you through."

Emotions fill me and I break down. I can't stop the tears. I can't stop the shoulders from trembling.

"Megan, it's okay now. You're safe."

"He made me believe."

"I know." She holds me and I'm not sure how long we stand in her doorway before she takes me inside. Sitting on her couch, she lets me cry until I'm cried out. By the time I'm finished, I'm congested and my head and eyes ache.

"Cherry, I'm so sorry for everything. You've been my best friend since we were kids, and I've been the worst friend to you."

She shakes her head still comforting me, but I pull back.

"No, I need to tell you this. I've been so selfish. Ever since I started dating Vincent, then Casper, I've treated you like crap and it's not fair to you."

"Megan, it hasn't been easy, I'll admit that, but I can't blame you. You've experienced so many traumas, it's only natural that you would...you know."

"Lose my mind. I let Vincent manipulate and control me."

"You didn't *let* him do those things. *He* did that to you. He killed so many people. Obviously, he wasn't right in the head. I should've been more of a friend to you, and I didn't see it. I never saw how he was with you. He was always so kind on the surface and seemed like he really loved you. I was wrong about Casper. I should've supported you more."

I let my shoulders fall, feeling awed. "None of this was your fault. I shut you out."

Cherry rolls her eyes and chuckles. "Aren't we a pair?"

I laugh with her. "Boys."

We're quiet for a moment and it's a little awkward. We haven't been close in so long it seems. Next year she'll be going to college. Pretty sure after my absences this year won't allow me to get into any college.

"Penny for your thoughts?"

"Just...thinking about next year and college. Doubtful I'll get in anywhere."

"You will and I can help. We can do it together."

"Yeah. Dr. Brown wants me to finish the story. She says it'll help me move on from all of this."

"Maybe it will help. What do you think?"

"I don't know. I don't want to relive anything, and I'm scared that if I go back to the story, it'll consume me again."

Cherry frowns. "Then you'll write it with me. Or at least, physically. I can't write a sentence to save my life."

I chuckle.

"Seriously, though. I'll help you stay in present time or whatever."

"I don't know why everyone wants me to write this."

"If you aren't ready, you aren't ready. I think in order to face your demons head on, you have to acknowledge them."

I nod and look up to meet her eyes. "I'm scared to let him go."

She frowns again and takes my hand. "I know."

"I fear forgetting the way he smells. The sound of his voice. The way he held me. His smile, the one that was only meant for me. I can't move on."

Cherry squeezes my hand. "You can. You won't forget any of those things. They'll be with you forever. Life is never fair but being miserable will never change that. Once you're ready, you'll write about the greatest love of your life. And the greatest loss."

I take a deep breath. "Cherry, I'm checking into the hospital. I need it. Maybe I'll finish the story there."

Her chin quivers. "Not long, I hope?"

"Just a few weeks, I guess."

"It's okay. I'll call you every day. I really am so glad you're okay."

"Me, too."

After leaving Cherry's, I call Spencer and ask to meet up at the park in town. He still makes me feel awkward, in a good way. Those butterflies still multiply inside my stomach when I see him. The guilt of liking someone else is beginning to subside but it's still there. Another thing I'm working on with Dr. Brown. One day at a time she tells me.

"You look great," Spencer says. His smile is sweet and sexy. I realize then how much I missed him.

"Thanks. You, too."

We're quiet for a moment. I bite my lip to keep from crying. I rush up to him and wrap my arms around him. He returns the embrace.

"I'm so glad you're okay," he says. "I wanted to go after you. Save you...or something."

Drawing back a little, I nod.

He tilts my chin up a little. "You are free, Megan. He can't hurt you anymore."

"Or you."

"I admire your strength."

I let out a small laugh. "I don't feel very strong at all. I told Dr. Brown I needed to stay in the hospital for a few weeks."

"You did?"

I nod, feeling embarrassed.

He takes my hand, and we lean against a rock wall staring out at the sunset.

"It's okay. I'm here for you."

"Thank you."

"For what?"

"For everything. For being there. For knowing exactly what happened to me. For not running for the hills."

He kisses my hand. "Never."

There is one more thing I have to do. No matter how much I don't want to, I have to. Driving to the cemetery, I park and inhale a shaky breath before I meander toward Casper's grave. I've been here so many times, but now it feels almost final. Of course, it will always be here, but I don't know if I will always be here. Either way, I have to say my goodbyes. Cherry was right. I never got to attend his funeral and I never got to say goodbye. Trying to push that pesky lump in my throat away, I stand in front of the marble headstone. I brought yellow flowers though I'm not sure why. I never understood bringing flowers to a grave. Does the dead really know we visit? Do they see us? Do they hear us? Somewhere deep down inside, I know we feel that they do. I know we want them to.

Biting my lip, I sink to my knees and set the flowers near the head. I hate seeing his name engraved. I hate seeing the dates. I hate how he died. I hate that he died so young. But most of all, I hate that he died.

"I'm not really sure what to say or even if you're really listening to me. I miss you so much, Casper." Losing the battle with the tears, I let them come out of me. "There isn't a day or second that goes by that I don't think about you. That I wish we were just holed up in your room playing those stupid video games. Or complaining about some dumb project we have to do for school. But I can't. I can't keep living in some fantasy world, no matter how much I want to. I have to move on. I will never forget you. You've given me so much and I never got to thank you. I never told you how much I appreciated you. But I do. I love you, Casper. Always."

Epilogue

Four Months Later

This year has been one of the most challenging years of our lives," I tell the audience of parents, siblings, aunts, uncles, cousins, friends. Behind me is a large group of anxious and excited students clad in black robes and black square hats. Graduation has finally arrived and by some miracle, once I returned from the hospital, I dove into studying and caught up and managed to graduate. Principal Pearson even asked me to give a speech today. For a while I wasn't sure what I would say. What do you say to a group of kids who have experienced so much trauma?

"We endured pain and loss and tragedy. We faced darkness so deep that none of us really knew what to expect or how to move on. But we prevailed. We fought back. We conquered our fears; we stood our ground and refused to let anything else stop us. While that day will always stay with us, it will always connect us; it will always be something that lets us know we can get through anything." Tears threaten to lodge in my throat, but I push them away. "That day has taught me to love more and to appreciate what we have. We must remember those we lost, especially for me, Casper Truitt. Sometimes I joked that he knew me better that I knew myself. He was the light to my own darkness. Casper saved me in so many ways. He saved me even in the aftermath. He never gave up on me."

I want to stop and cry, but I have to keep going. I take a deep breath.

"We have our lives ahead of us. Futures so great we can't even fathom. Nothing can take that away from us. We are strong and fierce, and we will persevere."

Once I finish, I hear the applause of the crowd as I return to my seat, trying not to be overcome with emotion. They call each one of us and we walk across the stage.

Afterward, I make my way outside to meet up with my family. Mom and Jonathan give me big hugs and I give Ron an awkward hug. Out of the corner of my eye, I see Dad.

Tears rush to my eyes. "Dad, you came." I curl into his arms, and he gives me the perfect daddy's girl hug.

"Hey kiddo." He hands me a bouquet of red roses and a card. "I'm so proud of you."

"Thank you. Thanks for teaching me to fight."

"Anytime."

"She's gonna need it." Jonathan grabs my head in an arm lock and gives me a noogie.

I playfully punch his stomach.

Cherry rushes up to me gathering me in her arms. "We did it!" she cries.

"I know. It still hasn't set in."

"Give it time," Jonathan says.

Just behind Jonathan, I see Spencer making his way toward me and I meet him halfway.

"Hey," I say.

"Hey. I really liked your speech."

"Thanks. Listen, I don't know what the future holds or whatever. I mean with college and all that. I want you to know that whatever happens, I don't want to lose you, Spencer. You mean so much to me and you've helped me through so much in the last several months."

"Don't think it was a one-way street. You helped me, too Megan."

We're quiet for a moment.

"Got any plans this summer?" I ask.

He shrugs. "Was thinking a road trip somewhere. You?"

"Well. I finished my book."

"Yeah?"

"Yeah. Gave it a happy ending."

"That's great. I'm proud of you."

"Thanks. But that book has ended and now it's time to start a new one."

"What will you write next?"

I shrug a little. "Maybe a book about a guy and girl road tripping together. A happy one." I smile.

My eyes meet his and I love the gentle way he looks at me. He doesn't look at me like some little girl who needs help. It's a familiar look – intense and loving.

"You're beautiful when you smile."

Heat rushes to my cheeks and I look away. He closes the small space between us and lifts my chin. My heart pounds and I want him to kiss me. Spencer's lips inch toward mine. I hold my breath. Waiting. Wanting. When his lips touch mine, my heart erupts. Fire surges within my veins.

"I think it'll be a great book."

I've spent my entire life feeling like I never fit in. I created a world that I could escape to and thought I fell in love with someone who understood that world.

He took it too far and I believed him. I wanted to believe it was real because it was better than the truth. It was better than living with the knowledge that I had lost someone so dear to me; that I never thought I could be happy again. I'll never forget Casper and who he was to me. How he saved me in more ways than one. He's the true hero of the story, and while I never see him in my dreams any longer, I still think about him. He will always be in my heart.

The End

PLAYLIST

Evanescence – Together Again
Blink-182 – Hungover You
Lord Huron – The Night We Met
Ocie Elliott – Run to You
Evanescence – Better Without You
Chevelle – Comfortable Liar
Of Monsters and Men – Destroyer
Gabrielle Aplin – Alive
Apocalyptica – Farewell
A Perfect Circle – Disillusioned
Death Cab For Cutie – Metal Heart
Muse – Something Human
Radical Face – Welcome Home
Breaking Benjamin – Far Away
Meg Myers – Desire
Aquilo – Waiting
Tori Amos – A Sorta Fairytale
Evanescence – Far From Heaven
Foo Fighters – Home
Sanders Bohlke – The Weight of Us
The Offspring – Gone Away
Jimmy Eat World – You Are Free

Carrigan Richards is the young adult author of critically acclaimed Pieces of Me, a contemporary romance, the Elemental Enchanters Series, a paranormal romance series, and January Dreams Series, a romantic mystery series. She lives in Atlanta, Georgia.

When she's not writing (which is rare), she's spending time with her family and friends, listening to music, playing with her furdog, Eli, or cheering on her Atlanta Braves. Carrigan loves hearing from readers. Follow her on Twitter, @carrigan34, Instagram and TikTok, @authorcarriganrichards, look for her on Facebook or follow her blog at www.carriganrichards.com.

www.ingramcontent.com/pod-product-compliance
Lightning Source LLC
Chambersburg PA
CBHW011138310726
48972CB00009B/2759